Andi knows being born an interse stay that way can have lethal consequences. After all, surgical assignment is mandated by law. But she ain't going to spend her life hiding from the Society, hooked on Flow, and wanking tourists just to make a few bucks. She's a member of the Trans Liberty Riot Brigade, an underground faction of Transgressors resisting the government's war on their illegal genitalia.

But it's not enough to tag their messages on shithouse walls and sniff down the next high. The government has found their headquarters, decimated their ranks, and they're crushing the resistance. Though Andi might be nothing but a junktard, she embarks on a desperate dash to stay alive and send a call for help before they're all killed—or worse, surgically assigned.

Andi, together with Brigade leader Elenbar, must get beyond the communications block preventing all radio transmission, which means crossing the seaboard Wall barricading the United Free States borders. It's designed to keep enemies out and the citizens in, but amid increasing earthquakes and deadly pursuit, Andi will discover there's a far more dangerous secret hidden deep within the Wall itself.

Published by
NineStar Press
PO Box 91792
Albuquerque, New Mexico, 87199
www.ninestarpress.com

Warning: This book contains scenes of drug use and gore.

Print ISBN # 978-1-947139-34-3
Cover by Natasha Snow
Edited by Jason Bradley

TRANS LIBERTY
RIOT BRIGADE

Book 1

L.M. Pierce

RESIST!

Matthew,
I really enjoyed
meeting + chatting
with you! Keep
writing! ☺

L M Pierce

Dedication

Trans Liberty Riot Brigade is a melding of many minds, hearts, and life experiences. This book was made possible by the support of the amazing Olympia Writers Group, who encouraged me (and Andi) from the very first page; Dante, my amazing BB4L and confidant who keeps me going every day; and my loving husband, Chris, with whom all things are possible, probable, and beautiful.

Most importantly, Andi's story is dedicated to Andrea Faye, whose experiences and questions were the beginning of my ongoing journey to understand and capture the many amazing ways we construct our identity and shape our presence in the world.

Table of Contents

A Sorta Prologue

"OH YAH? WELL, fuck off then, you cuck!"

He's a penny pickle dick anyhow.

I walk into the men's public shithouse and slam the door behind me. The splintered starburst of mirror glitters under the yellow lights. The reflection's sportin' a shaggy haircut like someone's gone faggin' buggers with a pair of kitchen shears. My pupils are blown black and wide with the upshot of Flow coursin' through my veins.

That pickle fucker ripped my shirt.

I examine the ripped collar in the refraction of the broken glass. My hair ain't too long, ain't too short. I'm still man enough, should someone, maybe Pickle Fucker, come pokin' around after me. Though, if I'm real honest, I'm gettin' sloppy. Just like Elenbar's always sayin'—*keep yer head down, don't draw eyes ta ya*—but it's a chafe to move through the world as a mere pockmark of who you really are. Yah, I'm still me, though they call me a "she," but if I keep hackin' at my hair, I'm gonna look more like the dangerous "Transgressor" news stations are always shriekin' about. But underneath it all, underneath the shag, that's what I am.

A Transgressor on a shithouse mission.

On the cracked vid screen in the ceiling there's some report about us right now—another undercover operation arrestin' a pack of Transgressors. They don't wanna get the snip-and-clip, the assignment surgery that'll turn us from who we are, into what they want us to be. They're reportin' two dead already—more to come, if you know news like we do. I shudder, imaginin' gettin' my delicates all mangled up by a doc with a blade and a twisted sense of divine providence.

I approach the urinals squattin' against the far wall. Smell of piss cakes and wankin' stains waft through the air, a strong reminder of this location's dual purpose. I peek under the stall doors, but there ain't no tourist trout loafers tappin' a signal for a blowie or a pop-off. Though pickle fucker was a bust, I'm still hopin' to cop some rand coins from a trout. Since I made the long trip and all. Don't matter, though. There's other work to be done.

I slip down my pants and jut my pubic bone and mini-man toward one of the white bowl interiors. Urine spurts, and I huff with relief. There ain't no company to gawk at me, and unlike squattin' in lady piss stalls, like a good li'l "she," this is good, it's good. Feels right somehow.

I zip up, don't wash, and at the exit, I whip out the chubby marker I carry with me everywhere. The embossed man symbol on the bathroom door gets a scrawled-on miniskirt, a crotch sweeper hardly proper enough for street walkin'. Though after I finish the big circle and the crosshatch over him, li'l man's got an identity problem, the blessed "he" symbol now one of those dreaded *Transgressors*. A *s/he*, they hiss in the not-so-quiet corners of the world. Well, the Society will be along to reassign *h/er* in short tit order, I'm sure.

I press a kiss on the new Transgressor. It's a tough thingtryin' to be alive these days.

I hear a whistle, the chitterin' bird call of my hip-mate. Waitin' for me to do what I came here to do. So I scrawl *TLRB* in big black letters on the door. Somehow it don't seem enough. So I write "A riot is the language of the unheard" next to it, one of my fav tidbits by a righteous guy. A guy who got gunned down for bein' the wrong color and bein' of the wrong mind. The Society don't like people of the wrong mind. Hey, I know, the message ain't nothin' fancy, but the truth don't have to be. It's just gotta show up.

The Trans Liberty Riot Brigade was here.

Lover's Quarrel

"SPARE US A Nut, would you?" Pint gropes at my chest, fingers searchin' for some sign of the familiar rectangular box. His head of orange pubey curls tickles my chin, and his eyes roll loose in their sockets, the corners beet red and weepin' yellowish slime. A puff of a Nutri-Stick could take the edge off a wicked withdrawal, but I ain't got any and push him away.

"Jesus, here, fiending like a puckerfucker. Yer an embarrassment." Elenbar flicks a Nut at Pint's feet and sweeps back her long red hair.

He drops like a Bridge Street jumper, kneecaps a dull smack against the pavement. Blood seeps through his pants, and he fumbles with the stick, hands shakin' with the withdrawal fever he's fightin'. He brings the white tube to his chapped lips and jams the button to activate a smoky flow of vitamins and downer. Helps with the shakes, the fever, the gut punches to come.

Bosco glances up from his readin' in the corner and shakes his head like he don't approve of people bein' alive at all. The whole room's hot, air thick with chemical sweat and the smell of Pint's sick body.

Everybody's quiet, watchin' Pint squirm and whimper on the ground. The small radio built into the wall of our headquarters mumbles:

"On this day, our Patriot's Day, we remember those lost in the Great War and those still fighting the Daesh Eye threat overseas. Thankful are we to the Wall protecting our citizenry as we are thankful to the Society who guides us from ruin. Patriot's Day of holiest remembrance, warriors of the Lord on High. Remember danger lurks not only abroad but within our own homeland. Those who would sow fear among us, the Transgressors who—"

"Turn that shyte off." Elenbar glares at the green glowin' light of the radio.

Bosco hops up from his seat and flips the switch to red.

"Faggin' cucks." Here I am, sittin' pretty on the upswing of a warm solid high and good ol' news from the Society broadcast gotta go bringin' me down. See, lettin' it get so bad is amateur shit for crotch sniffers like

Pint. "You know, you gotta pace that shit out, stay in control, Pint. Stay on top of it. It's how they get at us. If the Brigade's nothin' but a bunch of junk-tards twitchin' and blasted off, who's gonna listen?"

"Andi, just shut yer mawhole fer a pissy pretty second." Elenbar slaps my dome with the flat of her metal clunker hand and my ears start ringin'. "Weather's nice 'top that seat ya got? The pickle pricks yer sucking fer that seat? Brigade represents all people, not just the slick and squeaky clean. We're like this fer a reason, ya know that, so stop talking like ya don't." Elenbar's green eyes spark with rabid rage.

I rub my stingin' head and eye my shitkickers instead of meetin' her glare. "Look, I'm just gnawin' on it. We might be like this for a reason, but we'd howl the Society right down if we weren't just..." I need to drop it.

"Well, when ya get off and stay off the Flow perma-like, Andi, ya just fucking send me a postcard. I'll slap yer fruity dicklips on the cover of Brigade: The Softer Side. Yer a junkie like the rest of us. Ya ain't no better than any of us." The gravel in her voice hurts more than the slap. "Ya do the marks like I told ya?"

She points her bionic metal finger at the borough map spread on the center table, the corners weighted by beer cans filled with gravel. This cinderblock shack is the headquarter hub of the Trans Liberty Riot Brigade. We just call it the Brick because it looks like nothin' more than a maintenance shed. Basically is.

"Keepers. I marked up all the west front and the shithouses on the south."

"Heard ya was hooking on the run. Again." She flexes her right fist, curlin' the metal jointed fingers like she's testin' it. The bionic arm's a newly acquired thing and ain't none of us used to it, especially not Elenbar.

Bosco's eyes are on me, and I can't keep the red outta my cheeks. "Just once and didn't slop up anyhow. Just a tourist trout from outta the neighborhood."

"Didn't slop up? Then how ya think I'm hearing it? No hooking on the runs. Not ever, not fer nothing. Don't care if the president's begging ya fer a pop-off. Ya were seen, by one of ours, but ya might get remembered by someone else next time."

"But not this time." My beatin' ticker's takin' missteps all over the place. I feel woozy.

"No, not this time. But it brings too much heat, attracts all sorts of problems. Ya keep it clean and straight fer the runs. Now, head ta Lover's Lane with Bosco. He'll fill ya in as ya go. Fagging twat." She spits the last words and stalks outta the Brick, her lip wrinkled in a sneer of disgust.

Pint whimpers from his withered crouch on the floor. He tries to rock back on his feet but falls again. Don't think he's gonna be able to get up, and no one goes to help him. This ain't the first and it ain't gonna be the last time he's quiverin' on this floor. Pint's got the hook worse than most of us combined. Smoke snakes from his mouth like someone's lit him up from the inside. There are some things a good ol' Nut can't fix.

Elenbar likes to think I talk about things I don't understand, but I do. The come-down off Flow's some of the worst feelin's in the world. The tremors start at the edges of your peripheral vision, li'l specks of dark like you're rubbin' your eyes too much, but they stick around, get bigger. Soon it's rumblin' through the threadlines of your nerves and your stomach clamps on your sack of guts. If you don't rupture somethin' internal, you can usually ride it out. But too many of us drag or get dragged to Dr. Chambers, beggin' for a fixer. Most of the time he does us right, but he comes with a price. If you don't have the rands to pay, he does accept other kinds of trade. Right and honest maybe, but still a sadist fagger.

Flow also comes in waves, and the nods are comin' down on me, my body shudderin' and losin' some cohesion. I try not to let the fade happen too hard, or I'll be right next to Pint on the ground. Gotta stay on top. Stay in control.

"Heh. Andi's going wonky. Dr. Chambers'll take it outta your ass, for effing sure, you wanker." Bosco pounds me on the back, jerkin' me from the pleasant grayspace I'd slipped into.

The weight of the nods dissipates a bit. "Suck a dick duck, ya cuck."

He smirks, liftin' his eyepatch to wink at me with the perfectly good blue eye underneath. He's a faggin' anglosax dramatic, fancies himself a limey punk-riot pirate. "Knockers. You coming with me to Lover's Lane or what?"

"Keepers. Let's get this shit right, though. I ain't a fan of repeat business."

Elenbar's given us our instructions, and we gotta obey like the good soldiers we are. I try to pretend it don't matter, but a trip to Lover's Lane always gets at me, clawin' deep inside my fleshy core where my feelin' parts must be. I hate every minute, even though I ain't seen her prowlin'. Every time I gotta go back, the possibility of seein' her punches me straight in the mawhole. Nah, Lover's Lane ain't no love at all.

When we step outta the shack and into the night, I see Elenbar by the chain link, gazin' at the shoreline of the Anacostia River. The water's a shade of blotchy underpants, grayish yellow from the repeated wash and piss stains of the world revolvin' around it. Lights fester on the river's opposite edge, the shimmerin' world of the Uppers, filled with people standin' atop the shit crust of this Slumland the rest of us gotta live in. Elenbar cuts a statuesque silhouette against that distant glow.

Our little pocket of alleyway is littered with trash, knobs of it caught in the honeycomb fence line. You could follow that chain link all the way through the different sections of our quarter, if you wanted. Not that the fence serves any purpose. Rusted-away pockholes mean we could still duck to the water. Not that we would. The water incubates far worse than sewer sludge and dumped bodies, but there, across the rushin' river, is Elenbar's past, and I hope, someday, her future.

"Elenbar, you coming with us?" Bosco asks.

She wrinkles her nose at him. "I'll stay here with Pint. Needs ta get shored up with Dr. Chambers. Apparently, I run a goddamn nappy factory, wiping yer shitty asses."

"He'll be all right," I say.

Elenbar glares at me. "Aye, he will. But what about ya? Don't fuck it up, Andi."

Bosco touches my elbow, and together we slink back through the shadows of the alley, swallowed up in the bosom of the Slumland haze.

BACK ALLEYWAYS ARE transit of choice for scum breathers like us—like me—prowlin' among the rats, kiddy-diddys, and other junk-tards. For the rest of society, it's easier to ignore us, pretend we're not there. We don't fit into Temperance—the political catchphrase inflamin' politics like a mutated case of syphilis. And though it smells of jizz wrappers and moldin' dumpsters back here, I don't mind the alleys so much. Keeps the questionin' eyes away. *Is she one of them? A Transgressor? A s/he? Why can't they get h/er off the streets, reassign h/er like the rest?*

But there's more and more of us now. Some of us pass all right, wearin' proper lady locks and skirts or sportin' gentlemanly attire if such is our preference. But most of us struggle, eyes followin' us wherever we go.

Bosco's ahead, struttin' to a prick-bustin' beat pulsin' out the back end of the Loosey Goosey Club. The back door butts up against the alleyway, and it's here we come across Lucky Lips.

"Effing effer," he whispers. Then he cups his mouth and lets out a chitterin' series of bird calls. The ones we use to signal our hip-mates when we're runnin' our tags or an op.

She flinches and whips around like it's a pinch on the ass. Bosco chuckles and sidles up to her, greetin' her with a smarmy hug. His callused hands look like grease smears on her white latex dress. Lips's got a smolderin' Nut between her teeth, and she grimaces, pullin' away from him.

"You smell like shyte, per *ush*." Disdain strums her vocal cords, and she sounds prettier somehow, lighter and girly. Even her face, she's already pale as milk, but her skin's been painted ultra white, with large streaks of blue over her eyes. And her breasts, ones that don't come natural home-grown, are crammed almost to her chin. I try not to stare. I've never seen Lips look this way, with tits like this, and in a dress too.

"Naw, serious now, where you been? Elenbar had the whole Brigade on fire lookin' for you. Thought you up and drained out on us—you hawking Flow?" he says. His smile's playful, but she frowns like it ain't play at all.

Lucky Lips glances up the alleyway and drops her voice.

"Just shut it. I'm not *Lips* anymore. Name's Lucy. Now get outta here. I don't wanna call someone around, but I will if I gotta." She glances at the backdoor of the club, where a bulgin' beef steak stands with crossed arms. Watchin' us.

"What the eff?" Bosco frowns.

"She's been assigned." I put a hand on his shoulder.

He wrenches free of me. The rims of his eyes water with horror. The look you get when you realize someone's fallen beneath the waves and the person you've known and loved's drowned and dead forever.

"Lips. What happened? What the eff happened? Is that what this is?" He grabs *her* wrist, his mouth a cavernous black gash of rage. Her nipples are hard in the chill clip of night, and he pinches one. "You think this is real? That you can escape what you are?"

"Feck you! Feck you, aye? Tell Elenbar she's a fool. You all are now! How long can you go on playing at riot? It's all a joke, ain't—no, *isn't* it? It's all up someday, *isn't* it?" She jerks away, cheeks burnin' hot. Then she soothes her poofed dome of hair and nods toward the rump roast at the door. He slinks back inside, and she huffs an angry sigh. "Look, they patched me up. Got me off the Flow, and I can earn me some rands in a tight dress and clean hair. It's not so faggin' bad after all. Better than scootin' around, *s/he* arses in the dirt." Fury's brought out her accent, and she sounds like Lips again. The real Lips. But I know, understand real clear, that Lucky Lips is dead.

"*S/he?* Oh, *pardon,* like weren't a season ago you were swinging your pecker 'round the quarter? S/he now—look, Andi, we're just *s/he* scumsuckers to Miss Cock Queen of all the Land!" He laughs, lookin' crazy as he spreads his arms wide, and gestures to the grime of the alley we stand in. A roach sips from a puddle of gutter fly puke. "Society slut, you're just an effing Society slut. Gonna take that dick along with the poke of the Society stick?" Bosco grabs her arm again, twistin' hard, and Lucy shrieks, her wrist at a funny angle.

I grab his shoulder, tryin' to stop him because if he don't, they're gonna—

"Citizen, desist! You are in violation of the peace. Release her."

We all freeze. We are straight, lubed up, and puckerfucked. Bosco lets go immediately, his mouth a pinhole of surprise.

"All right, all right. We got heated, it's all right." Bosco raises his hands, palms out.

The clunk-a-junk Security & Citizen Enforcement officer glares, red glowin' bulbs where fleshy eyeballs would be. Assignin' security to portable lug nuts I guess makes sense from an Upper's point of view. No subjectivity, no bias. You can't bribe a clunker. They stand upright; a coffin-shaped reinforced body of painted steel, hidin' all the mechanical guts, nuts, and bolts of the system. The head's a calculatin' mass of probabilities and policy, enforcement and control. What made sense on an administrative level don't translate so well to us faggers who gotta live with it. They use human Enforcers in the Uppers. Down here in the Slumland? We got a robotic task force seemingly programmed to fuck us on the regular.

"Yah, he's right. We're leavin' Lucy here and continuin' on our way." I say it slow and clear. No misunderstandings. Tryin' to be cool, easy. But it ain't gonna fly. Not even a li'l tit bit.

"Ma'am, please resume your normal activities. Sir, please submit to a gender screening," the clunker buzzes, polite as pie, sinister as fuck.

"Ah. Well, I can't, things make me gag. I'm liable to throw up all over the place, all over you and the lady—" Bosco's green eyes meet mine. Ain't none of us want to be on the radar, gotta stay out of the system as much as possible.

I sprint towards Lover's Lane while Bosco splits in the other direction. The clunker processes for a second before rollin' after Bosco. Yah, they roll. Spry motherfuckers have got off-roadin' equipment, chains, and regular asphalt rollers. Ready to deal with any and all situations.

"Bye, Lucky Lips! Hope you choke on a bucket of dicks!" I shriek over my shoulder, reckless immaturity givin' me strength and speed. I'm still sprintin' because clunkers round up quick. No doubt, any moment, they'd descend on our location like cockroaches, infestin' the dark crevices of our back-alley world.

Mothers and Lovers

LOVER'S LANE: PLACE of sin and win. Though Temperance is determined to get us all back to America the Great, when everyone knew their proper place, certain allowances are made for the decadent pleasures of the citizens. Ain't no wine, women, and song either. The mostly male clientele could come and be men, get some, be boys with their boys. Funny thing about it, though, the underground's always gonna exist, and kinky flavors are always on the menu.

"Manly Breeze to Bring Them to Their Knees!" A billboard chimes across the square, a neon flashin' image of a cubi-square sweepin' some house-mama into his arms while she swoons. A newspaper crumples under the heel of my shitkicker boot, and I stare into the face of an advert for Lady Lace, a contour and reshape clinic for those who ain't come natural to bein' a "pretty lass."

But though the Temperance is a "he" or "she" world, most of us Transgressors don't really think about ourselves like that. Call it what you want, but all of us get called "she" because that's all we'll ever be assigned as. The sorta puckerhole fuckin' the Society is so fond of. I mean, I sure ain't a lass or whatever they call it. I'm a—well, I'm just me. All my bits and self equaling Andi. Just Andi. But no matter what we wanna be or don't wanna be, there's plenty of "hes" and "shes" who toe the Temperance line in the real world, and then duck down here for a taste of weird. For us in the Slumland, if you ain't gonna get assigned, if you ain't gonna let the Society clip you, then ain't much work in this world for you. Except to be here, turning out ass or worse. Supply and demand keeps the world spinnin', and there's plenty of demand from the Uppers and cubi-squares. Demand for a taste of exotic *Transgressor*.

"Score a Fist? Flow on the side?"

I flinch away from the simper at my ear, recoilin' from the lecherous grin of the Peddler.

"Come on, come on, score a Fist? Lookin' like death on stalky legs, love." One black eye twitches in the depths of his cramped face, skin like a fleshy paper bag. The other eyehole is a pock of blackened flesh and the shiny sinew of scar tissue. His whole quiverin' mass is a layered wrap of clothin', baskets, and tattered pockets containin' all types of secret delights. I try to avert my eyes, but I can only avert my senses so far; his pores exude rot and the acrid tang of a chemical sweat. He's with the Tivoli Clan, peddlin' their chemical Flow in Lover's Lane. He's also a pipeline of information even while festerin' with bacterium and malice. Been an informant more than once for the Brigade.

"Take your Fist with you. I'll have a knob of Flow, though." Hatin' myself as I say it.

He gropes through a pouch disturbingly positioned where his crotch oughta be and pulls out a plex vial, stickered with the black flag logo of Tivoli. He passes the small vial over. I already got my own aerator, and I slap a couple rands in his palm, tryin' not to touch the scabby skin.

Though the Peddler's got all types, I don't fag around with Fist or Lang or even Biff. They all got their different perks in my mind except for the motherfuckin' sewer of a Fist high. Think of a fist, a mighty lubed-up fist. Then imagine it's jackhammerin' through your skull, splatterin' your precious gray matter into puddin'. Doesn't get you jacked like Flow, but it does somethin' else. Fags up the mind's timekeepin' works; makes the world slower, longer, wider. Sexcapades lasts forever, but so does everythin' else. Keep pumpin' and it stays that way, your time placement gone, your anchor to the real world left on the seafloor. Days are years and reality fractures. Alice in goddamn Fist land.

"Ya lookin' for 'er?" The Peddler leers at me, the only expression made possible by the tight web of mangled tissue crisscrossin' his face.

"Nah, no one. I'm lookin' for no one." I try to load the vial into my aerator. My hands are shakin' though. The closer it gets, the tighter my chest. Muscle memory and anticipation wring me out hard, and I stop to breathe before tryin' again. The click of the vial snappin' into place makes my knees weak.

"No one lookin' for no one; ya still lookin' for 'er."

"Yah, no one." I try to ignore the intense stare he's givin' me. I bring the metal tube to my neck and depress the lever. There's a pop and my skin burns, but it's good. It's already in. My chest gets real heavy with a flush of heat, like breathin' in a bonfire, then it gets light, my breathin' loose and easy. There's a hot throb in my crotch and dampened panties to show for the launch.

I stumble away from the viral pile of human, the transaction complete, and lose myself for a while.

The wide avenue's drenched in a heavy red light, illuminatin' the shinin' flesh of the workers outside their indicated parlors. Most of them are Transgressors, but there's a few mainstream joints. Surroundin' the square, huge skyscrapers probe the thick nitrous sky, the metallic behemoths revelin' as kings of our polluted underbelly world. Their mirrored stances reflect the flashin' lights and the effect's enhanced by the Flow coursin' through me. It's comin' on hard, and I want to drop to the ground and finger-fuck myself until I pass out. Then there's a surge of giddiness in my crotch and dome. The spiralin' feelin' of goin' insane's always on the up, but it'd level out. It always does.

Then I remember. I scan the heated crowds for some slip of Bosco. It's hard to worry beneath a surgin' high, but I manage. He's not even a Transgressor, but his sister was. I say "was" because she's gone now. Found herself at the end of a stiff rope. Bein' clipped, the surgical assignment, well, it can warp the very mind. Not everyone can survive it, and so he's been with us ever since. That kind of loss fags with you too. Both of us got somethin' to prove maybe, takin' the shitty calls. Like this one. Sketchy info from an unverified source, and it's Patriot's Day, which means place'll be crawlin' with brass soon.

As though on cue, there's a loud rumble and the sky's a sudden kaleidoscope of fire, hot embers bloomin' as fireworks screech and pop in rapid succession. Red, white, and faggin' blue, of course. There's an eagle one. Oh, yah, there goes the Free States flag. It's the same shit every year, but the crowd's upturned faces and wide spinnin' eyes watch like it's the birth of the next comin' christ cracker.

The blast of colors and the peak of my high makes for a cool effect, but I'm bored of the slatherin' crowd's mania. I search for Bosco and there, from the farthest corner of the square, I see him sidlin' towards me, shifty as a tourist trout dodgin' his wife.

"Knockers, that's an effing omen if I ever seen it. Clunker on our rag already?" Bosco says as he comes up beside me. "And finding Lips— Lucy—like that? Shyte, keep your eyes open and stay up and up. Though looks like you're up and up enough already."

I feel the heat of his glare. Gettin' spun on a run? Just like hookin', gettin' high ain't proper protocol either, but it's gettin' harder and harder to give a rip shit about it these days.

"Right, keepers. Let's find it, get it, and lose it. I'm startin' to get a creepin' feelin' we shouldn't be here." Even through the shiny halo of the Flow, I can't shake the itch of bein' watched. I cruise the crowd again and meet fleetin' glances, most of them loaded or fadin' with wide pupils and pussy-lickin' smiles.

"All right. Thissa way." Bosco snakes his way through a throbbin' group of men in business suits, ties loose and pants unbuckled. These cubi-squares—men in suits and ties—are already well saturated with drink and they're takin' turns smackin' the bare ass of a mite who's hardly bleedin' age and that's with the makeup. The mini bulge in her princess panties tells me she's intact, a growin' rarity with the mobile assignment wagon visitin' the Slumland every weekend. "Bring your mite to keep them right!" Even though almost half of us are bein' born Transgressor nowadays, the Society keeps thinkin' up ways to clip more and more of us. This kiddo must be a gutter babe, hidden from the moment she popped out an unfortunate twat.

She looks over her shoulder at the growin' line of cubi-squares behind her, face burnin' with what looks like resignation.

"Effing hell. It's worse every time I show my mug here." Bosco grimaces. "Pixie's just a mite! Grown-ass men. What big men they be." He spits on the street.

I say nothin', keepin' my eyes steeled straight ahead. Though I wanna beat them down, sink my nails to the cuts, and count every bloody pulsin' spurt as they die, I know all too well: *can't save them and save yerself.* That's Elenbar in my ears. She taught me that hard. I finger a shiny patch of scar beneath my navel.

"What the eff!" Bosco smacks me on my dome. I snap back with a closed fist and cocked elbow, but he grabs it easy and twists me around.

"I've been saying your name. You here? You really here? I'm about to walk outta here and tell Elenbar you're too flat down to pull your head out. Gonna get us gagged and gutted," he growls in my ear. I struggle against him, a pleasurable tingle in my crotch because I'm so spun. Plus it bein' Bosco and he's always got a tingle effect on me.

But it's true, my mind is dodgin', hoppin' into pits and black holes. You start spacin' on the Flow, you'll get it comin' and goin'.

"Keepers, I got it. I was up and up, but it's comin' down now."

He lets me go, and I rub my wrist where he grabbed it. The skin's bright red.

"Right. It's your eyes I need up and up. This ain't a tourist grip and trip." He winces and grabs his side, teeth squeakin' as he does. I've been so up and up I hadn't seen the black scorch mark blazed across the right side of his rib cage. My heart, already aroused by the Flow, begins to pound in a painful staccato.

"Fuck, you all right? Did they shoot you? Are you shot?" I'm grabbin' at him, tryin' to see it, but he pushes me off.

"Nah, it's the damn tazer plate. Sheared right to the white. Heh, deflected that clunker's blast right off, though." He can't stomp the grin.

I smile too, but I know what's gonna happen when we slink back to Dr. Chambers. I've seen them remove a taze plate once. Things'll save you from a direct killin' blast, but the heat fuses it right through your flesh. The whole plate'll rip everythin' back when you get up the sack to peel it off. Skin goes, sometimes parts of the bone. Leaves scar tissue fuel for shiverin' nightmares.

"Knock the cock, it's fine. Let's keep moving," he says.

I follow him in silence as we weave through the crowds. The hour's growin' later and more throngs of cubi-squares are emergin' into the district. Some got a few ladies with them, quiet movers, lookin' to score some chems or kink it up for the evening. Some are even with their fellows for some couple's therapy. There's two of them squattin' in a back alley, a huge man plungin' his stallion cock into a lady's bare ass, panties around her ankles. Right beside them, her fella's knockin' his knob, like the sound of her screamin's all he needs to get through his day.

But shit's always like that here. Only place folks can be their kind of folks. Rest of the world's so locked down, you can hardly rip a fart without bein' ticketed for it.

Josiah's ahead of us, still the same with his long jesus hair and flowin' floral silk robe. I elbow Bosco. He's seen him too, and we slow, tryin' to make a casual approach. Without even lookin' at us, Josiah turns and walks inside his shop.

Bosco slings his arm around my neck, like we're lovers, and we slide through the entrance. The throbbin' lights illuminate racks of implements and tools for the adventures of Lover's Lane. Pussy willows, one of those spiked paddles, and varyin' lengths of whip and rope are the main trade, but in the back behind grated cabinet doors are finer toys: glass fists, splintered clubs, even an Eve's Apple. Bosco's already leadin' me on. I follow close, aroused and confused by the head of Flow that's makin' everythin' more hyper-surreal than it already is.

The crammed front of the shop opens up into a hallway with lots of doorways, most shadowed with panels of fabric and sheer tapestries. Behind them or peekin' out are the painted faces of the nighttime nasties, the Fist Royalty so many come to see.

Ya lookin' for 'er?

The Peddler's words are ringin' in my ears, and I try not to see her face, willin' us to go on and never see her there. But I already know, don't I just fuckin' know? The Flow's already whisperin' what I'm about to see, and when I do see her, her face pale and slick with sweat, I almost toss it, blow my guts all over the floor. Instead I let go of Bosco's arm. He turns, his mouth open to speak, but I don't pay him no mind. My eyes are on her, and the shiny white mucous of her foggy gaze swallows me up. She reaches a hand toward me, and I take it, hypnotized by the insanity, the nightmare I can't wake from.

I let my mother lead me into her lair, the smell of spunk and incense makin' my stomach lurch. Mydome's spinnin' as she leads me to the bed. Her every step is so slow, so deliberate, it's almost special. Like she's drawin' it out just for me, though it's actually the Fist and what it does to your mind.

"Lie on...well...lie on the bed." Her voice's a quiet slur, and her painted lips are smeared, like a cock's already been squeezed between them. She's comin' toward me, disrobin' in that slow, deliberate way. I catch a glimpse of her saggy tits, the wrinkle of her nips sad and shrunken, like a grandma twice her age.

"Ma. Stop, I—"

She stops, and she tilts her head.

So slowly, so slow.

I imagine her eyes clear. I imagine she sees me, sees me at last. The li'l Transgressor baby she left on St. Aggie's doorstep so long ago, a scrawled note tucked in its tattered blankie. The Flow is really muckin' me up, or maybe it's the fumes of the thick incense. She's topless already and slidin' her hand between her own soft legs. I see a delicate blush of fine blonde hairs on her unshaven legs and then I do lose it, upchuckin' my guts all over the floor. She stops and tilts her head again.

"Effing goddamn effer." I hear Bosco's voice, but my eyes are squeezed shut. I let him jerk me to my feet, draggin' me away, somewhere far away. I land somewhere soft and warm and empty. Everythin' goes quiet for a while.

When I wake up to the smell of flowers, I sit straight up. I'm still in one of the Fist Royalty rooms. My brain feels like it's gonna spin outta of my eye sockets.

"Peace, it's all right. You're safe, it's all good."

I see a spiral of gray smoke in the corner of the room. Josiah's puffin' on the end of a regal looped pipe, which looks like an antique outta time and place, and with the dim gloom lightin', it's like I'm in another world entirely. Like there ain't no Lane right outside the door, we ain't in the Slumland, and there ain't no Society, Brigade, or worries in the world.

"Where's Bosco?" The Flow's still with me, but it's come way down, and I can control it. My mouth tastes like an outhouse turd.

"Well, he came for something, I gave it to him, and he went back to Elenbar. Isn't that how it works? Well, usually." He gazes at me with placid eyes, and they look like they might be blue, though in the haze, it's hard to say.

"He faggin' *left* me here?" My voice pitches, and I hate the childish squeal of it. "Fuck, what happened?"

"Rose told me she had a child once. She's not always like this, you understand. Once, in those rare moments, fleeting between one Fist bump and the next, she did tell me. Told me about you, as it so happens. Bosco had to go. The brass were sweeping the square, but I told him I'd stay with you, just 'til you came back. You're back." He rises to his feet, readjustin' his long robe.

"Wait, has she, uh—ever wondered about me? What'd she say?"

"No. Never mistake the ramblings of Royalty to mean somethin'. Fist is her world, everything else too frightening to imagine. I had her tied after you. Won't be any more of you to dump on the Sisters." He sighs. "Wish we could tie more of them. No need for more lost babes like you in the world. All alone."

My gut heaves, his words punchin' through the haze of Flow. I spring to my feet, hot, yes, tears, stingin' my eyes. I push past him, through the hallway, not lookin' at any of them fuckin' Royalty bitches as I do. The throbbin' light of the street almost blinds me as I burst out into the grime and dinginess of the square, but I'm relieved. I slap myself once and begin to jog toward the distant skyline.

There's only one place I go when I feel this way.

I can find Hanger's Hill from any place in the whole Slumland. As I stagger up the steep incline, I suck in deep whooshin' breaths. My lungs feel like they're full of splintered glass, but they're always like that after a good run.

The Hill's a large one, givin' a full view of the skyline and distant lights of the city and surroundin' quarters. A few shadowy figures dot the trim soft grass, and I might be surrounded by shaggin' couples. Always that way at the Hill, but it's one of the best places, well, to just be, so I come here a lot. I seat myself away from the gyratin' anonymous shapes in the dark and suck in the air that's somehow fresher. Even with the stench waftin' off the Anacostia sewer-swill River, still got a bit of breeze rufflin' up here.

A rumble bellows below us, a groan of shiftin' earth as a quake rolls through. A few of the gathered silhouettes freeze mid-action, but it's over in a minute. They come more frequent, the quakes do, like grumblin' titans sussin' out territory deep under our feet.

But it's all peaceful again, and the lights keep sparklin' across the river. There's a whole world beyond, though I ain't ever been beyond St. Aggie's. And beyond the erect spire of the cathedral—you can see it from the Hill—rises the stark crisp edge of the barrier erected against the even bigger world Outside.

The Wall looks like hardly nothin' from here, but we all heard the stories. Sheer as a cliff, taller than most the faggin' buildings in the Uppers or the Slumland. Except a few of them cloud stabbers with fancy lights and view portals. Yah, the Wall don't look like much, but someday I'll go. I might just go all the way there, and who knows? Someday I might even get beyond it.

A Transgressor can dream, can't she?

If You Tell Me How

THE ALLEY'S QUIET by the time I get back, and even some of the trash looks like it's been swept up or somethin'. My skin's hot, and I try not to lose my head. I'm twisted about Bosco leavin' me and the knob-gnashin' I'm gonna get from Elenbar. Pumpin' Flow like that on a run? It ain't hookin', but it ain't good either. Fear's hot in my gut, and between that and the Flow, I'm worried I might shit my pants before I even see Elenbar.

The quiet continues even as I'm steps away from the front door of the Brick.

"You made it." Bosco emerges from the shadows, puffin' on a Nut. His one uncovered blue eye glitters in the streetlight, but he ain't smilin'.

"Why you just up and leave me there?" My voice's a whine, but I can't help it. "Let me get scooped like that?"

"Josiah wouldn't let no harm come to you. Quit sniveling. Clunkers were cruising the Lane after the firelights, and I figured I'd better get scarce." He points to the wide white bandage wrapped around his torso.

I cross my arms. I'm poutin', but feelin's are like that. Irrational bits floatin' around gettin' all butt hurt about shit. "You all right then?"

"Yah, weren't so bad this time. Popped the plate off clean." Bosco flicks the Nut to the ground and stomps it out. "Hey, you ain't been right these last few runs." He steps closer to me, so close I can smell the antiseptic whiff of his bandages and a touch of chloro-juice the doc uses. "Are you all right? For real all right?"

"I'm fine." I don't want to, but I take a step back. The li'l part of me wantin' to curl up against him and be close is the same part bein' a li'l bitch and cockin' up all the runs. That li'l part can go fuck itself. "Just all these runs and the sweeps last month. Seems it's all gettin' tight somehow. Like a squeeze we're about to get stuck in."

"Yah, the sweeps, it's all savvy, though. Most of our lot cleared out. You cleared out." He rests a heavy callused hand on my shoulder.

I shiver. "You and Pint got the worst of it."

"Spendin' a night in the Clunker Hut? Shyte, best meal I've had since New Year's. Advantages of having a proper dong swinging down south. Not much reason to hold two fellas caught hanging out in a shit shack."

I huff a sigh. He's right of course. We had the warnin' and, when the clunkers and brass came to look for the Transgressor supposedly hidin' out at the Brick, wasn't no one but Pint and Bosco to find. But they'd never come so close before. Not right into our center like that.

"Faggin' hell." I shake my head, and shove his hand off my shoulder. "Fine. Knock the cock. Elenbar on a tear?"

"Knock the cock, she's definitely gonna beat your ass." He smiles, and I swear he's winkin' under that eye patch.

"Let's get it tit over tit then." I grab the doorknob and mutter a hope before walkin' in. Bosco follows right behind.

My eyes struggle to adjust. It's dim as a sewer pipe except for one lantern burnin' on the tabletop. Everyone's here. At least, all twenty of us who're tight in the Brigade. My heart starts riotin' in my chest, and I wonder if I'm gonna get kicked out after all. Maybe even stomped down. Elenbar's standin' at the far end. She looks old in the flickerin' light, creases and gray pools in the crevices of her face makin' her skeletal.

"I'm glad ya made it, ya twat." Elenbar's voice's sharp as a prison shank.

"Well, beanbag Bosco left me and—"

"I already tore his arse up about it. But ya had no right ta go about it like ya did. That's the truth." Elenbar sighs, like I'm a damn nuisance and a child. "But one can't always be on, especially seeing what ya did. I'm sorry. Family's the hardest."

Mydome might explode, everyone starin' at me like I'm a prancin' prick pony. The sick is one thing, humiliation's another. I drop into a chair, my gut shiverin' because along with humiliation, the come-down off the Flow's startin' to happen.

No one talks for a minute.

"All right. Now we're all here and it's the right time ta really look at what's going on. And it's something big. From what Josiah said, there's been a reach-out. We've never had such a contact, right in the belly of the beast. The Society won't be able ta stop this charge if we get what I'm thinkin' we're gonna get. But there's a catch," Elenbar says.

"Ain't there always?" Pint's lookin' finer than he did when we left, though his booty-sore frown tells me Dr. Chambers got paid.

"There is. We have ta go ta the source. They can't come ta us, and it won't be as simple as popping ta Lover's Lane. The contact's in a secure location." Elenbar crosses her arms.

"W-w-well, how you proposin' we gonna get it?" Teeny whimpers, her voice whistlin' through the big gap where front teeth should be. She got thrown durin' a run-in with a clunker last year. Knocked her front teeth the fuck out. Lucky she didn't lose her damn head or end up with a nip and snip between her legs.

"We'll have ta go in deep. Now, I know we've had some burning licks this year. It's been hard on all of us. So I won't ask anyone ta go who don't wanna. I'll go myself, since I've been there before, but I need another ta come with me. Just in case." Elenbar's arms squeeze tighter like she gonna suffocate her own damn self.

"Well, to where?" Pint's lookin' more and more pissed about it.

"The contact is at the Farm, and I—"

"You up-ending bitch, you're crazy as a fuck fly's shit!" Pint's on his feet, lookin' ready to swing at her. P-Hat's entire six-foot-plus frame is up, her barrel chest a vertical wall, and she leans straight into Pint's face. Then they're throwin' elbows and—

"Tha's a faggin' trap, gotta be a trap, why you go right into a trap like tha'?" Teeny whistles again, her eyes blurry with tears.

"Right, it's gotta be a trap. Effing place'll snap you up, and you'll be gone for good." Bosco ignores P-Hat and Pint, who break a chair with their tusslin' bodies.

"Sit down and hear it, ya twats!" Elenbar stalks over and twists P-Hat's ear almost off her damn head, and she lets Pint out of an ugly headlock. "That's why I said no one's gotta go who won't. I'll go, since I got a pretty good grip on the damn place, don't I? I'm asking fer a volunteer. Which obviously won't include ya, ya crazy shithead." Elenbar spits on the ground a li'l too close to Pint's feet.

Pint slinks back into a chair, face red as his hair, not sayin' nothin'.

Everybody else is quiet. I wonder if anyone's crazy enough to volunteer. Minnie chews on a glittery fingernail, not lookin' at anyone. Pint's glarin' at Elenbar. Bosco's starin' at me, a smolder of—yah, he's probably thinkin' about dip-stickin'. We been hittin' it more regular than usual, and my crotch tingles with the pleasant recall of our fav back alley.

P-Hat's rubbin' her ear and grindin' her oak slab jaw. The others might as well be shadows, silent and set back from the pool of lamplight.

Then, because I'm amped and twisted and still thinkin' of my ma—well, I raise my faggin' hand, don't I?

"Fuck off, Andi, you ain't goin' anywhere. Junkie can't stay off the juice for a sec to do a damn run." Pint looks ready to punch me from across the table.

"You're rich one to talk about any sorta shit. How is Dr. Chambers anyhow? You gonna be able to pop a squat anytime soon?" I can't keep the slit-lickin' smirk off my lips.

"I'll fuckin' gut you." Pint jerks to his feet, comin' at me, but Bosco shoves him back into his chair and points a finger at me.

"You ain't ever been to the Farm. You got no idea what you're volunteering for." He glares at Elenbar. "You can't let her. She don't know." It's almost like he's, well, pleadin' with her. Rage and humiliation boil in my gut.

"He's right. Andi doesn't have the experience to understand what that place is like." P-Hat's thick velvet voice booms over the others.

"Andi'll do fine." Elenbar's expression is all pissy vinegar as she stares at me. "If yer feeling up ta it."

"I'll do it. I can do it, serious, I can." There's that mitish squeak again.

But Elenbar nods anyhow. "Besides, they'll scrub us out at the Farm, and sneaking product in is the least concern ya got once yer inside. So ya'll be sober whether ya want it or not. Though, listen ta this, Andi, I can't control what's gonna happen once we're in. We find the contact, then try ta escape as hard as we can. But, and this is fer real, ya could get assigned. It happens. If we can't get out, if we can't escape—"

"I know." I say it, but I don't. I have no faggin' idea, but it's real clear I'm gonna, and soon.

"All right then. P-Hat, ya'll hold it here and wait fer us ta make contact." Elenbar like she's comin' down off the mountain, tablets in hand.

"I'll hold it down, I'm always down fer it." P-Hat scratches the back of her neck. "But, and I don't wanna say it, but I've gotta. What if ya don't get back? What if it all goes to shyte? The Brigade's gotta go on. Just thinkin' we gotta have a plan in case it, well, goes wonky."

"Well, ya'd take it over, step up, and do what ya gotta do. P-Hat's in charge if I don't come back. That's how it is, so no bullshyte about who's gonna rise up. P-Hat's got the most experience, outside me, and all the other oldies are about gone or drained out. That's how it's going ta be." Elenbar glares at everyone around the table, and the assembled Brigade is silent, gazin' at us with a funereal finality. My skin prickles. I'm already wishin' I'd shut my damn mawhole like Elenbar's always tellin' me to. I'd been lucky, mostly lady-lass enough to dodge most the bio screens and hightail it when I didn't. I'd never been to the Farm, never been picked up, but it happened to a lot of us. P-Hat's come real close a few times. Lips...I mean, Lucy, weren't an exception really. More the eventual rule. If you got picked up, shipped to the Farm...well, they'd do what they do best. Elenbar's the only one I'm sure ever escaped before gettin' clipped. Her sister weren't so lucky. Jane went from Transgressor to just "she" before they could get out. But that's how it is. With a slice and dice, you'd be short half of yourself.

I stand up, open my mouth to speak, and puke all over the faggin' table.

Coulda, Woulda, Shoulda

"YOU CAN'T DO this, Andi."

I'm tryin' to block out Bosco's voice, but bein' laid on Dr. Chamber's table makes it hard. The doc is futzin' with somethin', and I wish he'd hurry with the shit so I can dodge Bosco's lecturin' monologue. I'm feelin' sick, but I done puked up all my innards on the way over here. Overamped again. Happenin' more and more these days.

I force my lips to form words. "It's gonna be fine. I'm with Elenbar. She'll keep it right."

"Elenbar's getting reckless; this is reckless. Ain't no information worth the risk she's willing to take, the risk you seem so set on taking."

"All right, ya cock bumpers, back up." The doc plants a hand on Bosco's chest, givin' him a proper shove. Bosco looks like he's wantin' a fight but steps back.

"Andi, Andi...what we gonna do with ya? Overamping's a good way to wind up on the cold slab, ya know? Heart's gonna rocket right outta yer ears, and no one to blame but yerself." He leers at me, his double row of black stubby teeth makin' me stifle a cotton-dry retch.

"Give her a Nutri-Shake and a drip." Bosco cracks his knuckles like he always does when he's stompin' down mean words.

Dr. Chambers eyes him suspiciously. "Ya got the rands? I ain't taking credit, 'specially not from this scab here. I heard what she been up to with Tivoli. Scabbing on Tank. Tsk. Word's no good from a junkie."

"I got your rands right here—"

"Shut your face." Bosco glares at me. "Here, and I'll get you a watch from my stash." Bosco drops a few rands into the doc's hands.

The doc counts them carefully, then nods. "All right, drip and sip it is. Don't forget that watch, though."

Then he's hummin' because it's damn good deal he's got just to do his faggin' job. Though, I'm just grateful I don't gotta stretch my puckerhole for his more unusual trade requests.

"I saw what you wrote. A riot?"

The way Bosco says it makes my heart stutter.

I shrug. "What? I always throw some shit up when I'm runnin'."

He shakes his head. "It's more than that. It's like, you got something, something real good inside you, Andi. I mean, you're an effing effer on your best day, but you got some poetry in there." He taps my chest. "Poetry that needs to stay in the world. I'm serious about this. You got no idea what you're walking into, what the Farm is really like. If something goes wrong and you can't get out, you'll get snipped. Won't be anyone there to stop it from happening. No one can get to you deep in there like that." Bosco's starin' into my eyes, and I can see the pleadin', the worry, but I'm so sick it's hard to feel nothin', except about bein' held down and getting' a poke in the—

"Faaaag it! Whatcha usin'? A harpoon? Butcher!" I hiss as the doc digs at my thready veins with an awful sketchy lookin' needle.

"Ah yuh, it's in already, ya wailin' babe." Dr. Chambers hooks the straggled line to a sack of drip and squeezes the pouch a couple times. "Ya'll be right and ready to go kill yerself in new and creative ways, I'm sure."

I got a powerful urge to bite at him, but the warm rush of the drip's already makin' me feel more teddy squishy than grizzly.

"Andi, please." Bosco takes my hand, his rough skin like a cat's tongue.

I feel the tingle again. Annoyin' because I'm tryin' to edge him off, get him to let it go. Because don't matter what he's gonna say, I'm goin'.

"Nanni went in there, and you know what happened to her." He flips up his eyepatch and levels both his blues on me.

I hate it when he does that.

"Your sister ain't got nothin' to do with this."

Bosco's upper lip lifts in a snarl. "Don't she? Getting clipped and coming out like she did? That shit changes you. What I told Lips—Lucy— that's true. You can't escape who you are, no matter how they rearrange the pickle bits."

I'd forgotten Nanni was in with Jane and Elenbar. Another snip-and-clip. "Hey, it ain't gonna happen. Elenbar clapped it outta there last time, intact. She's got this figured, what we're gonna do." Bosco's sweaty hand makes me want more, but maybe that's the warm crotch fuzzies the drip's givin' me.

"They didn't get out in time. Not for Nanni. I gotta watch you blow your own brains out too?"

Faggin' hell. His blue eyes look so sad I wanna kiss them. Oh yah, that's definitely the drip doin' its work. "It ain't gonna be like that. I ain't gonna... I wouldn't ever..."

"But if it does. If that happens...I know you. You won't hold for that. You couldn't stand for that. Just like Nanni. She couldn't either, bein' all cut up and half herself. It drove her insane." His neck's a web of tendons, and I watch his god-given apple bob with the force of stompin' back a knot of tears. "Andi, it'll eat you alive, and all's left is bones. You just— look, you just can't do it."

"You sayin' I can't take a wallop? That I ain't got what it takes?" I snatch my hand outta his, a flare ignitin' in my chest. "Ain't like you holdin' Elenbar's hand, beggin' her not to go, not to take the risk."

"You can't even straighten it out for an effing clip through the Lane!"

The doc scowls at us, and glances at my drip bag. "Hey, y'all twats need to save it for yer lover's hole. This is a proper medical joint, ya faggers."

Rage percolates like black sludge in my chest, muckin' up my breathin' even with the fuzzy warmth of the drugs. "You don't think I can do it, ain't that right?"

"I don't think it. I know it, Andi. Because I know you, don't I? You gonna get yourself up and killed just to prove a stupid effing point about your ma and the whole—"

"Fuck off then, yah? Don't worry about me since I'm all a write-off anyhow. I'm just a slug ready for the salt!" He reaches for me, but I slap him away, rakin' him with my nails. "Get pissed and let me go my own way, straight into the grave you so ready to stand over. I ain't whacked out like Nanni."

Words sometimes spin outta your mouth faster than you can crank on the reel and ain't no way to bring them back to the private shoreline of your mind. Once it's out on the water, everyone can smell the rottin' stench of your inner shitty self.

"Right then. Guess that's what it is. You effing wanker. Don't die, yah?" Bosco don't even look back as he storms outta the tent.

"Goddamn soap vid. This is a proper medical facility, filled with criminals and peckerwoods." The doc shakes his head, and holds up a vanilla and chocolate Nutri-Shake. "Now, ya want the chalk or wood-chip flavor?"

The Right Way In

"YA SURE YER ready fer this?"

Though Dr. Chambers brought me around with the drip, I'm still shaky and feelin' sick with the come-down off the Flow. My mouth's dry from the Nutri-Shake, and it's helpin' but it's nerves still makin' me sick.

"This is the way in, then?" Of course it is. We're standin' like sewer turds in front of the Central Enforcement office—already a couple clunkers have eyed us up and down as they rolled past. We're about to walk right inside and turn ourselves in. For what, I ain't sure, probably just for bein' alive, bein' a Transgressor, but the thought's makin' me queasy. This is it, though, the fastest way into the Farm and the fastest way to get to the contact.

"Come on." Elenbar walks up the concrete steps to the office. The sign in front glows underneath big yellow lights, neat fancy letters informin' us of the rules and expectations for local citizenry:

TEMPERANCE SOCIETY TENANTS OF HARMONY
1. Obey all Security & Citizen Enforcement officers. They are here for your protection.
2. Comply with all requested biological screens.
3. Restrict out-of-quarter movements after 9:00 p.m. Keep crime at bay!
4. Report Transgressors to your local Social Care office. It is for their protection.
5. Beware of subversive or political incitation! Report those who threaten Temperance and endanger your Society!
6. Association equals prosecution. Know your neighbors, know your Society.

We all knew them well, even riff and raff like us. Signs are posted outside every faggin' neighborhood in the Slums. I've heard the Uppers don't got signs all around like we do here, but maybe they got their own set of rules. Or maybe there ain't no room for signs with their fists shoved up their asses.

Fuck, I'm tryin' to swallow back the bitter slick at the back of my throat. We're at the door and then we're steppin' inside. I swear I almost turn a virgin tail and run. Elenbar's ball-shrinkin' glare stops me.

"Citizen, do you need assistance?"

The voice buzzes from a female-version of a clunk-a-junk Enforcement officer, metallic engravings clearly meant to look like a dome of luscious curls. Even the glowin' eyes are soft and a blue color instead of the angry red of the males. It's all about the "binary gender" as Elenbar always says, like that song from Primary:

Girl and Boy dance together
Happy and merry forever and ever
Hand in hand, heart in heart
Marriage, babies, they'll never part

I really am gonna vomit. I gag a li'l and clamp my fist against my mouth. I muss their shiny clean floor, they'll probably bend me over and fine me for the pleasure.

"Yes. We're—we are turning ourselves in." Even Elenbar sounds nervous.

The officer at the front desk don't respond for a few moments. Then it says, "Do you wish to report suspicious or criminal activity?"

"Well, yes, our own criminal activity. We mugged a woman last night."

The officer again is quiet for a moment.

"When and where did this incident take place?"

"Uh, well, it happened on Eighth Street around seven p.m. We grabbed her purse and knocked her down."

The Enforcement officer's blue bulbs flicker.

"There is no report of illegal activity occurring on Eighth Street at seven p.m. nor any reports in the vicinity. If you do not have suspicious or criminal activity to report, you must leave."

Elenbar glances at me, and I feel a squirm of unease in my bowels. Didn't think it'd be hard to get snatched up. I mean, look at us. Here we are, bold as bourgeois titties, and the damn box of circuits can't comprehend we wanna get snatched.

"Look, we mugged a lady, we stole her wallet even. Bought drugs with it, actually. Flow, Fist, the whole works. We're a damn menace, and if ya don't arrest us, we're gonna go right back and do it again."

"There is no record of theft or assault taking place during the specified times. There is no complaint or response from local Enforcement. Citizen, you must leave this building."

"And what if I don't?"

"Citizen, you will be escorted out by our security officers. Have a nice day." The officer rolls away from us.

Elenbar looks a little panicky, and I'm just as confused. How's a person supposed to get snatched 'round here without actually breakin' a damn law? Elenbar thought it'd be best if we didn't commit real crimes we might actually be called to pay for later.

"Wait, I—we are members of the Trans Liberty Riot Brigade!" Elenbar suddenly leaps up on a chair, spry as a whacked-out gutter fly. "We will fucking burn this place down, ya fascist oppressors of the UFS, eh, ya—ya turd squad!"

Apparently "turd squad" is the magic words to get snatched because out of nowhere roll seven angry-ass Enforcement clunkers. They cuff and shackle us faster than I can breathe. I'm so surprised, I forget to be sick. We're hustled into the back, where apparently gettin' snatched takes you. Elenbar looks pretty pleased considerin' we're bein' scooped, and somehow, I got a terrible feelin' about how it's all gonna play.

Havin' never been in an Enforcement office, I don't have a damn idea what to expect, but I certainly didn't expect boring cell blocks like from an old vid, minus the McFatFat sheriff and a swingin' swag of janglin' keys. I saw an old Western once, snuck in with my friend Oi, back when we were sneakin' outta St. Aggie's. That's before I got signed up with the Brigade. Gettin' snatched over a movie is somethin' we generally try and avoid as part of bein' subversive and stuff.

We shuffle down the concrete hallway, and I instantly see grates in the floor where bathrooms coulda-woulda-shoulda been. Unease cramps my guts worse, and I'm worried I'm gonna be usin' one of those crusted-lookin' waffle holes. The doors and walls of the cells are a mesh metal and they look sturdy, and Elenbar and me get shoved into separate ones. There's a li'l relief in that, that maybe Elenbar don't have to be nose-deep in my shit when it comes. Because it will.

"Citizens, you are bein' detained under suspicion of violating Society Law 5. Please do not resist. Stand by for collection and processing by local Enforcement." The clunker glares at us like it's angry, though it ain't much different from how they always look. We don't say anythin', and it rolls away, single file with the rest of the squad.

"I think I'm flattered," Elenbar says across the hallway. "Didn't know the Brigade left so much an impression. Wasn't even sure the fucks would recognize the name."

"Maybe they weren't sure, just snatched us in case it was somethin' real."

Elenbar's eyes widen, like she hadn't considered that. "Okay, suppose that's right. Well, we're in. Andi, ya done real good, and ya'll stay down as we go, keepers? Don't open yer mouth for nothin', don't answer questions, don't acknowledge anything. When they collect us, we'll be headin' ta the local Farm, and we'll have ta go through some shyte ta get there, but it'll be all right."

"What's it like, the Farm?" I mighta-coulda-woulda-shoulda asked that before agreein' to this death march.

"It's nothing. Big compound, kinda like this place. There's lots of buckets, but more human Enforcers, too. Mostly ya gotta sit through lectures and classes on how ta be right with the law, why it's bad ta be what we are. That's before they ship ya on ta Integration."

Integration. Other than that, it hadn't sounded so bad. I mean, long as we cleared out before we ever got near the snip-snip part, we'd be right knockin' the cock, and besides, Elenbar'd done it before. We could do this. For the first time since leavin' the Brick, I feel things might be all right.

Fag it, though. Should've known the Farm weren't lettin' us leave so easy, not without dear payment to the worst sort of devil.

THE NIGHT SNAILS by, and I end up shittin' and pukin' in that foul piss hole in the floor. The Flow's mostly outta my system, and when it's really gone, I'll stop oozin' out both ends. Though, even after that, there'll be the quiverin' shakin' hands, the crawly feelin' under the skin. I can't help itchin', though Elenbar snaps at me to quit it. As dawn creeps through the hallway portholes, a buzzer sounds, and water hisses across our cell floors, washin' most of the stink and shit away. Not all of it, but it's sweet fuckin' relief to my nose, and I'm less sick without the constant smelly reminder. The bracelets 'round my wrists and ankles chafe like the burnin' piss disease, and I itch at all that, too.

Elenbar heaves a sigh, about to speak, but the bang of the hallway door stops her. We both jerk upright. A muscle in my back contracts from us bein' crouchin' on the floor. My heart's thrummin' away like a buzzin' fuck fly, and I wait for lights to come on. They do in one painful snap, floodin' the corridor with white-hot light; it seems brighter than it'd been the night before. Comin' down the hallway are two Buckets and two human Enforcers. Their uniforms are smart and clean, and the lead, a lady fashioned in brass and black, looks sinister and sexy as fuck. Too bad they were on the wrong side of things. Friends could be made. Coulda-woulda-shoulda.

"Citizens, please rise and prepare for transport," the sexy lady says. I drag myself to my feet, my muscles flarin' with exhaustion like I hardly slept, because I hardly did. Tit to tit, though, I'm glad to get out, glad to be moved, if only to get away from that waffle of shit in the cell floor.

The door sensor beeps and slides open. The sexy lady checks my bracelets and jerks her head, indicatin' I should start walkin'. I obey, glancin' back at Elenbar, who is bein' sussed up by a manfolk type, also in brass and black. She follows behind, and we head back through the office.

The cool air smells like freedom, and I gotta stomp on an insane urge to run, to flee this whole crazy scene. It's too late for all that. I wouldn't get far with bracelets, and besides I couldn't go back to the Brigade, not without Elenbar. P-Hat would shank me and filet me for the evenin' meal, and I wouldn't blame them one bit.

Parked at the curb is a square vehicle, no windows, and it's familiar. They cruise around from time to time, and the Security Enforcement logo is all the authority it needs. Nobody gonna fag around with that mess. Now I get to see what's behind that shiny sinister veneer, and the thought terrifies me. Though Elenbar assured me with all her knowledge and experience, fear still jangles my nerves, amplified by the withdrawal from the Flow. I want a hit so bad I can imagine it, feel it snakin' through my veins, and it brings me some comfort all while makin' it worse too.

We come around the back, and I see the one grated tinted-black window. The door swings open, and inside there's another human Enforcer. This guy's a cum spot, barely a fertilized egg, like he just graduated from a bein' a shit-piece single cell. Ain't even got face fuzzies, and I try not to laugh. Not exactly a terrifyin' figure of authority. He must see my inner and outer sneer because he grabs my bracelets hard, and I almost knock my teeth out on the back bumper of the jail-mobile.

"'Ey! Faggin' shyte, I'm comin', aren't I?" No one acknowledges my protest, pushin' me forward until I've stepped up and in, seatin' myself on a cold plastic bench on one side of the big open square. On the opposite side's another bench, and the whole place could hold maybe six people side to side. The Enforcer sits on the opposite end and glares at us; Elenbar's pushed in beside me. I'm relieved to feel her arm against mine, and it radiates a comfortin' heat, a reminder that I ain't in this alone. The back door slams, and we're plunged into semidarkness. Small lights flicker along the floor, markin' where the benches are, but it ain' much.

As soon as the door closes, cum spot slouches a li'l. He pulls out a com pad and fiddles with it, ignorin' us both completely. The mobile jerks as it starts rollin', and Elenbar elbows me hard. I start to say somethin', but I see she's starin' at me intently. I look out the back window. She's tellin' me to pay attention, so I do, the faint world beyond the window tint sweepin' past as we drive toward the unknown.

We're out of the Grayland Quarter, our corner of the world, within minutes, but it takes a while before we're passin' through unfamiliar country. There's been so many turns and side roads that I'm not sure I could replicate it should I get to. Elenbar's lookin' at cum spot. He's sleepin', his chin on his chest, bobbin' with the sway and lifts in the road.

"We're outta the city center, entering the outer quarters."

It's been so long since anyone spoke, I flinch at the sound of Elenbar's voice. I glance at cum spot again, but he's still snoozin'.

"I ain't never been beyond the Hill."

"Well, now's yer chance to see it clear. Ya can see the fields and farming communes out here. Not much but families and small towns, living off the Society tit in exchange fer slave labor. Still, could be worse fer them. Least the air's a bit fresher here, isn't so much brass, might even feel a little like freedom sometimes."

Somehow I doubt this, but I don't say nothin'. Elenbar's on a roll.

"Look, up ahead, there's some turns I wantcha ta remember. Once we get back out ta the main, I should be able ta turn us back. But last time I got out, I wasn't in any condition ta remember how I stumbled to the road."

"How'd you make it, all banged up?"

"I had help. Jane and Nanni led me out—being half-blind and sick, I don't recall much, but I can get us across the bridge and back ta the Brick. So help me remember this next part."

We've bumped off the main road, as can be seen by the swingin' angle of the back end and the crunch of gravel and loose rocks beneath the tires.

Elenbar ain't wrong. We start takin' a lot of turns, and I try to remember. Right, kinda right, left, right, left, sorta left, semicircle loop, maybe? Right. Already I'm gettin' jumbled, so I just try and remember the feelin' of the turns instead of the words so much. Ain't sure if it's any good, won't until we actually got a chance to act on it. My gut's crampin' again, I got a cold sweat on my brow, and I'm thinkin' I might get sick again.

"Hang it out, they'll scrub it down when we get there; then things'll feel clearer. You won't be so sick, and we can focus then."

"But how'd you actually get outta the place?"

"I know the layout pretty well. I was here fer a while before we made a break."

"So you remember the way out?" I'm hopin' for a plan, for her to tell me the way so in case we get separated I might still be able to creep my way alone. Fear and pain's still hot in my bones.

Elenbar glances at cum spot and shakes her head slightly. I shut my trap.

We've been on a long straight stretch for a while, and we lurch forward as we come to a quick stop. Cum spot jerks awake and shoves his com pad into his uniform pocket. He glares at us like we been dip-stickin' while he's snoozin', and I glare right back. This panty stain can go fuck himself.

The back door pops open. It's gotta be almost noon, and we've been drivin' for hours. Two human Enforcers approach, with two brass rollin' and clunkers beyond them, all wearin' matchin' expressions except for the glowin' red eyes. The closest to me, a piss-haired sap of a man, grabs me by the bracelets. My wrists seethe with pain, and I step out, right onto piss-hair's shiny black boots. I'm grinnin' at my sass, when I hear Elenbar shout my name. I look up, right into the black swingin' stick smashin' into my face.

Lessons for Students

I WAKE UP in hell. The pain screamin' through my brain works its way outta my mouth, and I'm howlin' when I come to. Everythin' is all blurry and hard to see, and I'm freakin'. Maybe I'm blinded for good. Nothin' comes to me at first, and I think I'm in a gutter somewhere, up and drained out maybe.

"Andi! Andi, fucking stop screaming!"

That's a voice I recognize. It's Elenbar, and I try to stop, my bitch-wails fadin' to bitch-whimpers. The pain is so intense, I roll over and retch hard, black splotches explodin' in my vision as I do. Everythin's still kinda blurry, and I squeeze my eyes shut. Elenbar's strokin' my hair, and I'm half curled in her lap, like a vomit-smeared plushie. I try to pull away, but Elenbar holds me firm, and I'm glad for it.

I'm maybe sick a few more times, but everythin's fuzzy so I can't really tell what's happenin'. I think of Ma, of her mucousy, foggy gaze, and I cling to it like a raft in the middle of the roarin' sea. Not that I've ever seen a sea, but the stories at St. Aggie's made it sound mighty fierce, so I imagine I'm on waves and flattened against a whippin' wind. Just me and Ma in a leaky boat, storm swallowin' us all up.

Eventually I come back to myself and the pain's ebbed some, though there's still a throbbin' in my temple. I'm curled on the floor and I open my eyes, slittin' them in the bright light.

"Andi, ya coming back now? We gotta get it together. It's all wrong, I gotta talk ta ya before they come back."

Elenbar's voice is like a streetlamp, and I try to follow that light, not comprehendin' what she's sayin' at first. Then her voice is next to my ear, and I gaze up into her wide green orbs.

"I'm sorry. I thought they'd scrub ya out. This ain't how it was last time. We're in some holding pen, been here fer three days. Do ya remember?"

I don't, but I nod, tryin' to be helpful.

"I know yer hurting like hell, but ya gotta get up. We gotta figure this before they separate us. I'm not sure what's going ta happen, okay? They gotta come back soon." Her voice shakes.

I notice a white film on Elenbar's lips, white and cracked and the overwhelmin' smell of shit and vomit in the room. It's me, my own drippin' mess all over myself. I groan and claw at Elenbar's hand. She grabs it, and I squeeze hard, hopin' she can tell I'm listenin', even if my brain ain't all the way in it.

"Aw, Andi, fuck. Last time we went straight ta the clinic, got cleaned up, sobered out. Not like this, not anywhere like here."

The words flush over me like a deluge of fuckin' firehose rain. I'm cold and tremblin' hard. My body's reawakening, and I wish it wouldn't, the threads of agony makin' me want to retreat back into darkness, into sleep. But a fierce desire to hear Elenbar, to sling my arm around her and comfort her somehow, overtakes me. Painfully, I push myself into a sittin' position. I have to close my eyes again, fightin' the terrible urge to vomit, though somethin' whispers I ain't got nothin' to give up anymore. Besides, if it's been three days, ain't water to spare. As my mind grapples with the words, I realize I'm lucky I woke up at all. My tongue sticks to the roof of my mouth, and when I speak, I'm terrified by the sound of its raspin' whisper.

"How?" It's all I can manage.

"I don't know how. I was spitting in yer maw fer a while, but I ain't got no spit left myself. But it ain't good, Andi, we gotta get a doctor in here. Someone's gotta mend yerdome." There's a strange whine in her voice, real raw fear. I ain't ever heard Elenbar talk like this, but I'm too wrung out to feel much beyond the pain and exhaustion cloudin' me. She touches my temple, and sharp heat twists 'round my head like a bandsaw. I scream, can't help it. She jerks back, blackness on her fingers. Old blood.

"The bleeding's mostly stopped. Shyte, there was so much. I thought they knocked ya outta the world fer good. T—t—they'll be back soon. They gotta come back now."

My eyes are open again, and maybe it's just now I'm seein', maybe I wasn't so clear before, or maybe I just didn't wanna see it, but...somethin's happened. Elenbar's face is like wet newspaper, wrinkled and gray. And it ain't just the cracked lips and pallor of faggin' death; she's hurt or somethin'.

"Are...you okay?"

Elenbar barks a laugh, an ugly dry one. She strokes my hair and looks towards the wall, and I see, well, there's fuckin' chains. Bracelets and shackles mounted to the wall. There's a table too, and the table is smeared with red—with blood, Elenbar's blood, even though her face is all right, and I can't really see...

There are moments you want to forget, times that you wish the mind would up and swallow you, take you away and hide you like a bad kid in a closet. The blood ain't from her face, probably ain't from any so obvious part, that's true; a wet drop, a tear, slips down Elenbar's cheek, and she wouldn't waste no water unless it was important.

Ain't like none of us been raped before. Shit, I been raped before. Life in the gutter means there's a tit for tit chance it's gonna happen at some point, but not like this. Not locked away in some damn dirty hole, surrounded by Enforcers, who are supposed to be keepin' it all locked and safe. No friends to speak of, no one to hold you up, or track down the fucker and curb-stomp their dome into brain pulp. Only me, dead and dyin' in this corner while Elenbar's up on that table, maybe even shackled to the wall. My mind fills with blackness, an angry hollow that must be like goin' crazy, because I feel crazy, the closest to madness you can get without gettin' stuck. Like I might stand up and stagger to the door and find the energy to kick in some marble sacks when they come back. Though it ain't so, couldn't stand if I wanted to, my mind is purrin' deep from the bottom of a well of rage, and rage don't know reason.

"I'll fuckin' kill them."

Elenbar stares at me, and there's no sign of the tear. She shakes her head and pats my back gently. Not much more to say after that.

IT'S HOURS LATER when someone does come, and though my mind still seethes, my body's givin' up, for real this time. I'm shakin' so bad my teeth are clatterin', and though I don't feel no cold, I must be. I'm wonderin' if I'm really gonna die here, curled up in Elenbar's lap, when I hear the footsteps outside. They're heavy and loud, and I'm amazed we haven't heard them comin'. They're right outside, and the door beeps before sliding open.

Four Enforcers step inside. One's the sexy brass bitch from before, and there's a man in a tan suit, lookin' like an Upper cubi-square ready to cruise the Lane. He's got a bald spot on his dome and thin glasses that gleam like water in the light from the singular bulb hangin' from the ceiling. He glances over at us, and his lip twitches. With a smile? A sneer? Disgust? He turns away and motions to the Enforcers accompanyin' him.

Two step forward, and Elenbar flinches like they've up and shot her. I squeeze her hand hard, and one of them wrenches it away. They jerk me to my feet, and I go limp, crashin' back to the ground. The Enforcer shouts somethin' and cuffs me on the ear. I must black out because a few seconds later, I'm being half carried to the door and the Uppers man is shoutin' at the Enforcer, his face a splotchy purple. He looks ready to fuck some puckered ass for all they're clearly screwin' up. Their words all rush together. Elenbar's ahead of me, and we're all shufflin' down a bright hallway. There's doorways, several of them, and then we're outside. The sunshine hurts, my eyes rebellin' against the glare, but even with them shut, the light sears through the thin skin of my lids. My feet are mostly draggin', and the Enforcers' hands dig into my armpits. I want to fight, to bite, to try to stop this insane march. But I think about Elenbar, about what they did to her, so I don't, and I hate myself for it.

There's a beepin' door again and the light vanishes and my feet are bumpin' against a threshold. I open my eyes a bit. We've entered another building, and it's definitely a clinic of some kind. People are dressed in white, bustlin' around like sanitized angels or somethin'. Boxes beep and IV lines pump saline, and it's all like the kinda stuff Dr. Chambers used, but its newer, nicer—shit you see in the Uppers. Elenbar's led to one gurney and sat down by the Enforcers, who look pissed at bein' here, and I let them drag me to another gurney, across the walkway from Elenbar. At least I can see her, but she ain't lookin' at me. One of the Enforcers leans into her face and growls somethin' I can't hear, but she's listenin' and gives the smallest of nods. I've watched Elenbar knock a clunker on its back and beat a gutter punk to a bloody pulp...but I ain't ever seen her capitulate like she is right now, and somethin' tells me she's scared and this Enforcer gave her reason to be. The Enforcer stands up, straightens his jacket, and glares at me. His face twists with, yah, that's definitely disgust, and there's a scar across his cheek, old and mangled, like a bad burn from long ago. I try to glare right back, but I ain't sure what my face looks like right now, so I try my best at a grimace. It probably hurts me more than it hurts him because he stalks off like I ain't nothin' but the wall. Elenbar's gaze is on the ground, and the Enforcer who dragged me is already gone too.

Two nurse-types are talkin' to a couple people who are on gurneys on the other side of the ward. The place could fit in beds, but there's just a handful of us and most of them are lyin' down, maybe sleepin'. I wish I was sleepin'. Or dead. My head throbs like I got a woodpecker jerkin' his knob inside my skull. I lay back and give in to whatever's gonna happen because at least this place seems a lot safer than a bloody table, a bare lightbulb, and Elenbar's tear.

I wake up a little later to a nurse gently touchin' my shoulder. I flinch because it hurts, and she flinches like I'm gonna hit her. I feel bad about it, so I try to smile. Her gaze susses me up and down, and she shakes her head, producin' a needle that's about to go in my arm.

"Wait," I murmer, and then she does smile at me and it's warm, like a bath full of bubbly, and so I just let her do it, and as I sink into the sweetest sleep I've ever slept, I wonder if she might just be sent to kill us all, injectin' us into the afterlife with that sweet, sweet smile. I'd be okay with that, I think.

What We Take With Us

WHEN I WAKE again, I don't feel anything. The pain's burned through every synapse in my body for so long that to have it gone is almost a sadness. Almost. Like a missin' limb or losin' an eye. Chronic nigglin' discomfort's a sensation I'd come to rely on, and I ain' talkin' just the pain of gettin' banged in the head and all the crap from bein' in that concrete hole with Elenbar. *All* of it's gone, even the pain from livin' in the gutter, rippin' from Flow hit to hit. The shakes, the burnin', the pinch of want in my gut; all of it's just gone.

Jesus christ crackers, this bed is so soft... It's a tug off a synth stick or the fuzzy warm when you finally get the wank off. I almost don't want to open my eyes, suppose it's all some amazin' dream, feels too good to just chance lettin' go. I wiggle my toes and flex my fingers, and let my eyes peel open to the world. The room's bathed in soft white light, sunshine streamin' through large windows, curtained by wispy fabric, like steam risin' off the Anacostia River. It's like some version of heaven, the place where God takes pipe rips and passes judgment. St. Aggie's tells a different kind of story, but it's all about the same in my head.

Elenbar. But I'm alone. A couple beds share the room, but it ain't like the great infirmary hall. This is a place to pop a squat, squeeze a nap, curl up for the night; almost like a dormitory at St. Aggie's, but white instead of the gray soap scum of the convent. I manage to clench my gut and force myself upright. Shit, I might even stand up. My bare feet are cold against the white tile floor. Everythin' is so faggin' clean, it's unnervin', but in a comfortin' sorta way. I slip outta bed and stop. I'm... I'm dressed in a...a *frilly* nightgown. My face goes all mad at it, like the place bent me over and puckerfucked me while I was out. Someone, somewhere, stripped me, and stuffed all my sausage bits into the almightiest *froufrou* I've ever been in, and I don't like it. Not one tit bit.

I search for my clothes, but ain't no sign of them, so I turn to the small stand next to the bed. The drawers are stuffed with folded white things.

I pull a few out, open them up, horrified at the amount of lace I'm seein'. I drop them on the floor. It's worse than the doily encasin' me at the moment. I check for any kind of escape. This place is becomin' a Fist nightmare, and I want to find Elenbar and bug the fuck out.

I wobble over to the front door, ain't all steady on my feet yet. I throw it open, half expectin' Enforcers to pop outta nowhere and cuff me or beat me down. But there's no one, and I'm hearin' music, a piano somewhere, and singin'. Lots of singin', like a fancy chorus I saw once on a vid at Christmastime. I mean, the Sisters sang in front of their piano, but it was all black habits and clam faces. "Lift your voices to the Lord." But damn if they didn't look somber as dumpster porkchops doin' it.

I follow the sound of music, and the hallway spits me into a wider one, doors off to the sides. Wide windows face the hall, revealing each room as I walk past. I like this, bein' able to see what's happenin' without havin' to go in. The first two are empty, but there's books and shelves and pictures on the wall. The third room is full of people. Full of...well, of women. They're probably all Transgressors, but they don't look it much. They're standin' on one side of the room, all neat in rows, mouths flappin' all pretty, singin' all pretty, and these powder puffs are dressed in soft white frilly gowns. Like me.

Clearly the faggin' uniform for this place.

Two other ladies, dressed in soft pink, stand at the front. One of them's seated in front of the piano, fingers flyin' like sparrows, while the other leads the singers with dancin' hands.

Then I see Elenbar. She looks like a different species, but I can tell she's Elenbar because she's starin' right at me, green eyes blazin' like she's tryin' to send me messages through my brain. I wave through the glass and she frowns. Her hair is all brushed and...she looks like a vid star, long red hair all washed, and clean, and curled all pretty-like. She's dressed in the same wispy shit we all are, and I ain't ever seen her look anythin' like it. Don't look like the steel sack leader of a subversive underground, of the faggin' Trans Liberty Riot Brigade. She's like a regular girl...maybe not regular, maybe a lot better than regular, but a faggin' *girl* anyhow.

Somehow that shakes me, makin' me cold and prickly inside. She don't look like Elenbar at all.

The conductin' pink lady turns and sees me, her smile stretchin' like it's gonna break her face in half, so big are her teeth, so wide is her smile. She drops her hands and the singers snap their mouths shut. A few grimaces indicate they're grateful for the interruption. It's pretty and all, but *damn* they do sound like a pod of beached whales. The lady opens the door and motions for me to come inside. I ain't sure what else to do, so I enter the room. At least bein' closer to Elenbar makes me feel like I'm doin' what I'm supposed to.

"Do you sing, dear?"

I shake my head so hard it might snap off my twig neck. Last thing I'm gonna do is get up and sing with them. The thought is horrifyin', terrifyin, and all sorts of no-no-hell-fuckin'-*no*.

"Well, maybe next time then. We're almost finished, so please sit with us." She's gesturin' to a chair alongside the wall of the room. The woman turns back to the chorus and lifts her hands again. They all burst into song right in sync with the plinkin' piano, as if they got all the words memorized and know exactly what they're supposed to sing. How they do it I ain't sure, because the song ain't nothin' I've ever heard before. They sing for a few more minutes while I fidget, unsure where to put my hands because the cobweb nighty ain't got no pockets. I'm a bit fuckin' pissy too, as the faggin' thing's sheer in the bright sunshine. Everybody's starin' at my Mister when they're supposed to be singin'. I cross my legs and flip a few of them not-so-subtle high birds. When they stop, the lady turns right back to me and smiles that big face-splittin' smile again.

"Now, let's go find you the proper daytime clothes, shall we?"

Elenbar's stare burns the back of my head as I follow the lady toward the bedroom and, I just know it, back to those drawers full of Sunday supper finery.

I DON'T SEE Elenbar again until lunchtime. The pink lady from the singin' room won't leave me alone and instead bores me with all sorts of talkin'. Mostly lots of talkin' about things I don't understand, like the *fun* classes about how much dick the Society likes suckin'. Right, not really, but it's all a bunch of stuff about how *fun* it's gonna be learnin' about bein' a proper tight twat lady. They even got classes on pluckin' your facial hair and how to host a proper Upper-twat dinner party. Like we gonna be hostin' sandwiches and tea in the faggin' alleyway Brick. But she goes on and on about the *fun* activities we're gonna do. So many *activities*.

My stomach's howlin' by mealtime, so I'm relieved when she leads me into the cafeteria. It's a big wide-open room with one side all windows facin' the greenest patch of earth I've ever seen. Loads of blooming flowers grow in the manicured beds, and the whole thing's so much like a creepy dream it's hard to pay attention to all the little things. Elenbar would be tellin' me to watch what's goin' on, keep my eyes open and such, but I'm so damn lost and feelin' so damn good I've just been floatin' through most of the day.

A line of Transgressors shuffle past trays of food, servin' themselves, dainty as springtime posies. Ain't much talkin', most of them focused on the food, and I see, with horror, there's hardly nothin' on their plates. Tiny scoops of stuff hardly fit to feed a squirrel, much less full big people. Elenbar sittin' at one of the long tables in the middle, and she jerks her head toward the line. I pick up a shiny white plate and join the slow shuffle toward the food. The plate's so light and so clean—I don't think I've ever eaten off somethin' so clean—and then I look at the trays of hot food. I don't recognize half of it. There's lots of colored bits I think are types of plant stuff, and tiny humps of bright white chicken. Stuff you see on vids. Most everythin' I've eaten comes from a can or as a supplement shot, so this all looks weird and too colorful, like a pack of crushed-up crayons. I watch the others, at how they're scoopin' the food, and I try my best to do as they do, though I'm grabbin' bigger scoops because I'm so faggin' hungry, I'm tempted to squat down and start eatin' right in the line.

"A lady must always watch her figure, mind her weight, and maintain buoyancy."

I almost drop my plate. Another pink lady's standin' there, starin' at me. She doesn't have a big splittin' smile, but she's got a small one. Her brown hair is pulled back into a fancy-lookin' tumor at the back of her head.

"I'm so hungry." It sounds faggin' dumb, even to me.

"Hunger will pass with poise and concentration. For now, focus on nourishing your body, and we'll practice more at the next mealtime." The lady moves on down the line, glancin' at plates and not seemin' to care too much about what's happenin'. She speaks to a couple other ladies, and I hear more stuff about *buoyancy,* whatever the fuck that means. I'm so relieved when we reach the end of the line I almost forget how hungry I am. I hurry over to Elenbar, who scoots over to make room.

"Holy horse fuckin', I'm glad to see you." I say it in a whisper because a couple fairies are starin' at me like I'm a floatin' shitbuoy, come up from the toilet to sit at the table with them. Even Elenbar's sittin' like she's got a splintered paddle up her ass.

"Andrea, you need to be careful." She sounds weird too, and she ain't ever used my full real name. Not since St. Aggie's. It bugs me more than everythin' else about this damn weird-ass place, and I wanna shout at her for bein' so fuckin' weird when I need her to not be weird, to tell me what's happenin', to make me feel like everything's gonna be fuckin' okay.

Instead I say, "Okay, what're we gonna do?"

She shakes her head slightly, and a pink lady glides by, head swivelin' like a security cam as she surveys the room. I realize we're the only few talkin'. Most of the others got their heads down, focusin' on their food, takin' tiny bites and chew, chew, chew, chew. I poke the colorful lumps on my plate with the spoon I got and then shovel a good bit in my mouth. I almost spit it back out. It's tasteless. It tastes like nothin'. No salt, no flavor, nothin'. It's pretty, but it might as well be water on my tongue.

My look's gotta say it all, because Elenbar just grimaces, and shrugs, takin' another bite of her own food.

AFTER OUR "MEALTIME," they lead us into the outside. My lacy dress chafes, but when I scratch, people look at me uneasy, so I try to stop. Once we're outside, Elenbar starts talkin', and I'm relieved she sounds more like herself.

"Things aren't anything the same from last time I was here. Well, first with the hole and now here. These...pinkies weren't here fer one thing. It was all doctors and teachers sussing us up. My contacts, who used ta be here—well, they're gone now, ta where I'm not sure. Andi, ya gotta be careful. Don't talk ta no one, don't tell no one anything about yerself. When we were in the hole, I convinced 'em we didn't have any idea, nothing about the...ya know, but I don't think they really believe us, so they'll be watching. They wouldn't shut up about it, were real fucked off."

"Because we said we're Brigade?"

Elenbar's eyes bulge at the words, and I glance around frantic, but no one's close by.

"Don't fucking say those words out loud. Not ever, not here."

"Okay, okay. But is it?"

"I think so. I'm not sure what's happening, but everybody's on edge. What they did ta us when we came in—I didn't expect that, didn't see that coming. Normally they bring ya right in ta the infirmary, scrub ya out. Ya feel good, yah? Fixed yer dome proper, didn't they? Upper medicine will fix just about everything that ails ya."

"Oh cuck suckin' yesssss. Ain't felt so good since I was a mite really. But damn if I ain't still hungry."

"That's all part of it. The poise, being a lady, eating trim. Ya'll never be full, they'll lecture ya ta death about bein' a lady, try ta get ya rehomed, tempt ya with a job on the outside. They want ya ta *want* ta get assigned. Makes it easier, so ya don't go all crazy and kill yerself once yer out."

"Like Nanni."

"Yah, like that. Wait until we get ta classes, if we get that far. I gotta find our contact, then we gotta get out of here. Everythin' feels wrong about this. Things are different and... I'm sorry, Andi, I shouldn't have gotten ya into this." Elenbar looks so sad I wanna loop my arm around her, but I don't, because another pink lady walks past us, starin' at us hard for some reason. She ain't got no smile.

"Look, where's the contact at? Do you know where he...or is it a she...is supposed to be?"

Elenbar shakes her head. "I was supposed ta meet them at the Central Plex, but it ain't even here anymore. Well, not proper. The building's here, but it's closed off, and no one's allowed inside. Looks empty. It isn't good, Andi. How the faggin' hell can I see the signal if I can't get inside? And the contact might not be in there, they might've been moved too, so who the hell knows where anybody is in this damn place? I can't see what ta do, and I never thought I'd come back into this place without a tit tight plan. Not like this."

"It's, well, it's gonna be okay, we'll figure a way outta this. You got out before. I mean, there's a way, we just gotta find it." And the look Elenbar gives me, it's enough to make me cry, though I don't. Tears shimmer in those big greens of hers, waitin' to fall.

Now I understand, and it scares me near dead: Elenbar's terrified we ain't gonna get out at all.

Friends in the Right Places

I'M GONNA GET inside that buildin'. It's my mission.

Elenbar's right. Whoever's inside's probably gone on, been moved elsewhere, but I don't wanna get snipped. Don't wanna be here another goddamn minute. It's the second day in this pit of pink snakes, and I want out. My skin crawls with the wantin'. I've had four meals taste like water and air, and my gut growls with constant hunger. A pink lady scolded me for my grammar—apparently "ain't" ain't a word proper ladies use, and it makes me wanna do it all the more. Elenbar and I are in different Sleeping Wards, and truth to tit, they're conspirin' to keep us apart because I almost never see her at all. Just at lunch and the brief time we get to walk around outside. They're big fans of us practicin' our buoyancy.

"It's time for Domestic Arts," a pink lady chirps at me. Hard to tell them apart, they're about all the same. This one's got bright pink lipstick on too, and I wanna tell her it makes her look like a Lover's Lane Cock Queen, but if "ain't" isn't fit for proper ladies, talkin' about whorin' in the red light definitely *ain't*. So I nod, grindin' my teeth like the dull axe I imagine crackin' her tumor-bun head. She leads me toward the Domestic Arts buildin', and I wanna break into a full-out run, but instead I practice bein' "demure" as they told us in "Bein' a Proper Clam Cunt" class. That ain't the real name, but it's the one that fits.

Maybe I been quiet too long because she tilts her head and reaches toward my face. I flinch so hard I almost fall on my faggin' ass, but she just touches my hair, which is almost as bad. When I woke up in the Sleeping Ward, it became obvious not only had I been stripped and changed into dolly clothes, but they'd mucked with my hair. My blunt-edge shaggy hair is—it's like a wad of dead puppy in my throat just talkin' about it—I woke up with ring-a-ting-ting curls. They'd made it all funny too, like the curls don't come out neither, even scrubbin' at them like I been doin'. And my hair, it's—oh fuckin' god, it's—

"Your hair is just darling, Andrea. Really. I mean, blonde is just so coquettish. So *Monroe*." The pink-lipped Cock Queen flutters her eyelashes at me, but her smile's a smirk. Because I don't look *Monroe* at all. More bleached crack baby stuffed into a frilly lace bag of cross-stitch. I will *kill* this bitch.

She turns away, and I force my feet forward, imaginin' I'm kickin' her face in with every step. We're walkin' past the Socialization Center, right next to Domestic Arts, where we practiced dancin' and talkin' pretty and proper. It's a death march, though I feel so healthy I wanna run circles around the whole place. Maybe launch myself over the nearest faggin' fence and run right back to the Slumland, back to the Brick. The whole Farm is actually fenced in, but they're put up in a way that you don't see them proper until you really look.

But the buildin', the buildin' where the contact's supposed to be, well, looks like all the others. Painted white with pink shutters, but no one comes in or out of it. It's got a digital door too. All the pink ladies got badges to beep through, but the buildin' might not have one that works because ain't no one gone inside yet. Somehow I gotta get a badge so I can go in and check. Just in case.

"Andrea, how are you enjoying your time here with us?" The pink lady stares at me, blinkin' her big hollow doll eyes. They're bright blue like sky, and it gives me pickle skin.

"It's nice here. Very clean," I say, tryin' to remember to be proper and stuff.

"Yes, we work hard to keep it that way. Hard work is the foundation of all happiness, and you've done very well. I'm proud of your progress and watching you brings me such joy. In fact, after today's lessons, we'll be moving you forward. It is time for you to go to Integration. You are a capable and bright student."

"Integration?" The word makes me scared, though I ain't sure why. I block her out, and as she talks, I think about the buildin'.

"Yes, it's the next phase to reintroduce you back into Society; to make you whole and well again. It's the most exciting part of your journey, and you're fortunate to be able to move forward so quickly."

"Well, okay, but what about Elenbar?" As the word leaves my mouth, I realize I've crossed some line, some invisible barrier, maybe the *real* barrier that separates the pink ladies from the rest of us.

"Elenbar? Oh. You mean, Elenora. She had...troubles the last time she visited us. Really, I must say this—for your own good, you should really try to break those associations. If you want to ever be able to go home." She says this with the same creepy doll smile, but there's an edge of ice in her voice, tells me there's a threat there. So I nod, and lucky as a fuck fly on a turd, she leaves me.

The Domestic Arts building is right ahead of me, and I see the doors, painted cheery yellow, as though they promise somethin' fun and excitin' inside. Primary paint or not, ain't nothin' there for me, nothin' there for us, and it's like I'm just rememberin' what the hell we're really here for. Because if Elenbar ain't comin' with me, I'm not goin' nowhere, so I walk away from the door, like maybe I just remembered I gotta piss or somethin'.

I sidle along like I know where I'm goin', and I do. Walkin' with purpose, pretendin' to be where you belong has gotten me so far, and it's a skill that's kept me from gettin' snatched and kept me out of all sorts of trouble. It's helpin' me here too; pink ladies glide by with prim smiles on their faces, not noticin' or just not carin', and either is fine for my purposes. I pass the Socialization Center and slow down because there ain't nothin' this way so if someone sees me, I'm gonna have to pretend I'm lost. I turn the corner around the long side, hidden away from view from the other buildings. Here I'm pretty close to the exterior fence, a mesh-grated length overgrown with vines and grasses, topped with razor wire. The windows are all dark, and I press my face against one, shadin' my eyes against the glare of daylight. The place looks deserted. There's lots of boxes and stuff like storage, mainly. I step back, gut churnin' with the leftover bile of fear.

Overhead, somewhere way high up, the white trail of a plane passes. I wonder where they're headed, who they might be, and what it might be like to fly above it all. What this fuckin' place must look like from the land of clouds. A land of heaven. I get caught up, almost wave, but...I flip them a high-top bird instead. It's stupid, but I'm so disappointed and fucked off about everything, I don't see the brass bitch with the perky tits and pretty face until she's right on top of me.

"What the shit are you doing back here?" She grabs my arm and scares me so bad I bite my tongue, and it's bleedin' and throbbin', and my plan crawls right up my fuckin' ass.

"I was ju— checkin', ow," I mumble, tryin' to pull away.

She glares like she's gonna bum-fuck me with her clubbie and then glances around all suspicious-like. "You aren't subtle, and you've both been a pack of fools. You're lucky contact is even being made. Shouting to clunkers you're all Brigade? The hell were you thinking?"

I realize who she is, who she must be, or I'd already be gettin' a beat down. I open my mouth to speak then, but realize in the same breath it might be a trap. I choke on spit, and my tongue is throbbin', and I'm so confused and lost I'm sure I must look like a drained-out gutter corpse.

"Come on, ya fagger," the brass mutters. She's gotta be from the Slumland. Ain't no one talk like Slumland talk.

"We didn't have a choice. Things, well, things've changed in case you ain't faggin' noticed."

"Augh, your Elenbar tell you that? Yah, she would, spent a pretty time here last time. Look, the contact's been moved. I can't get to him from here. I haven't spoken to him in months; don't even know if he's still in or if he's been transferred. They're getting...*tetchy* around here. Paranoid, doing random checks, and their shitholes were foaming at the thought of the Brigade rabble bein' here."

"They almost killed us when we came in. Worked Elenbar over, hard." I swallow the splintery glass of rage back down into my gut. "I guess that explains that."

The brass bitch sighs, glances around again. "We can't talk. But I wanted to tell you, I've got them convinced to move you on, forged some papers to get you to the next level. I think he's in the Integration Ward now, but you'll have to be careful."

"Yah, they just told me I'm goin'—just before I came out here. But Elenbar..."

"Let me worry about Elenbar. You just focus, move on, make contact. He'll reach out to you. He knows you're in here. I'll try and get Elenbar on this end. I'll try, no guarantees," she says, spittin' into the grass.

"Not very ladylike." I can't help a booty-lickin' smirk. I like her. The feelin' ain't mutual because she gives me a sneer, like I'm a hobo pisspot and turns to walk away.

"Wait! Who's the contact?"

She glares at me like I'm the smallest-minded bean in the whole faggin' pod. "It's Dr. Ellison, 'course."

Integrate

TURNS OUT INTEGRATION *is* a scary thing, and it makes the rest of a Farm look more like a warped sort of heaven. They blindfold me, along with about five other of us lacy train wrecks, and we get loaded into another padded van. My heart's poundin' so hard it's tickin' in my throat. Leavin' meant leavin' Elenbar, and maybe I won't ever see her again. Trustin' brass bitch don't feel right, but there ain't much choice about it, and Elenbar told me to go on too.

When we get to Integration, they pull off the blindfolds. We're in a slick enclosed compound. My stomach cramps harder than the Flow come-ups, and I feel like I could be sick. How the liver-spotted hell are we supposed to get out of here? It gets worse when they open the thick steel doors and lead us inside. The other lacy "ladies" look pale and nervous, but I must look shades from death, just guessin' from how I feel. The clean hallways echo with the distant clang of closing doors, and from somewhere deep inside the steel belly, someone's screamin'.

"Against the wall, slugs," growls a bulbous cyst of a man, his cufflinks gleamin' against the strain of sausage wrists that don't quite fit the uniform. We line up all quiet-like, against a wall, and a pecker squeaker starts takin' pictures of us.

"We'll be taking your measurements, and don't be trying to squirm and get out of it." The Fat Fucker hoists his belt higher, leerin' at us like we're freshly lubed puckerholes. "Well, come on then, take them all off."

I don't look at him as I slide the frilly gown off and let it fall around my feet. The others do the same, and we all stand there, gettin' pickle skin in the cold air. Someone's still screamin' in the distance. My head's funny, and everythin's too bright under the faint flicker of the sterile lights. I look down at my legs—haven't run a right blade over them in months—and at the tight patch of crotch fuzz allowed free rein most of my grown-up life. Nestled in the soft grass of puberty is my mini-man, my Mister, the thing that makes me a Transgressor. A dreaded *s/he*. I didn't ask for it, didn't ever have a choice in it, but it's there all the same, and for the most part, Mister ain't never done nothin' to make my life any worse. Except bein' the reason I'm in the Brigade and why I gotta live in a shit gutter. Oh, and the whole faggin' reason I ended up here. But other than that, I mean.

I peer sideways at the others. The first of us, shaped like a manhole, is cryin', her pudgy cheeks strawberry red and sweatin'. Fat Fucker draws his clubbie, a long black rod, shiny and sinister as a fist fuckin'. He pokes at her thigh.

"Spread them, sister. No one's got any secrets here." He's grinnin', and I bet he's sportin' a righteous stiffy. A sickenin' cramp pinches my gut again, mingled with molten rage as I think about that one tear slidin' down Elenbar's cheek. I clench my fists to stop them shakin'. Don't want Fat Fucker seein' it.

Manhole's cryin' and shakin' her head. "Please, no, please—just leave it, just leave us alone!"

Her head whips back like a crack of lightnin' as the clubbie snaps across her forehead. She collapses like she's been shot. We're screamin', surprised at it bein' all sudden. Blood's poolin' around her, and one of the other brass, the pecker squeaker that ain't takin' pictures, shuffles forward and tucks his hands under her fleshy armpits. He drags her like a sack of rotted meat, gruntin' and sweatin' as he does. A thick smear of freshly pulsatin' head blood streaks in her wake. Fat Fucker's already moved on to the next of us, who spreads her legs without him even askin'. We all know what's what now.

"Ahh, big pecker, you are. Surprised you didn't get shuffled in with the gents. Not that there's any of them, am I right?" Fucker chortles with malicious glee as he eyes her Mister. Of course he's right. None of us get sorted as menfolk. Elenbar tried to tell me once about why there ain't no male Transgressors, somethin' to do with world population bein' all slanted, and honest to tit, I was too spun to hear it all proper.

Fat Fucker's buck teeth poke out beneath his top fleshy lip, and I envision stuffin' my fist in his gut, rippin' out his insides, and feedin' them to his fat fuckin' face. Then he leans forward, producin' a tape measure from his pocket. She squeals as he—I wish I couldn't see it—as he grabs her mini-man and stretches it as far as it'll come easy. It's like a shriveled prune and it's tryin' to hide, tryin' to retreat back into the body where it's safe, but he yanks harder. She's really cryin' now, knees quiverin' like a newborn calf. He stretches the measurin' tape alongside it and clicks his tongue. His assistant, a big hulkin' brick of a man, punches the numbers into his com pad.

Fat Fucker's on the move and I look away. I mighta once been curious to see what others got swingin' between their legs, but not anymore. This is just the worst sorta fuckin'. I been held down behind Jerry's Pub more than once, cursin' beneath the gleeful grimace of a tourist trout, but it ain't nothin' like this. They can rape the body, but it's the mind that is a fragile, fragile thing. Livin' in the gutter, you learn to live with the desecration of your goodly bits; it's just the fact of life's shittier parts. But you learn quick to guard the mind, to build walls to keep the rest of you safe. Long as you got space in your head, you'd get by.

This is so much fuckin' worse.

"Hey, you right cunt. Spread them."

I don't look at him because I don't wanna see that shimmer of excitement swirlin' in his piggy pockholes. I spread my legs and clench my teeth.

"My, oh my, what a lovely pecker ya got there. Truly, a gem. Smallest of the lot, a mere kernel." He pinches it, hard, and I can't hold back a groan, pain shootin' deep inside my skin pouch. I glare at him, so pissed I'm tempted to let him knock me flat just for the pleasure of sockin' him one, but he's lookin' right back at me, and I see he's darin' me to. He *wants* me to. Then I know. What must happen to those who get knocked flat, and I won't do it. I ain't gonna let this sweatin' pig have the body too, not if I can help it. I stare down at my pecker instead.

Once he realizes I ain't gonna do or say anythin', he measures it. The assistant punches in the numbers, and they move on to the last of us. Soon it's done, and they shuffle us forward, naked, through another set of locked, grated doors. Here it's a long hallway with li'l rooms on either side. Somewhere someone's screamin' again. They're cells; we're in a prison. They shove us into them, one by one, and I'm surprised to see I've got a roommate. She might have long curly locks, but she's all butch.

"Well. You're just a little peachfuzz, aren't you?" She grimaces and tosses a set of clean pressed white scrubs at me.

I dive into them so fast I almost trip right on my faggin' face. She doesn't say anythin' for a while, lyin' back on the bottom bunk and starin' up at the ceiling. I'm grateful for it, tryin' to get right with myself, tryin' to settle my heart and the pain in my gut. I'm fuckin' hungry too, like rage has carved away the last of the water calories.

"It gets worse," she finally says.

The screamin' in the distance stops with a squeal, and the cell block is plunged into somber quiet.

"The fuck is all this anyway? The measurin'? This...prison thing?"

"They gotta remind you who's in control. Besides, I think security gets upped because, if you knew what's coming, you'd climb any damn fence trying to get away," she says.

"And what is comin'?"

"Well, they're going to cut your wanker right off."

I feel a squirm of sick, but she's right. That's exactly what they'd do. Lucky Lips—I mean, Lucy—had it done. Gone from she to a real *she* with one snip. I mean, but you sign up for that shit, they make you want it, like Elenbar said. They work on you until you're ready as you're gonna get. They don't just... Well, they do, as it turns out.

"I mean, they can't just do that. They try to break you down, convince you to give it up, ain't that it?"

She looks at me the same way that brass bitch did, like I'm a dumb peapod. "Choice is the greatest illusion ever perpetuated upon men," she says. "Look here, peachfuzz, you ain't got no choice. They try to wear you down, sure, to try to keep you from offing yourself once it's done. They'll start the injections, get the hormones going, and eventually, once they think you've given up, they'll take you in and complete 'Integration.' Trust me, it's the only way outta this fucking place."

Is this the only way I'm gonna make contact? Get reassigned, lose my Mister, become like the masses? No longer Andi, a Transgressor, a...a...for-real she, trapped in frills and lace, servin' throbbin' pricks in booby bars? A slag for the Society, livin' off the tit, doin' their biddin'? Like Lucy?

I try to stomp on Bosco's voice, itchin' at the back of my brain like an oozin' scab, but it's the itch of someone else bein' right. And of you bein' so faggin' wrong.

"Have you...you know?"

"Hell no. Wouldn't be here now, would I? They move you past, into another ward to recover and begin the transition process back into the world. Last stage of indoctrination. Nah, I keep 'em guessing, telling 'em I'm fantasizing about death." She holds up her wrist, and I gasp. Black ugly stitches squirm through the pale skin.

"Had to really convince 'em too. But I think my time's about up. They've been pumping me so hard with the psych drugs it's hard to think, hard to piss, and I can't rub a decent one off in months. Ain't a life worth living really, and I don't want to be here anymore."

"Where is Dr. Ellison? Is he here?" My throat's slick with traces of comin' vomit.

"Well, I mean, yah. He's the one who's gonna cut it off, ain't he? He's the only doctor in this place."

Cut it off. Then I do vomit, and it's clear and like water. Just like the food, just like everythin' about this nightmarish hole I've come to live in. My roommate grimaces again, but she don't act surprised. She hands me a fresh folded pillowcase, and I wipe my mouth with it. It smells like bleach and perfume.

"My name's Tandy," she says.

THE MORNING SIREN goes off. The whole block is still pitch-black, and I stumble off the top bunk, bangin' my shin hard on the metal rail of the bed.

"Fuck, fuck, mother fuck!"

"Watch that mouth, Miss Sass." Fat Fucker is outside our cell, us bein' the first on the row, and I shut up, not wantin' to give him an excuse to come inside. Tandy's already up, quietly makin' her bed in the dark. I grope for my sheets, doin' a messy job of it. The lights snap on without warnin' and I groan, blinded by glare.

All the doors open with a digital chime, and we step out. I follow Tandy, watchin' her for what to do. She moves with a familiar step, casual and calm. At the end of the hall, a whole crowd of Enforcers stand with arms crossed. At the opposite end, there's more there, too. They lead us through another set of doors, deeper into the guts of the buildin', and it's even darker and colder in here. We walk through a couple more blocks, filled with Transgressors just like us, gowned in white linen scrubs. Then we enter a wide room with spigots on the wall. It's a damn shower room. I shudder at the thought of Fat Fucker gettin' another free show, but Tandy is already naked, not payin' any mind to anyone, so I follow her lead.

The water is fuckin' frigid. I turn it all the way over and look at Tandy. She's scrubbin' with the tiny hand towel they give us, ain't no soap, and she don't even seem to notice the cold. She's done in less than a minute and shuts off the water. My teeth are already chatterin', and I try to scrub but my muscles are seizin' from the shock of the cold. Finally, clean as I'm gonna get, I shut off the water. The others from the block, maybe twenty of us altogether, are standin' there, a few of us shiverin' with blue dead-hooker lips. The rest already got the routine, and like Tandy, they don't seem to feel the wintery chill. They usher us into another room and then step out, leavin' us alone a brief moment. A whoosh of air, not quite as warm as the air off a sewer drain, rushes over us until we're dry, and I'm grateful for it. Then it's on to the next room, where there's new clean linen outfits piled in neat rows. The Enforcers move with a practiced gait, like Tandy, but always with one hand on the butt of their clubbies. I wonder how often they get to use them.

The next room is the cafeteria, and I give quiet thanks because my gut is hissin' and yowlin' with hunger. It's the same setup as the Farm, and I fall into line, surprised to see cheese, gravy, and other decadent eats. I heap it on and see others are too. No one stops us. There ain't any pink ladies floatin' around, tellin' us to watch our waistlines. This might be hell, but hell's got damn good food.

I wander over to where Tandy's sittin' and plop down. I shovel the first bite of food in my mouth and moan. It's delicious, fuckin' delicious. No vapor here, no watery, tasteless substances. It could be Ma's cookin' if I ever had a ma off the cock and pipe long enough to cook, and it's far better than anythin' at St. Aggie's.

"It's good, huh, peachfuzz?" Tandy's face is frosted with sweet amusement.

"Oh, it's so good. I could stay stuck here for a while with food like this."

Tandy shakes her head. "Not once you realize what it's all about."

"Huh?" I mumble through a mouthful of mashed potatoes.

"They're feeding us a rich high-calorie diet so we can be flush and ready for the surgery coming up. There's all sorts of vitamins, supplements, and hormones in the food you're eating. They work hard to make it taste good."

I stare at my plate. Hormones, supplements, vitamins... It looks like nothin' but plain delicious goddamn food, and I'm pissed because it's so obvious. Of course they would. Eat as much cud as you want, you faggin' clueless cows.

"Go on then, nothin' you can do about it. Starving yourself won't do any good. They'll just strap you down and tube-feed you. I tried that. Might as well enjoy while you can." She takes another bite of her creamed spinach.

I sigh and shove another bite of potatoes into my dry mouth. It don't taste so good this time.

Human Contact

"ALL RIGHT, GET up and keep your hands up." Fat Fucker's standin' outside the cell, and he taps the bars with his clubbie.

"Where are you takin' me?" I try to keep my voice neutral, but my heart's tickin' in my throat.

"Doc wants to size ya up, make sure you're in good health. We live to serve around here, or so they say." He chortles like a ruttin' pig.

I glance at Tandy, who shrugs. Ain't nothin' else to do about it, so I keep my eyes on the clubbie, put my hands up, and approach the door. They beep it open, and waitin' for me are two more Enforcers in the hallway. Place is crawlin' with faggin' brass. I follow Fat Fucker, and he leads me through a side door, instead of toward the showers. The door opens into another hallway, and there's a few turns before we come to another clinical ward, like the heavenly-lookin' place I first woke up in. Smells like antiseptic and clean cotton, familiar smells, and it comforts me a bit.

"Now sit down and don't cause any trouble for the doc. I'll beat your damn head in if you do." He wags his clubbie at me, and I nod. He motions to the nearest gurney and then turns and leaves. I'm surprised by this, but the door beeps locked behind him. Two nurses mill about, checkin' on the other patients. They're awake and alert, not lookin' like people who've had their willies nipped off. One, lookin' hardly old enough to bleed, even laughs, talkin' to the nurse. I fidget and swing my legs over the side, feelin' like a mite waitin' for a checkup.

"Hello, Andrea."

I whip around. A man stands there, with rimless spectacles, dressed in a doctor's coat and carryin' a com pad. A small badge around his neck identifies him as Dr. Ellison.

"I'm sorry, I didn't mean to startle you," he says, brows arched with concern.

I must be gawpin' so I pull myself together. "Uh, no, I'm sorry. Tired's all." Again, I try to sound neutral, try to sound like "Hey, I'm not a secret resistance fighter here to make contact with you." Not sure it works, but Dr. Ellison smiles and steps closer to me. He looks at his com pad and taps the screen a few times.

"I have here that you are nineteen years old. Is that correct?"

"Yah, that's me."

"And your ident is 346721?"

"Uh-huh."

He frowns as he reads somethin' else. "It says here you have no residential address." He glances up at me, and his light blue eyes are penetratin'. "Are you homeless?"

"Uh, well, um. Yah, kinda. I guess." I'm turnin' red, my cheeks burnin'.

"It's all right, many of our patients who come here are. I want to make sure we connect you with a residential coordinator who can help you get back on your feet, find you a place to live, maybe help you find a job?"

I don't say anythin'.

He nods as if I've agreed. "So, we're here to do an initial exam, address any health concerns you may have, and discuss the transition process that is coming up for you."

"You're going to cut it off," I say flatly. Ain't no point beatin' around it.

Dr. Ellison frowns. "The removal of the secondary genitalia will help you in many ways."

"Oh yah? Like what?"

"There are many possibilities, depending on your unique physiology. There are additions and implantations we can provide."

I think of Lips, I mean, Lucy—her tits snug as a fist in a puckerhole. "Like, uh, givin' me a bona fide rack?"

The doc doesn't smile. He adjusts his spectacles. "Some women regain menstrual cycles with removal, even without hormonal supplementation, though most do require an ongoing maintenance dose. Many of you also do not have fully developed reproductive organs, but with surgery we can shape a new system, allowing you to participate in the PERMIT program and maybe have children someday."

"All these are soundin' like bold-ass negatives, Doc. I ain't a—I mean...I'm not a woman. Ain't gonna be, no matter what. It's up here that matters, yah?" I point to my head in case the doc's slow in translation.

The doc crosses his arms and nods. "The mind isn't something we can replace, no. We can't fix how you perceive yourself, which is why transition is so hard sometimes. Remember though, you were always meant to be a woman." He holds up a hand because I'm about to drop some truth on him, and there's—well—there's somethin' in his eyes that makes me stop. A glisten of...well, of somethin'. "Nature is not always perfect, Andrea. Nor are people. But we can give you all the resources for a healthy and happy life in the Temperance Society. And after all, it's our duty to our species." He smiles faintly, and the glisten in his gaze is gone. "To preserve the integrity of the female sex, these surgeries are essential. There are hardly any natural-born females anymore. If we didn't— Well, it isn't an option. These other biological benefits may seem lofty, but the most basic benefit to you, of course, is bringing you in compliance with the law. This is not a punishment, though it can be a frightening prospect for new patients. We are here to support you and get you through this."

"But I ain't just a female. I'm... Look, I'm Andi. Rearrange all you want. Ain't gonna change what I am, natural or not."

Damn, if he really is the contact, he plays slick. I watch for some sign, some betrayal of his alliances, but there's none. He's calm, collected, and completely well-versed in his role. I'm gettin' nervous. I wish Elenbar was here, here to tell me what to do, to talk to Ellison herself. My head's spinnin'.

"Are you all right?" He peers at me closely, lookin' genuinely concerned.

"Yah, I'm all right. I just feel a li'l woozy."

"Yes, after mealtime, that can happen. I'm sure they've told you about the supplements and hormones you're receiving?"

I nod.

"There will be some dizziness and there may be soreness and changes in your breasts as the treatment continues. There may be effects upon your menstrual cycles, if you currently have them, which we will monitor and provide support for. These are all normal and to be expected. We will do what we can to make you comfortable, but most of the side effects resolve themselves in a few weeks."

"Weeks? How long am I gonna be here?"

"Had your parents brought you in and had you undergone assignment at birth, it's hardly an overnight stay. I'm—and I apologize for the assumption, but I assume your parents are also transient?"

I don't know all the words, but I get the gist. "My ma's a hooker, if that's whatcha mean."

He nods, lookin' over his glasses at me like I'm somethin' fascinatin'. "Well, sometimes people are woefully uneducated about what assignment really means. But in answer to your question, puberty complicates things. What I mean is, your timeline depends on your progress, your compliance, and our surgical schedule. There are many young ladies here like you, and it can take time to get everyone scheduled accordingly. We do strive to have patients transitioned out of the facility within six months."

"Six months?" My heart is poundin' hard again. I don't wanna be here six months—shit, I don't wanna be here another six *hours*. "Look, six months is—it's... You can't make me do this. Really." There's a click in my throat, and I hate the whine I hear. But what Bosco said is true. I can't—I *won't*—let this happen.

"I understand it is scary this early on." Dr. Ellison leans forward on his elbows and gazes at me through his spectacles, his eyes doin' the shimmer again. "You will adjust, and we do try to have ladies transitioned sooner. Again, this is not a punishment, only a program to help you come into compliance and rejoin Society, achieve Temperance." He smiles then, and it looks so sincere he must believe it.

Desperation sets in, and I gotta try.

"Doctor, um." I look at my feet, grapplin' with the right words for what I gotta say. "You ever heard of this group, they call themselves— uh, what was it, uh—the Brigade?" I look up and try to give him a pointed look.

"Never heard of them," he says, face placid.

My gut cramps, and I got a bad feelin' about this. About all of this.

"Now, shall we get started?"

Precious Intel

TANDY'S CHEWIN' THE nail of her index finger, reclined on the bottom bunk like a prison Queen, when they usher me inside our cell.

"How'd it go?" she asks, gazin' at her fingernail like it's a steak dinner.

"Uh, fine. The Doc seems nice enough, considerin' he wants to chop off willies all day." I scramble up to the top bunk and huddle on the thin mattress. Truth is, my head's spinnin' terrible with anxiety and fear. Dr. Ellison didn't give nothin' away, and this whole thing's seemin' a right mistake. *What intel am I supposed to be gettin', anyway? How the tit-fuckin'-hell am I supposed to do it with my willy still attached?* I wish Elenbar was here, and the wantin' is so bad I bite on a knuckle to keep the sob tucked back in my throat.

"Well, I don't know about that," says Tandy from below me.

My brain starts whirrin' and thinkin', interruptin' my pity party. "What do you mean?"

"About wanting to cut off willies. Doing his job, isn't he? He's getting along to get along, I think. Maybe just wants to make sure it's done right. There's horror stories, about other doctors who were here before him. Mangle you so bad you'd be lucky not to die of infection or worse, be crippled from the waist down. Might never leave the infirmary."

"If he didn't want to, he'd find a way to leave. He'd find a way to escape this place."

"Have you? Even with the burning desire you got to escape, have you? From what I've seen, and I've been here a long time, none of them are allowed to leave. The staff, I mean. Everyone's the same, except some of the underlings get shuffled out now and then."

I'm quiet because I'm thinkin'. Tandy might have more info than she even knows she's got, and I gotta get what I can, but I've gotta be careful too. *Trust no one.* That's Elenbar in my head again.

"Tsh. He seemed pretty up in the business of gettin' it done." I try to sound a faggin' prat about it.

"Well, he's been working with me a long time. I've been here a while, as I said. Been here since before he came along, and he's much better than the last sadist here. One tried to convince me to let him sew up my twat and scoop out all my inner lady bits. Said it might chill me out some. I got a knock on the head before they could pull me off from stompin' his kidneys. He wasn't here long after that."

"Faggin' tit shit. How long you been stuck in this sewer hole?"

"Mmm, been almost three years? Dunno, time goes by slow and then real quick."

I'm glad I'm on the top bunk so she can't see my gapin' mouth and look of pure fuckin' horror. *Three years? How could anyone stay upright and sane?* My respect for Tandy blows out the goddamn roof.

"That's...impossible," I breathe quietly.

"Yeah."

We don't say anythin' for a while, and I manage to doze off for a while, before jerkin' awake to a sudden rude bangin' on the bars. Fat Fucker jitters his clubbie across them like bowstrings again.

"Get up, bitches. Mealtime, oink, oink," he says before continuin' down the line.

I swing off the top bunk. Tandy's risin', serene as a fuckin' paintin' of sunset. It annoys me bad.

"Has the doctor ever said anythin' about you gettin' out? Without gettin' the chop-chop, I mean."

Tandy stares at me and don't say anythin' at all.

I SEE DR. Ellison again the next day. He's hummin' when I come in, reviewin' stuff on his com pad. He looks up and smiles like he's really glad to see me, like a straight-laced grandpop from a store ad. Gray hair and spectacles make him look harmless as puddin'. And everyone likes puddin'. Hard to believe he's the one doin' the snippity-snip business. It's nice, li'l creepy, but makes me like the nutcracker a bit.

"Hello again, Andrea. Please have a seat if you're comfortable. I'd like to do another examination and have some blood drawn. Is that all right?" He motions to the bed sheathed in white paper. We're in our own room this time, off the main clinic.

I squirm a little, rememberin' the exam from yesterday. Wasn't much, just pictures and measurements...again.

"All right."

He nods and smiles like a dandelion pokin' up from a sewer grate. I sit myself on the gurney and take off my linen uniform. Might be prison garb, but it's a faggin' lot better than the doily dresses at the Farm.

"Hey, Doc, I got a question for you." It pops into my head without takin' the time to squat, and I hope I don't regret my spurt of inspiration.

"Sure, ask away." He doesn't look up from the com pad.

"So...why's there, you know, so many uh, Transgressors now, anyway?"

Then he does look up and even puts the com pad down. "Well, that's a good question. There's a lot we're not sure about, even now. Around the year 2050, we began to see a significant uptick in the amount of individuals born with ambiguous genitalia, along with other intersex deformities."

I ain't ever thought much about other kinds of Transgressors bein' possible, though I know ain't all Misters look the same. *Huh. What other types of sorry sacks are roamin' the world with warped crotch parts?* But I don't wanna interrupt with stupid-ass questions.

"So we just started bein' born? Just randomly?"

Dr. Ellison smiles like I'm a quaint child. I wanna kick him in the head.

"Well, nature is rarely random per se, and there's a lot of questions regarding certain endocrine disruptors present in the food and materials we used a lot back then. But even after those were outlawed, the trend continued. It could be evolutionary, but there are other possibilities, as well." He turns and prepares some syringes. He's gonna be pokin' me good. There's a lot of empty tubes, lookin' like anal suppositories, and I'm glad ain't any butt stuff happenin' here. Anal's the worst.

"So then when did the Society start sendin' us all up to Farms?" I don't actually care why the fuckwads felt we needed to be rounded up, but I gotta keep him talkin' somehow.

"The Temperance movement had foundations as early as 2020, but the intersex trend added significant fuel to that fire." He scans a few of the tubes with the com pad, checkin' one of them twice, to be sure, before he continues. "There was societal backlash against the special interest parties and the gender politics of the time. They said people were becoming too flexible, and when the Wall was built, other social policies came under review. That's when Temperance and the governing body we call the Society was founded in earnest and eventually the gender assignment processes were put in place."

I mean, I guess all that's supposed to be interestin' and it's important, but damn. Dr. Ellison ain't ever gonna be teachin' history, I hope. I stifle a yawn.

"But why's it gotta be like this anyway? I mean, why's it so bad to be us? To be a Transgressor, you know? We were born like this, ain't done nothin' to no one." I'm thinkin' my way might be workin'. Maybe he'll reveal somethin' more, and I can suss out whether he's still with the Brigade or not.

But he don't even blink, just gives me that placid frog face like he's just waitin' for the next lily pad to jump to. I'm likin' him less.

"It's the law. Our duty is to be in compliance with Temperance and the Society statutes. It's the way it is. Now, Andrea, which arm would you prefer to have blood drawn from?"

Escape

WHEN WE GET to the cafeteria, the line is crammed with people already. More than usual, and there's some I ain't ever seen before. I glance at Tandy, but she don't give any sign she's noticed or cares. She's probably seen it all before.

"Bitch, get outta my way!"

Two spider-lookin' Transgressors are circlin' each other like there's a juicy fly about to get divvied up.

"If you don't get the fuck away from me, you're gonna be hard up with a pockhole fer a mawhole!" snarls the lanky blonde.

The other, a bullface with red hair, brings her tray up and cuts across, slappin' the flat end against blondie's angular cheekies. Then the fight's on for real. Blood's gushin' from blondie's busted nose. Enforcers trickle in, and they're wadin' through the surgin' crowd gatherin' to see what's what. Everyone loves a fuckin' fight.

"Cocking cunts, out of the goddamn way!" Fat Fucker's face is bright red, and he's huffin' as he pushes people aside, tryin' to reach the chaos in the center.

"Let's go." Tandy grabs my wrist, *hard,* and pulls me back toward the entrance. I protest, cranin' my neck to see what's goin' on behind us, 'cause shit, I like a good fight too, when the lights suddenly snap off.

The dark explodes with caterwaulin' and screamin'. A few flashlights snap on automatically, cuttin' thin laser points in the dark. Some are whoopin' and laughin'. Bodies writhe, and I smell pit sweat. Everyone's jostlin', and someone knocks a knobby elbow into the side of my head. I shout and stumble, but Tandy drags me upright, still holdin' my wrist in a deathly hard grip. My hand's throbbin', but I focus on followin' as close to her bulbous ass as I can. The large space closes around us, smaller as we enter the hallway. The digital door ahead blinks and turns green. It musta beeped, but I can't hear over the din of shoutin', screamin' curses, and laughin' comin' from the cafeteria. Tandy slides the door open, and the dark's real deep in here, no light comin' through any windows or nothin'.

"Tandy," I whisper, but she hisses at me, pullin' me faster. We're joggin', and it's a blind-man's grope because I can't see nothin' at all. Tandy stops, and I run into her, and we both almost topple right fuckin' over. We're at the second door, and we must've taken a detour at some point because this ain't the way back to the cell. The door's light is green, and it's quiet enough now to hear it beep.

"Where are we goin'?"

I'm ignored as Tandy slides the door open. As sudden as they went, the lights snap back on. I'm blinded, black fuck flies buzzin' in my vision. We both freeze, and Tandy glances around real quick before joggin' again. She lets go of my wrist, and we're sprintin' hard now, down a corridor with lots of doors on either side. Never been in here before. The digital door at the opposite end has a glowing red light, and through the square plexi window, on the other side...on the other side I see...

"Elenbar?"

Her big green eyes shine with somethin' like joy as she smears her palm against the glass. I grab at the pane on my side, imagine squeezin' her cold bony fingers, my heart about to explode like a bloated slab of road smear.

Behind us, two Enforcers step through the door.

"Hey, you stop right fucking there!" They're already drawin' their clubbies and one of them has a com pad and types somethin' into it. Everythin' explodes in a blastin' wail and red and white siren lights begin flarin' in the hallway.

"Andi, hang on! Just another second!" Elenbar yells at me, but I'm lookin' at Tandy who's glarin' at the Enforcers. Her eyes burn with a flare of hatred, white-hot hatred. She looks at me.

"When the door opens, you run and run hard. The doc'll meet you on the outside. Trust him, trust him with all you got. It's the only way out." Then Tandy rolls up her white linen sleeves and launches.

I can't help it. I turn and watch. Tandy's body becomes sleek and light, duckin' the first Enforcer who swings wide with his club. She's wide and bulky, but moves like a righteous angel layin' some epic jesus shit on risin' demons. It's like all the only good parts of the bible.

The second Enforcer drops his com pad and it's crushed beneath the soles of her stampedin' feet. She flings her large mass against him and sinks, shit, she's sinkin' her teeth into his neck. He shrieks so loud I hear it over the wailin' sirens. The other Enforcer comes up behind her, and doesn't miss this time. Tandy collapses forward, releasin' her jugular bite. Blood sprays in an arterial spurt from the chomped neck, and he claws at it, tryin' to stop it up with his hands. Their feet are slidin' in the spreadin' pool of hot black blood.

Then Elenbar's hands are on me, the door is open, and we're runnin', runnin', runnin' so hard toward the exit, toward freedom. *Tandy*. I hold her in my mind, say a silent prayer she somehow makes it, survives, and then focus all I got on the door ahead.

The outside entrance is a thick slab of steel, but it's propped open. Dr. Ellison is there, motionin' with his hands to hurry. He don't got glasses on now. We burst past him, and he falls in beside us, runnin' like someone a lot spryer and younger. The night is thick and cold, and it feels so damn good, tears streak my face.

"Where do we go?" Elenbar's breathy and anxious.

"There's a car, back here, we need to hurry. I was able to get the keys out of the security office, and they should still be there. Look, they traced the break in power faster than we thought. They'll be looking, and they'll see I'm missing when they bring the wome—people—to the infirmary." Dr. Ellison says it all in a rush. *People. He called them "people," not "women."* And he's ain't wearin' white scrubs anymore; he's in black slacks and a black jacket. He ain't goin' back. This is as much his break for freedom as it is ours.

"How? Wait, why?" The cold air chafes my throat.

"Because. We need to get you back to the Brigade, and then we need to move you all out. There's much more happening here than you think. A lot is moving behind closed doors, and they're about to start the sweeps." We follow him around the corner of a buildin', followin' the fence line topped with snarlin' barbed wire. Spotlights scan the perimeter. "I couldn't... I can't let that happen. People *are* listening. To the Brigade. Come on, keep moving. The car—it's over here."

My heart's poundin' so loud it might as well be on speaker. I wanna hear more, but I also want to get outta this puckered shithole so I say nothin'.

Elenbar is still holdin' my hand, and she squeezes it hard. My chest is gettin' tight. The car won't be there, it'll be gone, somethin' will have fuckin' happened, and damn it, *damn* it, they're comin'!

But the car *is* there, a gleamin' black T-Class model, and it looks like money because it is. It's parked among a bunch of other clean cars in the bright bold moonlight. Serious cash got dropped for this kind of shine, and I've only ever been in one once, when we boosted it for stash change from the Uppers.

Elenbar rips open the backseat door, and we dive inside. Still smells new, like a fresh cock rubber mixed with old cowboy boots. The Doc slides in front, pawing at the controls. He frowns and turns toward us.

"Get down, as low as you can. Try and disappear. I have to disable the system and drive it manually. It's—it's been a long time, so just hang on. I'll tell you when we're out. I'm taking a back road, through a side gate. Lillian said she would leave it open. They would never let me through the main gate." Seems he's talkin' to himself, his eyes wild and wide. He's scared, maybe even more than us, but we do as he says, curlin' up into the foot depressions of the backseats. The windows are tinted almost black, and it's a moment of comfort, bein' curled up in this space, just me and Elenbar, breathin' heavy in the quiet. But my head's imaginin' Enforcers rippin' open the doors, draggin' us out, and sickness twists inside my guts.

The car revs, and we skid hard, gravel plinkin' against the underside right under my head. We jerk and bounce as the doc rockets the car forward.

"Do you think we'll make it?" I wanna hear Elenbar's voice, want to hear her reassure me for real. My hand gropes and finds hers in the dark. They're cold.

She looks at me, close enough I can see tears shinin' in her eyes.

"I don't know. I don't fucking know, Andi. It's so much worse than I thought. Shit's outta hand, fucking everywhere."

The words flush me with cold fear. "What do you mean? What's worse? We're gettin' outta here. Once we're back to the Brigade, we'll figure it out. And we got the doc now. He'll tell us what's what." My words sound good to me. They sound good and safe and hopeful. Then Elenbar digs her nails into my arm.

"The Society knows, they've got eyes on everything. The Brigade might be scattered. Everyone's gonna be in hiding or maybe some got scooped. Might be...might be fuckin' dead. Look, I found out the Brigade...it's everywhere. Groups started springing up all over. That's what got the Society's attention—it's been growing. There's been rioting in some of the boroughs. Bombing. News got it locked down so we wouldn't know. Wouldn't..." She glances up at the doc's shaded profile, grim and determined as he jerks the wheel. "Wouldn't coordinate efforts. Look, the doc...he's... Well, he's got his own ta do. You and me, Andi, we're going ta the Wall."

"The Wall? What the faggin' hell for?"

None of this makes a singular lick of sense to me.

"Shit!" the doc yells as the tires squeal against asphalt.

We get thrown backward as he gasses the accelerator, and I'm so scared, here in the dark, can't see shit. It ain't cozy and safe no more. The car's a rocketin' portable coffin for the livin' dead. I get up; I have to. I can't die not seein' what's comin'. I peek over the door. Several cars weave through the night, their shinin' headlights like alley cats lookin' for rats. Lookin' for us. I peer through the windshield. Doc's shut off our lights completely, and darkness hurtles toward us. I let out a suckin' squeal of terror, and dive back down beside Elenbar.

"They're gonna catch us." My voice squeaks.

Elenbar's starin' at me, eyes wide. I want her to say no, to tell me I'm wrong, like she always does, but she don't. She looks like she believes me, and I hate myself for sayin' it at all. The car turns hard, and we come skiddin' to a halt. The engine dies, and I wait for the doc to holler surrender, to give us up, but instead he ducks, too.

"Stay absolutely silent. We're hidden in these trees, and with a lot of luck, they'll slide past us. Just stay quiet, stay calm."

We lie there in the dark, breathin' and starin' at the black windows, beginnin' to fog from our breathin' so hard.

We hear the car before we see its headlights, the sound of its tires churnin' against dirt.

"Well...shit." The Doc sits up. He straightens his black jacket like he's goin' to a meetin'. Like it's a day at work. Just another day. "Sneak out the back if you can, run straight north, and there's the river. Get in, follow it—it's your only chance. I'll try to, well, distract them, keep them busy. I'm sorry. Sorry I couldn't get you home. And...well, for everything else too."

I clamp down on the sob tryin' to come out between my teeth, drawin' blood from my scrap of lower lip. I grope for the door handle, the one opposite the direction of the oncomin' car. The creak as it opens sounds like a thunderclap, and I wriggle through, droppin' onto moss and damp dirt. My prison garb soaks through at the knees. My hands are numb. Elenbar's right behind, clippin' my back with her knee as she comes. I belly-crawl away from the car. But I ain't got no idea where the faggin' hell north is, how to find directions, what the fuckin' hell a gutter shit like me knows about findin' anythin' anywhere in the woods, in the dark. Panic's chokin' me. I can't breathe.

Elenbar punches my calf and I look. She points skyward. Up there, glitterin' in the night sky is a bright star. One of the few we can still see. Shit, well, it's the faggin' *North* Star, ain't it? It's like the story, a story Sister Jordana told me, about blackies crawlin' to freedom, with a North Star leadin' them all the way.

I crawl toward the star, freezin' and wet from grass, mud slickin' my arms and belly. I shut out the world, shut out all sound. Nothin' but the Star. Follow the Star. Somewhere, floatin' around in the world I'm shuttin' out, is the sound of the doc talkin'. The shoutin' for him to get down, to put his hands up. Then gunfire, and screamin', screamin' is all I hear, not sure if it's mine or the doc's, and suddenly I'm plungin' forward, tumblin' down an embankment. I hit my chin, teeth snappin' together hard, and stars are spinnin' over me, around me, then I'm plungin' into icy black water. I grasp toward the surface, lungs and body spasmin' in the worst cold I ever felt. I cough and suck in air, strugglin' against the violation of water tryin' to gush down my throat. I look for Elenbar, but water's in my eyes, my teeth chatterin'. The current is fuckin' strong, and I can't paddle against it. Can't navigate at all. There's a moment, a moment of fight, but then I surrender. I surrender to the all that engulfs me, to the nightmare all around me, and the bellowin' gnashin' river swallows me up into its cavernous belly, carryin' me to destinations unknown.

Elenbar.
Elenbar.
Elenbar.

Home Sweet Home

I'M AWARE OF it bein' bright, so bright I cover my eyes. My body's hot, skin feels too tight for my innards. I try rollin' over. Pain shoots up my spine, knifin' me like a switchblade, and I cry out. Smooth stones dig into my shoulder blades. Then I shut my maw because everythin's comin' back to me and I'm rememberin' where I am. The rush of river still roars in my ears.

And Elenbar.

"Rise and shine, ya sleepy maggot." Elenbar's speakin', and my eyes water and sting from the sun and heat. I sit up fast, though it hurts. Sun radiates from behind her silhouette like a faggin' angel of deliverance. Her dress from the Farm is smeared with mud and ain't white anymore, lookin' more like a toddler's underpants than lacey fashion. In her bionic hand, she's holdin' some black-lookin' berries and extends them to me. I shake my head. I don't feel no hunger yet, only pain in my back and hot syphilitic thirst ragin' in my throat.

"Where the bucket-fuckin' hell are we?"

"Ya don't remember? Ya saved my life. Dragged me up out of the river, and we've been drying up on the shore ever since. I'm guessing we're quite southwest of where we were."

"Where the hell is southwest?"

"Keep walking this way and we'll hit the Expressway. I think. We should get moving, try ta get back ta the center. Hitch a ride, maybe, if it's safe."

My head's foggy, but I remember the dark, the freezin' water, and maybe, yes, findin' Elenbar, grabbin' her head, and haulin' it up. It's all cobwebs, but my body's screamin' with pain, so I musta done somethin' drastic. I don't swim more than a limp-dick paddle in a kiddie pool. Fear's an amazin' thing sometimes.

I struggle to my feet like a hundred-year-old mummified sack of shit. Elenbar helps me, her metal arm flexin' and strong as a baby ox.

"Surprised the clunk-a-junk's waterproof."

"Wasn't gonna settle fer bottom-barrel tinker-toy shyte. Should've made ya pay fer it."

"I'm sorry for that."

"Yah, well, don't matter now at all. Though I thought ya'd stay off the juice longer, just outta respect, considering I'm always saving yer junkie ass from something." Her voice ain't hard when she says it, but my guts turn to lead. Because she's right, of course she's right.

"I need to drink somethin'."

"Don't drink that water, though we probably did enough of that last night. Stuff'll make ya sick. Shouldn't even be swimming in it, but can't be helped. Water's crawling with sewage sludge and the slough off the mills up yonder way."

"Lovely. I coulda done without any of that."

"Well, fuck it, we'll hose off when we're able and top off the empty tanks, keepers? But right now we gotta go. Gotta keep moving."

"The Doc? And, oh god, Tandy." My heart ticks in my throat thinkin' about that butch warrior goddess.

"They done their part, gave their lives like we woulda if it needed ta be done. Remember them, but remember them by doing yer part. We gotta live on, ain't no life going to waste."

"Are we too late? What you said, what you said last night about the Brigade... Is that up and up?"

Elenbar gives me a look chill as a fuck in a fridge. "Can't think on that. It's gonna be what it'll be. Lot of people gave their all ta get us this far. The Doc gave me what he could, and we'll use it as we're able. But he didn't—well, bein' stuck on the Integration Ward, he wasn't sure what the current status was." Elenbar sounds stronger, like she did before goin' to the Farm. Like bein' back in freedom's reminded her of what she is, a tiger back in familiar jungle.

She keeps helpin' me, and we hobble together, slippin' a little on the loose stones of the shore. The bank gets steep on either side, and we have to get on all fours and scrabble up the grassy slope. I'm exhausted and weak, like a bagged and suffocatin' fetus, newly born and dyin' all the same. We walk through a large field, and the grass is nearly as tall as we are. The sun's burnin' hot and strong against my neck, burnin' my chicken-pale skin. Ain't no buildings or smog to filter out the killin' sunrays. Fatigue chomps away at my vigilance, and I might not care if clunkers did pop outta the trees. Long as they brought bottles of water and let me lie down a while.

We come upon what I guess is the Expressway, though I ain't ever seen anythin' like it before. Only seen it on Brigade maps of the surroundin' quarters. It's huge and loud, cars flyin' by at speeds unthinkable. Elenbar makes us lurk in the brushy overgrowth a while, watchin' the types of cars drivin' by. She's watchin' for some sign of Enforcers or clunkers, but we don't see any. Whatever commotion mighta gone on, or whether they kept lookin' for us, ain't no sign of it. This makes Elenbar twitchier, and she flexes her fingers, poppin' them loudly until I almost can't stand it. I end up bein' the one standin' on the side of the road, universal thumb stuck in the wind.

A while later, a honkin' behemoth truck pulls over, and we climb up into the cab. Driver's a friendly sort, and he don't mind our stink and sweaty mucked-up mess. Fact, soon as we slide inside, he's chatterin' nonstop about everythin' from weather to his mother to his four kids and his cunty ex-wife. It's just as well because neither of us are in the mood to talk, so we let him go on and on. He even gives us some warm stale water from bottles that taste like there was booze in them once. Ain't until he wants Elenbar to take off her dress that we make him pull over and let us out.

We're in the Upper Subs already, and eyes are instantly on us because we stand out like dirty crotch sores between pretty legs. My linen scrubs are prison issue, and Elenbar looks a bit too much like a gutter slag who enjoys makin' mud pies.

"Just keep yer eyes ahead. Like we know where we're going and working on walking through," Elenbar whispers at me.

"The clunkers are gonna be on us, keepers. These pucker princesses probably got Coms to the brass right now." My heart's jackknifin' in my chest.

"Knockers. Just keep going."

We're slinkin' through some clean-pressed neighborhood where kiddos are playin' in a paved cul-de-sac, and I smell the twinge of smoke and sizzlin' meat. My mouth waters, and I'd trade all my Flow and a free pop-off for just a bite. I can't imagine havin' a BBQ in the Grayland Quarter, though gutter flies would be all over it and peeps'd be pinchin' your steaks right outta your teeth. We follow along fence lines and back alleys, stayin' outta sight as we're able, but everywhere we go, parents shift nervously, waitin' for some sign we're causin' trouble.

But soon enough the Burbs fade into more familiar streets, drifts of newspaper, pop cans, and liquor pop shop signs signalin' the change. Even Uppers gotta get their kicks somehow, and tucked against the edges, you could still get booze and some more basic delights. We sidle past a boobie bar disguised as a boxing club.

Then we hit the Slumland Bridge. The bridge marks the edge of the Inners, the Anacostia River creatin' a convenient barrier between us and the rest of them, and here, just to make it clear who we're faggin' with, is the Devil's Line. Of course, ain't no real devils except in the bible, but close enough. The steel cages sway a little in the wind comin' up off the river. The bones of the once captive are still inside them. A few leg bones and littler ones have fallen through, and the ground's littered with the bleached twigs of once-complete people. They've all been picked clean by eager birds, bugs, and the passage of time. The cages still hang from the upper rail of the bridge as a reminder. These are from the K Street Riots. A bunch of Transgressors and starvin' gutter flies rioted and tried demandin' food rations from the Society. Clunkers rolled in and caged up the whole leadership. The Society fuckin' lubes up with irony, watchin' starvin' people starvin' for complainin' about starvin'. Shit, been about ten years. I gaze in at one of the grinnin' skulls as we walk past, and when we step onto the steel platin' of the bridge, I salute them. I always do.

"Shit ain't shit, Andi. They're dead and gone on."

"Still. They were fightin' when we were just crotchspawn. Might not be us without them."

"They weren't any good at it, though. Rioting out in the open? No wonder the Society scorched them out, and look where it got them. I ain't ever gonna be up on this bridge. Ya neither." Elenbar spits off the bridge as we walk it.

"Least they did somethin'. Went out fightin' for somethin'."

"Nothing came of it though. A waste of lives."

I say nothin', though I don't agree. Elenbar's about results. Results that don't include hangin' until you're nothin' but bones. Can't fault her for that.

"Holy horse fuckin', smell's about ten million worse since last time we been here," I say, lookin' for a change of topic.

"Well, look at it." Elenbar gestures to the sludgy brown current below us. "A cesspool of waste and dead bodies."

"Like a dysentery diaper crawled right up my nose."

Elenbar snorts a laugh.

"Ya ever think about writing half yer shit down? Ya got a way with words. Slumland poet. Put ya in charge of our brochures, how about it?" She socks me in the arm, but I don't laugh because even though it does smells like shit, my heart purrs like a ruttin' tomcat. It smells like shit and looks like shit, but we're almost home.

Once we cross the bridge, we're only a thirty-minute walk from the old territory. I walk faster, the aches and pains of my body stretchin' and easin' for the first time all day.

"Wait, hold up. We gotta talk. We need ta figure our plan first." Elenbar's slowed way down, eyein' the streets with nervous anticipation, sizin' up every person walkin' past us like they got pockets full of pipe bombs.

"Right, right. What're we gonna do?"

"We gotta be careful. They might be surveilling the place, watching fer us ta come back. They might know about the Brick."

"Shit, I don't buy that. Ain't no one gonna tell them about the Brick."

Elenbar looks at her slippered feet, and I realize. I realize what's happened.

"You told them? *You* told them?" My voice squeaks with the shock. Rage prickles in my veins.

"Ya were out. I thought ya were gonna die. Maybe I shouldn't've given a fuck, but I did, and here we are. They piled a gang on me fer all my trouble, too, and ya almost died anyway. I'm a fucking twat. I know it." Her voice shakes.

Though I hate her just then, I also can't purge the image of that one tear, slidin' down her cheek. In a dark room sour with my own vomit.

Anger seeps outta me like a pair of crotchless panties, leavin' me nothin' but drained. I slip my arm around her shoulder.

"Well, thanks, you sentimental twat. For tryin' to save me anyway. Look, we made it. Even if they figured the Brick—"

"I didn't tell them exactly where we're all at," Elenbar says. "I told them we had a gang, the Brigade. I told them some stuff, but I tried ta play it down, tried ta...make it seem like, ya know, we were piddly road-gang cucks. I don't have any idea how much they believed, how much they...shyte."

I'm sorry for her, and I ain't ever felt sorry for Elenbar before. She'd be more likely to beat my ass for it, but now she's, well, washed out. Though my gut's sick at the thought of them gettin' scooped because of what Elenbar mighta said, I'm sicker about the one wanker who'd probably be fine if he got scooped: Bosco. I mean, if they don't string him up for runnin' around with Transgressors.

Already we're on the outskirts of Grayland Quarter, and we know the way home like we're already there. Takin' the side streets, we make it to the Brick as it's startin' to get dark, though we skulk in an alley across the way.

"We just gotta lay low fer a while. See if anyone's around or if they're still doing runs." Elenbar's eyes flick back and forth across the small courtyard where the Brick sits.

"P-Hat wouldn't leave for long. Not with you leavin' her in charge. She'd stick around." Just thinkin' about P-Hat's massive stacked body and square jaw makes me feel safer.

"Yah. She fucking better."

We squat and wait. Though I'm jacked with fear, fatigue is leakin' through again. My body's creakin' and new aches are howlin', but still no one stirs. No one comes or goes. Except for the roar of traffic from Previce Avenue, place mighta been deserted. My skin's crawlin' like I'm on the backdraw from the Flow.

Then, finally, a mop of tomato hair appears. It's Pint. He sidles out of the opposite alley and slips through the Brick door, which slams shut behind him.

Warmth gushes through me, and I'm so glad to see him, to see *anyone* from the Brigade, I break into a run. Elenbar don't say nothin', just follows close behind. I burst through the door, the sweet smell of familiar dust, dirt, and stale beer flushin' me with joy. Pint's eyes get wide as he sees us, and in two steps, I'm at him, throwin' my arms around his neck and squeezin'. Then I smell it. The tangy sweet ethanol whiff of Biff smoke. Biff ain't somethin' found much outside Lover's Lane or Tivoli land. It's pretty hard to score at all, but already my body's twitchin' at the thought of a hit, just one.

"Pint, you holdin'? It's good to see you, faggin' cuck!" I punch him in the arm. I'm lookin' for some sign of his aerator, a baggie, some sign of the Biff treasure coursin' through his puffy jugular vein.

He's smilin' at me, and then he sees Elenbar and grins even wider. His eyes are glassy and kinda wild. A chill passes over me.

"Pint, you all right?" I shake his arm a little. It's all quiet in the shack. The place is awful empty lookin'. No warmth from the barrel stove. No sniff of fresh pit sweat. Like no one's been here for a while. "Where's everybody? The fuck is everybody else?"

Pint starts to giggle, a maniacal crazy squeakin' giggle.

I look over at Elenbar, and her hands are shakin', face splotched red and pale white, danger simmerin' in her deep green eyes.

"What did you do? Pint! What did you *do*?" Elenbar stalks right over to us, and before I can say anythin', she swings hard, crunchin' his nose with her steel knuckles, powerful enough alone, but now fueled by rage.

Pint's blood spurts across the concrete floor, and I stagger back, watchin' her bionic fist rise and fall, again and again and again.

And again.

Keeping Up Appearances

I DON'T THINK Pint'll ever be the same. Elenbar beat him so hard my guts liquified, and I finally pulled her off, though I got a few knocks in my facehole for doin' it. We're pantin' and huffin' as Pint bleeds, squirmin' and moanin' on the ground. His cock-tip haircut's matted with thickenin' blood, like hair gel.

"Ele, what the fuck?" I can't remember last time I called her that. A li'l girl name, the name they called her at St. Aggie's. She hated it. Once upon a time, long before the Brigade, she was Eleanora, Ele, and I was Andrea. Now, I can't look at her. Too scared to look at the snappin' snarlin' beast standin' where Elenbar used to. Her muddy front, once a doily dress, then a gutter rag, now's a modern art piece, spattered with Pint's still-warm blood.

"Piece of fuckin' shyte, I'll gut ya ta the spine," Elenbar mutters and rummages through the shelves, cupboards, and backsacks scattered all over the faggin' floor. She snaps up a few scattered rands on the ground.

The place is trashed beyond understandin', beyond reason. Even if a pack of gutter flies and peeps had broken in, robbed the joint, it wouldn't've looked like this. Almost everythin' is gone. The books, the maps, the layout of Grayland Quarter, all gone. We never put down the names of our people, code names, and all that covert shit, but a lot of other intel and brain knowledge is gone for good. The Enforcers been here already.

"Fuck, fuck, motherfuck!" Elenbar kicks a piss bucket across the floor, and it clatters hard against Pint, splatterin' him with piss and more of his own blood. She crouches beside him and gnarls her fingers in his wavy dark hair. She jerks his head so hard I think she's gonna twist it clean off the bone stack.

"The faggity hell! He can't talk with you all kinked. Give it a second, let's think about this." I say it because Pint's one of us, been since I was a mite. We even dunked our chubbies a few times over the years. I gotta say somethin', have to, even if he's a bleed-out traitor.

But Elenbar's got eyes on me, and I don't like what's in them. They're burnin' hot, green and gold rage focused like laser points on my face.

"He let them in. Where is everyone, Andi? Are ya paying the fuck attention? Did ya not fucking *see* what's what at the Farm? How many dead just in the time it took us ta get outta there? Where is *everyone,* Andi? He's the only one left? Just hanging out in the Brick like he's king of this motherfucking castle?" She stares down at the crunched-up body of Pint. A spit bubble of blood pops between his lips. "This fucker, this dead faggin' fucker I'm gonna bleed out, but first he's gonna tell me where the *fuck* everyone is and what the fuck he did ta get them there!"

Pint blinks through the sheetin' red, his eyeballs rollin' in pits of coagulatin' blood. Elenbar squats and grabs him by the back of his hairy dome.

"Geruff...get 'reffs," he mumbles through swellin' lips.

Elenbar sneers and releases his head. It drops with a wet thud against the concrete floor. Pint, faggin' Pint, manages to roll to his side and spews a horrible soup of yellow foam, the Biff streakin' it pink.

"What happened?" I crouch beside him, eyein' Elenbar as I do it. With the rage flappin' her sails, I don't trust her not to kick *me* in the faggin' head.

Pint's eyes lock on me hard. "They...sefa fas'." Blood sprays as he breathes heavy, his nose a plug of mucous and shattered bone.

"They came in here, took everyone. How'd they find you? Where were you? Where are they, Pint? Where the fuck is everyone? Are they at the safe houses? Did they make it?"

But he's already shakin' his head kinda, though it's more like a lollin' flower head on a broken stalk.

"Did they get them? Did everybody get picked up?" My stomach clenches. They could all be headed to the Farm. They could all be right where we just were. All this just to trade the entire crew? I feel like spewin' my own addition to the soup seepin' down Pint's front and all over the floor. I don't got a strong stomach for most things.

Pint's eyes roll again like he's noddin' out good, probably gonna be gone for a while, but then he focuses and grabs my hand. His knuckles are scraped clean to the bone from gnashin' against the concrete floor.

"De— They dead. K—k—illed them."

Elenbar squeals a sound I ain't ever heard, a mouth suck of rage whistlin' out the smear of her twisted mouth. I don't look at her because

I'm cryin'. I was before he'd said it. Because of course they were. Of course they're all fuckin' dead. Found right in the Brigade center, not just a boastin' shit talk in a clunker station, but actual proof and presence. None of them woulda gone quiet.

We're crouchin', cryin', snot runnin' down our faces, and I think of Ma again, cobweb eyes, saggin' tits. All for naught. Wasn't that all it was? For naught? All the work we'd done, the raids, when we hit Second Avenue and smashed a clunker to the bolts, everythin'. We'd been so bold, so faggin' sure of our comin' victory, that knowledge would set us free. But we're done. All done.

"W-we gotta get outta here." My voice's a snotty snivel in the dead air. Everythin' smells like vomit and tears. Pint's passed out at some point, don't know if he'll be comin' back, but the hard pit in my gut tells me I don't care.

A clatter outside the joint makes us all jerk, even Pint, though all he does is moan. Elenbar's up like a Flow jacker and creeps to the door, hands clenched around a length of splintered wood someone ripped off the doorframe. We're still, waitin' for the proverbial dam, for the whole clunker force to burst forth, to crush us.

"'Ello?"

It's a mouse of a voice and it ain't no clunker. A face appears in the doorway, white as bleached bone. It's Minnie, and I let out a hard huff of air, hurtin' my ribs doin' it.

"The fuck? We're about ta be jumpin the river, ya shit rat," Elenbar hisses and snatches Minnie by the collar. She shoots one wild glance around the street before jerkin' Minnie inside.

"Peepers! I was hiding, waiting for someone to come back. T-they...everyone..." Her eyes are wet, but they ain't runnin'. Cheeks are whore rouged from the tears she been cryin' long before.

"Yah, so Pint said." I nudge him with the toe of my slippered foot. Still got Farm-issued pink princess flats on my feet.

Minnie glances down at Pint, shakin' harder as she sees the blood, then looks up at me, at Elenbar, like we're clunker spies. With Elenbar's splattered attire and my crack-baby blonde makeover, we must look like poor replacements for former steel-sack Brigade members.

"Minnie, what happened?" Elenbar's voice is real quiet, dangerous-like. My stomach's squirmin' as I hear her say it, and I hope Minnie's got sense in her bunny-fuck head. Her eyes get real wide, and she's lookin' at me again, nervous.

"Well, I think, I think they mighta been scopin' it for a while. Few days after ya all went in. Saw this Upper chumsucker hanging around on the street fer a few days, but he kept whistling at me and I figured he was looking fer some dip-stickin'." Her eyes are rollin', real nervous as she looks at the ceilin', the floor, anywhere but Elenbar's burnin' glare. "I ain't trying to run that no more, so I just ignored him, like, thought he'd go on and he did. Then the next day, they showed up. Elenbar, it was bad. I was just walking, about to go see Dr. Chambers. He's letting me help at the clinic now, did I tell ya? Gonna make me a real nurse—"

"Minnie, what happened next?" I'm tryin' to keep her on the road, her spinnin' glassy gaze tells me she's Flowed to the gills, and Elenbar's rage is makin' the room a hundred degrees hotter.

"Oh, well, I was walking and heard the yelling. They started firing right away, P-Hat was, well, yelling something, ain't sure what."

"What about Pint? The fuck was this motherfucker?" Elenbar wrinkles her nose and growls a wad of spit right onto his twitchin' body.

"Uh, he was inside when I was there. Don't know what happened after that. Ran, didn't I? There wasn't nothing I could do, Elenbar, I swear to Flow Jesus, I woulda helped, but I wasn't even holding a stick with me." Minnie's eyes fill with tears all new and fresh, like she's just again rememberin' everyone's fuckin' dead.

Elenbar growls like she's gonna kick Pint again, but she doesn't. She squats, glances around the place, and snorts. "Right—we're out then. Andi, grab whatever yer gonna need, and then we're gone outta here. Fer good."

"Where we going?"

Elenbar's eyes still burn with rage but mingled with somethin' else, a cold certainty that says she's got a plan and it's happenin' right fuckin' now.

"Andi, we're going ta the Wall."

"So you said before, but goin' to the Wall to do what?" My rapid heavy pulse makes my head ache.

"We're leaving, leaving the United Free States of Liberty fer good." Elenbar rips off her smeared dress and throws it at the wall. She's naked but for a pair of white cotton knickers, and somehow, it's all the more frightening. Minnie whimpers as Elenbar stalks over to a crumpled cardboard box in the corner and rifles through a pile of clothes, jerkin' more usual gear over her head. She hops into a pair of tight pants—look like they mighta belonged to Pint maybe—and for the first time since we went to the Farm, she looks like herself. Rabid, spittin', furious, but herself all the same. Panic is settin' in. I look at Pint, at Minnie's big dinner-plate pupils, and we're fuckin' leavin', really leavin', for good...

"Faggin', hey, wait, just *stop*! Just stop, for a—a second. Tell me what the hell is goin' on? I went with you, went all the way, and I still don't got no goddamn cockring idea about nothin'! *Why* are we goin' to the Wall, and why are we goin' right now? What did they tell you? What the fag we gonna do when we get there?" I'm squealin' like a trashbin baby, but I don't care a tit lick about that. My head and heart are poundin' in sync, and for the first time in a long time, I'm together, focused, and awake.

Elenbar stares at me hard, maybe sussin' up whether she can blow it off for a while. Then she sighs. "Come on, grab yer shit, and let's get outta here. It ain't safe just now, and I'll tell ya all I been told. They're gonna sweep back, especially with word of us escaping. They will follow."

She's right, but my questions are a load of splintered glass I gotta swallow . So I busy myself with dressin' and preppin' a backsack of my own, though I can't tell you all I stuffed in it, my head swirlin' with the questions and wonderin's.

Elenbar turns to Minnie, who's still leanin' against the wall, shiverin' and lookin' down at Pint's twisted beaten body. "Minnie, ya good? Ya got a place ta go? Ya need ta get outta here. Don't pock it for Pint. Seems he's got friends where he needs them."

"Yah, my ma's got a shop. I can hang it there fer a while. Ya'll really going, huh?"

I nod. "We're gone. But it'll be back. We ain't done, not even close. We'll be back in a big bang sorta way so keep your ears to the ground, eyes to the sky, knockers?"

Minnie nods, and I pull her into a squeeze. Her body's a chopstick in my arms, all hard and stiff. I don't blame her, not at all. I look at Elenbar and nod.

"We gotta go one place, though." I say it because it's gonna be my last chance.

"Huh?"

"I'm goin' back to St. Aggie's."

St. Agatha's Residential Home
for Needy Youth

ST. AGGIE'S IS a glorious heavenly spear juttin' from the mucky swamp of the Slumland. The Sisters told us it was the "Holy Spire," a signal some still wanted to suckle at the puckered teat of the divine. Well, they didn't say it like that, but it's around about the faggin' same. You can see the phallic tip from most parts of the borough. Those stained-glass windows are about the only bit of beauty in the whole Slumland, though it's tucked up on one of the nicer sides of it before you cross the bridge to the Uppers. Still, couple of those pretty windows are boarded up. Ain't everybody got respect.

"Hey, let's stop it up a sec. Before we go in all hell-bent, I gotta tell ya something." Elenbar touches my arm, and we slink up against the brick façade of a line of row houses.

A couple peckerwoods are slingin' a block down from us. Their thick hair's pulled back into a bulbous scrote on the top of their domes, a mark of the Tivoli Clan. Keen eyes rake over us, but then they're lookin' on for customers sneakin' in on the block. A couple Transgressors ain't no threat around here. We were customers once too, and I feel a pull of wantin' because I know they're hawkin' Flow.

"Andi?"

She's been talkin' at me.

"Sorry, what's the faggin' waggin'?"

"Look, at the Farm, after ya left, after ya went on, I talked ta that brass cunt fer a bit. She weren't the contact, but she knew a pinch about it all. Least what she knew most recent. I'm gonna guess the doc weren't able ta tell ya much?"

"Not a tit bit. We didn't talk about any of it, it all happened...too fast." My gut clenches, rememberin' the smell of new car leather. Gunfire. A freezin' river. Drownin'. "What'd she tell you?"

We pause as a deep-seated rumble begins, the familiar growl of shiftin' ground remindin' us of the tectonic world still deep below us. A few windows rattle in their frames, and an old yellowin' one shatters, sprinklin' the alley below it with shards of glass. But the earthly growl passes like all the others do, nothin' left in its wake but a few squealin' car alarms and a cussin' Italian woman, examinin' her broken window.

"There's been a lot of movement up top. Orders come down from the Society—sweeping out the Brick's part of that. They're gonna start them up again. Traitors to Temperance, executed without trial. Remember the Charlie Riots?"

I nod, though it's from before I was even a knocked-up egg. The stories live on.

"And they're making moves—now, look, don't go all crazy, knockers?—but they're gonna sweep the other parts of the network." Elenbar rests her hand on my shoulder.

"Keepers..." I don't like where this is goin'.

"They know about Josiah and even Dr. Chambers. So, yah, they got info on St. Aggie's too. They might even know about yer ma. Look, now, *look* at me, Andi."

I hear Elenbar, but I don't either. My head's sloshin', and I'm thinkin' about cobweb eyes... Elenbar shakes me, hard.

"Right, okay, right."

"When we go in, we've got ta be quick out too. They might've hit it but maybe not, and they could still be watching. Are ya sure we gotta do this? We can't get pinched up here."

"We've gotta tell them. If they don't know. There's...fuck, there's li'l mites in there. What's gonna happen if they don't know? I couldn't carry that on. They're just babes. Li'l ones." St. Aggie's is just across the street, and I'm sweatin' like the walls and alleyways got eyes on us, but I gotta go tell them. They might still be able to get out.

"Knockers. That's why we're going ta the Wall anyway. There's a— well, intelligence has been saying fer a while that there's a radio tower on the edge, outside the Wall, and outside the interference the Society pumps across all the band lines. That's why no one calls in or out. All those Coms? We're only getting what the Society wants us ta get. We've snipped little pieces here and there, but most our intel comes from in-person contacts."

"I got it, least I got that much." I'm lookin' at St. Aggie's, wantin' to ditch the talk, but we might not get another chance so soon.

"So we're sending a call fer help."

"To who? Who the ruttin' hell we gonna ask for help from?"

"I got, there's...yah, it's a long story anyhow, but I got contacts from long ago. Old friends who know what's what. Remember what we've said about the blockade sittin' in that ocean out there? The thing blockin' the UFS in and keepin' us from skitterin' away in boats? Long as we don't get scooped, we can get through the Wall and get ta the radio tower... Look, I'm not letting the Brigade go down without a fight. The intel I got, it's old maybe, but it's what we got. What the doc said, about the Brigade spreading, more people startin' ta rise up and fight? Now's the time. We're not backing down, we're not going ta hide. Not when the word's gotten out and others are fighting fer it too."

"So we're gonna go to this, uh, radio tower and hope someone's still listenin'?" This plan sounds like a gutter fly's shit sack, undigested, and pocked with poor plannin'.

"Basic like that. We've gotta try, Andi." She don't blink.

Well, I've always been a fan of bad ideas, and this whole year's been a long string of them. "Right. Well, knock the cock. Let's get goin' before I change my faggin' mind."

I glance across the street and then back at Elenbar. She's ditchwater pale under the light of the overcast sky. We ain't eaten since—well, since a while, and the runnin' and fear gnaws at us. But ain't no time for none of that.

I step outta the alley and make a straight approach to St. Aggie's. Figure ain't any point bein' coy about it. If they're watchin', they'll see us anyhow. Elenbar's at my back, and I hop up the long stone steps in two strides. Fear's loosenin' my bowels.

The smell's somethin' you don't forget. It's a sliver of memory embedded in your core, like a hangnail in that soul they're always talkin' about. Stale Sunday incense and mildewed tapestries linger, like nothin's ever happened but church within these walls. But any of us who been here know that ain't true. Beyond the stacked stone walls is the true miracle. It weren't pretty, but for most of us, St. Aggie's was sanctuary.

I search for some sign of a Sister, a bobbin' blackhead somewhere in the pews, but there ain't none. This makes me more nervous than anythin' else. I glance back at Elenbar, but she's watchin' the doors we came through, jittery like we just ripped off a tourist trout.

"They might be at the school. Or back in the hall." I say it in a whisper, not sure why, but it don't seem like normal voices should be allowed in here. Especially not now. We move like thieves in spotlight, waitin' for some shout, some sign we're scooped, but all is quiet. We make it all the way to the rectory door when the bells start gongin'. The reverberation of the bells makes the fuzz on my neck bristle like a five-o'clock shadow.

"Andrea?"

Sister Jordana is just outside the rectory door, and her eyes are wide pools of dark brown, just as I remember them. She extends her arms toward me, and I ain't sure why, didn't even know my soul was tremblin' at the thought of them bein' all caught up, but I run to her, throw my arms around her thick waist. The habit is rough against my skin and smells like the church. I catch a whiff of the rosemary soap they make to raise money for the orphans. Orphans like me. Sister Jordana crushes me against her, and it feels so faggin' good, so like comfort and home, I cry a li'l bein' held like that.

"Andrea, are you all right? It's precious good to see you." Sister Jordana's words are like cream, swirlin' to sweet butter in my ears.

I knuckle away a couple tears. Ain't time for berry pickin' down memory lane. "I thought—thought they might've come already. I was scared." I sound like a faggin' five-year-old mite, but I don't care. "Sister, they're comin', they're comin' for them all." I force myself to let her go, to look at her hard, to make her understand.

Her eyes are wide and clear and deep. There's yellow spots of age in the corners of the white.

"Who? Who would come here? Are you in trouble, Andre—I mean, Andi... That's how you are now, isn't it?"

I nod, touched she would remember my chosen name, the one I insisted on carryin' into the world. "The Society. They've sprung it. Somehow, everythin'—it's all fucked up." I say the last part in a whisper, but she still looks surprised at the vulgarity. Not much I can do to help it, so I just go on. "They know about the mites, the kiddos. They're gonna sweep through. Things're bad. They sent me to the Farm."

She touches my arm again, and there's fear pulsatin' in her chocolate-brown gaze. I fight back tears.

"You've gotta get out of here, gotta get them all outta here."

"Andi, thank you." She squeezes my arm, then beckons. Elenbar's been standin' way back, watchin' the entrance, but she follows as we enter the rectory, crossin' into the back world, which was home for us so long ago. Well, not so long ago for me, longer for Elenbar.

We hear them, voices floatin' to us down the hall. They're singin', so dinner must've been done. Singin' always comes after the supper. Shit, what time is it? I try to remember the gongin' notes, but all that flew out my brain pan when I saw Sister Jordana. I'm followin' close, my hands sweatin' because the thought of seein' youngsters makes me nervous somehow. Li'l mites, baby Transgressors, with no idea about much, except that they're bein' hidden from the Society. Sittin' through the sermons and stories of the Sisters, who think Transgressors were lovingly created by the Lord. To teach us humility and unite the sexes. The early education about how to practice silent resistance to the Law of Man. After all, only thing the church cares about is the Law of God.

No, these mites got no faggin' idea about anythin' at all.

The hall opens up to the dining room, and heads swivel toward us. A whole crowd of big buggy eyes stare. Some of them got boy haircuts, some look right girlish, but they're all Transgressors bein' hidden from those who'd do them harm. God, they're so young, like we once were, and my gut quivers thinkin' about the world they'll walk into. The world I walked into. St. Aggie's may be sanctuary, but it ain't forever.

"Oh, Andrea!" Sister Faline rushes me, drawin' me into a hug almost as hard as the one I gave Sister Jordana. Then she rushes Elenbar who looks nervous and uncomfortable at bein' all squeezed.

"Ele, dear Elenora, it is so good to see you." Sister Faline always was the fussin' type. I still feel those mites' eyes borin' into me, wantin' to know who I am, what I'm doin' there. There's a couple of them with bright red hair like Pint. I try not to think about the price redheads fetch in Lover's Lane. There's li'l mites like Pixie who ain't lucky enough to get dumped at St. Aggie's, who instead get forced to turn out ass for pimpin' parental profits.

"Sister, we need to move the children. I think it's time for a drill." Sister Jordana speaks with measured calm. Sister Faline's eyes widen, and she looks at me and Elenbar.

"Yes, of course. I thought—maybe once, you might come to visit us. But yes, of course. We need to move them right away." Her face is pale, her ivory hands shakin'. She turns away from us and faces the children, her smile ampin' up about a million watts. "Okay, everyone. Your beautiful voices bring us such joy! Now we'll need to be going, all together to a special place. I need you to go into your rooms and get your go-quick bags. Hurry now. We'll come around to help you get ready.

Please, be quick!" Her voice is cheery and bright, but a couple mites already look mighty scared like the roof's gonna cave in on them any moment.

"But—but what about my sissy?" A small mite with white-blond hair and who's got the requisite boy haircut stares up at us. "She won't know where to find me."

Sister Faline squats beside him and rests a hand on his shoulder, smilin' all the while.

"Why, she's going to meet us there. Isn't she, Andrea?" Sister Faline looks at me, noddin' encouragement.

I nod because what can I say? *Hey, kid, she's probably all scooped up already. Maybe even dead. Tazer to the baby brain.* My gut twists even as my inner-self prattles on. "Yah, she is." I swallow the lie like a sock full of crusty marbles.

The mite keeps watchin' me even when they coax him up and lead him toward the back dormitories. The others, a couple lookin' just old enough to be gettin' ready to go out into the world, follow the Sisters obediently, whisperin' to each other. Fear's got a taste, and the whole room's swelterin' with the tang of sour sweat. None of these crotchspawn got any idea about what they're afraid of, but everybody knew, when you were at St. Aggie's, danger's always at the door.

"Okay, we came, did it. We need ta blow outta here," Elenbar hisses at me. "Andi?"

She's right, but I run ahead, catchin' up with Sister Jordana.

"Look, we—"

"You have to go, yes. We'll be all right, Andi." She touches my face, and I flinch, because it's been so long since someone touched my face like they wanted to love it. "Oh, my dear. Remember this, the Lord works through us all. I know you don't feel that, but I do for you. He brought you here and He'll watch over us. I pray He'll guide your way as you do what you must. Where will you go?"

"To the Wall." My five-year-old voice is talkin' again, but Sister Jordana just smiles as though it's the most perfect plan in the world instead of rabid insanity.

"Yes, you must then. You must reach the world beyond. Will you say a little prayer with me before you go?" She takes my hand and starts murmurin' the Lord's Prayer. I know it, but I can't hardly say it. My tongue's dryin' to the roof of my mouth like a sticky rubber. Then, about the moment she gets to the part about bein' delivered out of evil and not bein' a twat or some such shit, we hear a loud bang from upstairs.

"Children! Come to me!" Sister Faline calls, emergin' from one of the dormitory rooms, the blondie mite in tow.

Elenbar pushes me. I slam against Sister Jordana and we almost fall. I smell smoke and grab the Sister's arm. Then we're runnin', flyin' down the dark passage to the tunnel, the tunnel everybody knows about but hardly ever gets used. Except for times like this.

The tunnel leadin' to the catacombs.

Bodies of Rats

THE TUNNEL AIN'T much, mostly paved and slick marble except for the bits they tunneled beyond the tourist circuit. Folks used to come slack-jawed at the monument to the dead and the rooms dedicated to them, though that's all long ago. Not many frequent the echoes of the past anymore. Bit too many bones rattlin' in the dark.

We shuffle together, quick and quiet. Elenbar's hand is in mine. It's like holdin' a warm tropical toad. I'm havin' flashes of memory, of long-ago. The practicin' the Sisters had us do, just in case, bringin' us into the tunnel. But in my day we had never used it for real. Not until now. The dull fluorescent lights are scummy green against the white tiles and walls. The children rush ahead of us, like scamperin' rats, danger right behind. Along the walls, the placid gazes of painted Saints follow us, onlookers at a funeral. Goose pimples prickle my skin.

All's quiet from up above. We knew, when we heard the bang, they were gassin' the place. Clunkers love gas of all sorts, bein' immune to it themselves, and it's a faggin' good way to snuff out large groups. I'd been gassed—most Brigade been gassed at some point—but that's more riot-crowd stuff. They use other shit to clear out vermin. That vapor will turn you inside out and you'll do the flip-flop in a puddle of your own piss-and-gut perfume. That's the kind I'm worried about now.

The lights flicker, then all goes dark. A few of the children shriek. I squeeze Elenbar's froggy hand.

"It's all right, it's all right. Just hold on a moment," Sister Jordana says, and she's right, because dimmer lights snap back on along the floor. It ain't much, but it lights the way to walk. We've come to the end of the hallway, and somewhere far behind us is a monotonous bangin' sound. It's comin' from the door we came through. Just behind where we stand.

"Quickly, come on. Andrea?" Sister Faline touches my arm. The cadaver white of her face is shadowed by the curve of her habit, and I shudder. Feels like the dead still walk and one's touchin' me, but I follow the children who are disappearin' into a wall where a large flat stone's been moved. The stone's too ancient and far too massive to be moved by human hands, but it's a catfish trick; the stone is on a hinge. The escape leads into tunnels far reachin' through the underbelly of the entire City. So we move quiet and keep our feet light.

The mite with the blond hair is still holdin' Sister Jordana's hand as she guides him through, and I follow right behind. The other children follow at my heels, with Sister Faline at the last. She pauses and fiddles with a control pad on the inside, and the stone begins to grumble and shut. It seals itself into place, and the small tunnel, barely large enough to pop a piss, seems smaller than ever. The control panel beeps three times, then goes dark. The Sisters light hand torches. As a child, it had seemed like a cavernous wormy belly, promisin' unknown excitement on the other end. I didn't understand the world then. Shit, I don't understand it now.

A few of the older children whisper to each other, but the sound is muffled in our tight space. I block out brain images of collapsin' tunnels, about bein' crushed beneath tons of dirt and the asphalt streets way above us. It's hard to breathe, like there's a horny tourist trout sittin' on my chest. But I ain't on my back and I sure as shit ain't gettin' paid.

"Just up here. We're almost to the end, children. We must all use our eyes and our minds." She points at her eyes and her temple, as though it's an anatomy lesson on terror. "Hold your friend's hand, and let's see what we can see, yes?" Sister Jordana manages to sound cheerful in the drear darkness. We slow to a walk and then stop. Ahead she peers up at the tunnel that leads us back to sky. Back to the world. Back to freedom. It's probably hidden, a pipeline to the underground web of safe houses mobilized for times like this. Times for hidin', times for fleein'. Maybe it's the beepin' of the control panel, maybe it's some other signal, but the tunnel leadin' to sky opens, floodin' the tunnel with the light of day.

"You all right? Drilling?" someone calls down to us.

"Angels." Sister Jordana doesn't say anythin' else. Must be the code word, and I hear the person shout, must be to others waitin' up top as well. Sister Jordana looks back at us and beckons, to me maybe, or to Elenbar. We wade through the tight space, through small knobby mite bodies until we get to her.

"You go on. You need to escape out of here. They cannot find you here in our company. Other things we might explain. The Trans...the Brigade, we could not. Bless you and all that is within you. Both of you." She smiles tensely and squeezes my hand, then Elenbar's. I look up at the gritty runged ladder leadin' back to the world, up into the face of a dark-haired woman with pale lips. She reaches for me, beckons. I start climbin', Elenbar at my ass, nearly ready to crawl up it.

It's only seconds to the top, and the stranger helps us out. Behind her are others, tense and uneasy as they scan the neighborhood surroundin' us. A couple men, a couple other women. We've emerged from underneath a carousel in a run-down park. A couple swings squeak in an unfelt breeze. Sister Jordana is already out and takes the hands of a girl-lookin' mite, then a boy-lookin' one. I'm sure neither got a nip of crotch hair. Their wide eyes devour the world they stand in. Maybe this is their first time "drillin'."

The explosion knocks me flat onto my back. Dirt and dust sprays across my face. My ears are twin gongs, bongin' my brain full of noise. Hands are on me and I fight them.

"Andi! Andi! Get up, get up, come on, ya twat!" Elenbar lunges at me, and I grab her hand, staggerin' upright. A couple people are crowdin' the mouth of the tunnel, pullin' another kid up. A dusty vortex swirls up out of the hole.

"The tunnel's collapsing! Move it! Go!" the woman screams down at them. I shove Elenbar away and dive toward the tunnel, reachin', clawin' at another kid body. The mite screams as I wrench the lithe body and shove them away from the hole. *No, no, no, this can't happen.* Sister Jordana's at my elbow, snatchin' the kids as we pull them up. My head's throbbin'. I still can't hear right. My mouth tastes like suckin' copper pipe. I'm starin' down into Sister Faline's face. It's covered with dirt. Her habit's gone and her black hair's a bramble mess. The little blond mite starts up the ladder and she's below him, shovin' him up. He cries and slips on the metal rungs, his arms looped around the next step above.

I reach for him.

A loud roar shakes the ground beneath me. I lunge at empty air, snatchin' at the boy. Sister Faline yelps. The last thing I see is the wide-mouthed cry of the boy as he falls. Elenbar bites my ear as I buck against her, tryin' to fight my way back to the edge.

It's not too late, it's not too late, it's not too—

The ground caves with a deafenin' whomp. My legs kick in empty air. Elenbar's arms wrench hard into my pits and lift me back and over the solid edge of the earth. There's a giant crater where once there was an exit. The air's choked with dirt and screamin'. My eyes are blind, I am blind, all is blindness.

But I can hear the comin' sirens.

When You Need 'Em

FAGGIN' EYES ARE mud. I'm blinkin' against thousand-grit sandpaper. Someone's got me by the hand. Hope it's Elenbar. Even if it ain't, I cling to the bony fingers like they're the last vials of Flow in the known universe. The sirens grow louder, wobblin' in and out my muffled eardrums. The invisible hand jerks me hard, and I almost topple over. Sudden cold water sprays my face, and I swallow a mouthful before I get good sense to splash it in my eyes. The world looks like smeared anal sludge, but yah, the angular sack of bones in front of me's gotta be Elenbar.

"We—a—back." My throat's a clot of gravel, and I lean at the waist, spittin' dirt. Try again. "We gotta go back. Sister. The boy."

"Andi. They're gone. We gotta get split and gone. Brass are comin'."

My eyes burn, and it ain't the grit no more. The wide mouth, the boy's final scream. Faline's squeak. Collapsin' earth.

It's too late. It's way too fuckin' late. I know it. Elenbar sure as sucklin' tit knows it. I sink my chompers into the slug of my tongue.

"Come on—we gotta git. This place'll be swarming with brass and clunks. Say a prayer, and get it outta yer mind." She grabs my hand. I let myself be led on. "I need ya here with me, Andi. Ya hearing me?"

I nod because my tongue's bleedin' and there's more dirt in my mouth than any spit's gonna fix.

My sight's gettin' better, though my eyeballs probably look like scratchin' posts for rabid tomcats. We've plunged into the thick of the neighborhood, swallowed up by apartment blocks. The sirens are accompanied by more, gatherin'. Soon we hear the thwap-thwap of a helicopter. We duck between dumpsters. Smells like egg foo yung and jizz wrappers. Elenbar rifles through one of them as I watch the mostly empty streets of the neighborhood. A couple boys scamper by in knee-highs and flat caps. My chest aches. These boys ain't never had to worry about a world tryin' to snip them, bein' born natural in the world. Girls ain't got no such luxury. One of them shouts and points to the sky, where the swoopin' shadow of the helicopter is passin'. Afternoon's fadin', darkness is comin' to the land. Wonder if any of us'll live to see tomorrow.

"Hah, a couple rands just sitting here. And hey, this looks good 'nuff." Elenbar tosses me half a spongy apple that looks like a Flow jacker's mouth. Pocks of black rot and all. She's already munchin' the other half.

My gut's rolickin' like a spin cycle, but it ain't the meal. Truth is, the apple might be a haunch of beef far as my shriveled gut sack is concerned. But while hunger's got a magical way of pushin' out the shit storm of life, my mind's got a powerful need to self-flagellate. My ears still carry the echo of a screamin' boy. The white in Faline's eyes. I coulda done more. Coulda-woulda-shoulda.

"'Ey! Eat that shit. We gotta find more. The Wall ain't no buffet line, ya know? Here, these egg rolls are square. And look, fortune cookies!" She shoves the bounty in my face, smilin' wide. She's tryin' hard, like Dr. Chambers when he's shootin' your ass with the anti-clap. But it helps, somehow. Just a li'l.

"Fuck." I stuff one into my mouth. Force it in. The steel trap of my guts slam shut around the slight musk of mold, sinkin' into the fried mystery meat and slop of soggy veggies. I chew twice then swallow, and though it's like a chafin' brick on the way down, my body receives it like ambrosia. Then the apple's in and smushin' between the good teeth I got left. My gut rumbles ominously, but I suck air through my nose, hard, and it stays down.

"Yukin' yuk, ya faggin' twatter beeeeens!"

We snap around like the ground's a pit of snakes. Down the alley, a bulbous bunny of a person's comin' toward us, totterin' fast on the knee stubs where full legs and feet once were.

"Puddin'? Shyte!" I grab her up in a big-armed scoop, liftin' her up and around. She squeals. The pop-can nose smudged in the depths of her piggy face wiggles, her smile barely able to push against the fat cheeks tryin' to swallow up her mouth hole entirely.

"Taut-tat ya'll deeeead. Aggie's boomed up ta da Kingdaam!"

"Ya piggy-wiggy fucker, what the fuck happened? Where were ya?" Elenbar's a fallin' sledge, grabbin' Puddin' up by the neck. Her blunt knee stubs flail in air.

"Squeeeeeeee—no—no—no!" Puddin's face turns fifty shades of naughty girl.

"Ele! Stop!" I lunge at Elenbar, slappin' at her arms. Don't realize the name's slipped out again until Elenbar spins around and clops me straight in the face. I'm caught without feet, slammin' back against the hard rough steel of the dumpster.

"Hey! What the hell y'all doing back here? Y'all get out of here 'fore I call the brass around, ya hear? Fuck off!" One of the servin' twats from the Chinese joint's come out. Bushy eyebrows wag in disapproval, and he don't look faggin' pleased, not a single eggy bit.

I stagger to my feet, head spinnin', my nose hot and wet. Elenbar's already draggin' Puddin' along, though her stubs are back on the ground. The snufflin' squeal she's makin' tells me Elenbar's still clampin' down on her. We move outta the alley, but we step out onto a wide avenue. Too wide. Too open. Even with my bleary eyes stingin' with tears from the facial assault, I can see too many people suddenly starin' at us.

Elenbar straightens up and lets Puddin' go. I straighten up too, and we three start walkin' like we supposed to be there. Migrate ourselves up onto the sidewalk. Blendin' in is just about pretendin' you belong. Sometimes. People are still watchin' us, but they start shufflin' about their business again. The sirens still wail in the distance. We're not in the Slumland fringes, we're mainland now, and behavior counts.

"Answer me," Elenbar hisses at Puddin', and I take a couple quick steps to come alongside them. Puddin sweats like cold pisswater set in the sun.

"I—I weren't dere wen all wen down. Ween on da run-run fer Chambur-son. Shured up afta 'n Peeent's sailin' on da Biff-tiff. Baabblin' like hee dun got ta deeel. Dink hee wen ta brass? I skooted ta Red Line ta weit fer ya all ta come on back."

I fuckin' hate it. Puddin's talkin' sounds like a stuffed-up glory hole. Hardly understand her drawl, but not every mite ends up at a place like St. Aggie's. Some mites never get any kind of schoolin' at all. Puddin's legs got half-lopped off in a Spades bet gone wonk. Li'l bit of schoolin' might've done Puddin' a whole lotta good. Two legs' worth, at least.

"Shut up then. Who's still floating?"

A baby cries, and I take a two-step scoot away from a spermy wormy pushin' a carriage. Lady eyes me like I'm a plague rat walkin' on two legs. I waggle my tongue at her, and she struts away, tuttin' like a teapot.

"Bom-bom, den dere's Meenie, Peexie, Tank, and dere's—"

Elenbar rounds on Puddin', and we stop in the middle of the walk. "Wait, hold up—where the fuck's Tank?"

Puddin' blinks, lip tremblin' like she's waitin' for Elenbar to lop her nose off.

"Spit it, piggy Puddin', or I'm going ta make a fucking piggy *pie*."

"Tank's gune undergrune. Seen 'im last at Red Line heedin'."

"Fagger, *no*. Please don't tell me we're hoppin' to Red Line. Thought we're goin' to the Wall?" My heart's clip-cloppin' because I already know. Don't I just fuckin' know?

"Tank's family all worked on building the Wall, didn't they? He can tell us the best way ta get inside."

"Ohh, no. No nee's no gud."

For once, I agreed with piggy Puddin', glory hole and all.

Red Line

PUDDIN'S SNUFFLIN' GOES on and on and on. I'm surprised the crotch stain can even get around, much less keep up with half legs, but she does just fine. Elenbar's three steps ahead, forgin' on like a mongrel prick seekin' precious bitch heat. Though Red Line ain't anywhere I'm wantin' to go and Tank ain't exactly who I'm wantin' to see.

I charge up until I'm stridin' alongside Elenbar. "Why we gotta get to Tank? You were all rip-tip to go to the Wall before we heard nothin' about Tank."

"Our odds will be...better if we get more info."

"You don't know how to get through. That's the faggin' truth, ain't it? You were gonna drag me out and wing it?" My voice's pitchin' high, but I don't care.

Elenbar turns on me, side-eyein' a paper boy wavin' the daily news. He drops the paper and steps back from us. She's got that effect on people. Or maybe it's the smeared blood and bein' covered with a sheen of dirt and sweat that's doin' it.

"Ain't no one know how ta get all the way through the Wall. Ya ever heard anyone coming back from it? I got all the info from the Brigade's operations, up here." She points at her temple. "And we gotta get it out there. So means dragging ya ta the Wall and winging it if we gotta. But I hear Tank's floating around? I'm gonna snap up all the info and help I can get."

Elenbar's right, but I don't wanna hear it. Not really.

"Nee's gunna be darn peeeeesed."

"Gee, thank you, Puddin'. I wasn't faggin' sure until now. Yah, he's gonna be peeeeesed when he sees me." Can't keep the salt outta my voice.

Elenbar glares at me. "Ya jacked him of a stash. Ya pay yer dues, suck it up, suck it in, whatever ya gotta do. I ain't skipping intel just because yer a shit junk-tard."

Her words slide into my belly like ice. Tank ain't the forgivin' sort, and I dodged him too many times before all this. Ain't sure I'm gonna have the opportunity to suck up anythin' but my own teeth off the floor.

"Here. Let's grab the forty-four. My feet're dying and dragging this piggy sack around's taking too long."

Together we board the bus that's pulled up. Elenbar nips a few rands into the coin dispenser. Ain't a pleasant ride, so most prefer to walk. We enter a haze that smells like sewer and lunch meat and slink to the back to find it occupied by a... Yah, there's a drained-out gutter fly there. The cold vacant eyes are half-mast, like the last glimpse of the world weren't much to see. His clothes are stained yellow, and it smells like all the body fluids are makin' their final seep. Probably won't clear him out until the bus gets back to station, so we sit in the midway seats.

Outside, the St. Agatha Quarter is slippin' away. We'll cross the Liberty Bridge and enter new territory. Well, new since the last time I'd been here, which was right about the time I jacked Tank's drop-off point. Yah, this ain't gonna be good at all.

The people change, in subtle ways at first. Haircuts gettin' more frequent, less questionable stainin' of clothin'. Children runnin' around under the watchful eyes of parents who took classes and got permits to have them. Not like gutter babies. Or dumpster babies. You could have as many of those as you wanted. Even the streets get a li'l cleaner. I stop countin' beer cans and switch to countin' cars with both headlights still workin'.

Once we hit the Liberty Bridge, the whole bus starts hummin', wheels thrummin' against the rough grates of the lanes, a rhythmic rumble threatenin' to lull me to sleep. Too bad my nose's still squirmin' with the smell of corpse juice and crotch sweat. It's an almost scenic thing, the water spillin' beneath you in a swampy foamin' green. Stretchin' out in a shimmerin' avenue all the way to the Wall itself, where the river hits the vertical concrete barrier, sloshin' down into giant whirrin' fans at the base of it. Supposedly creates electricity for the whole faggin' city. Elenbar told me that once. The water's left green ring marks along the concrete, markin' its decline over time, the thrashin' death spasms of a dyin' supply. Elenbar told me that too.

I look over at her and see she's starin' at it all like it owes her somethin'. Maybe it just owes her freedom. Or maybe she's imaginin' the ocean spreadin' beyond it. Been told enough and seen enough maps to understand that beyond the Wall is the Detachment Zone. You go there, you're gone from the United Free States of Liberty for good. So say the Society. Ain't no comin' back from it. Not ever.

The change in borough is real clear once we bounce the last steel grate and hit real asphalt road again. On either side of the highway are erected pikes with strange signage hung from them. The letters ain't all English, but some of it is. There's bright red paint slashed across ripplin' ripped black flags, like they're pirates from old-world novels. It's all written in some strange half-mouth talk, and it's the markin' of the Tivoli Clan. All upside this bridge is Tivoli. They're a patchwork mottled gang of all colors, who came together and made up their own language, mixin' together bits of others.

"You got a plan? Any kind of plan at all?" My words intrude upon the pungent air, and I try not to imagine particles of dead man shit gettin' sucked into my lungs as I speak.

"Besides tossing ya ta Tank and hoping fer the best? Not really."

I let out a single-syllable laugh and see she ain't even crackin' a smile. It gets real hard to swallow my own spit.

"Nee gonna beeee peeeeesed. Nee gunna durn y-y-ya out, wurk yer ass wit da bom-bom geeng," Puddin' says helpfully.

I wonder if I can crush her trachea with one hand.

"It's—" Elenbar sighs then, long and deep like she been forgettin' to breathe all day. "I'll talk ta Tank. I will. But ya gotta know, the time ta collect may come around now. Ya two gotta work it out. If it means we bang out of there at the last sec, then we do that, though I don't want Tivoli trailin' us all the way ta the Wall. We got enough heat ta scorch half the mainland already."

"Fag it. I know. Don't I know? But I'm tellin' you, it ain't goin' to be good. Not at all."

"Knockers."

"Kneekers."

I might be able to kick her from here.

THE RED LINE ain't cozy. It's a big sprawlin' marketplace of sorts, butted up against a tall squat buildin' decked with the same Tivoli jargon we saw at the bridge. We pass by tents and hollerin' women, most with hair wrapped up in colorful scarfs and heavy-lidded dark eyes that follow us as we go. Others are flecks of chalk weavin' through the place, baskets of apples and leafy vegetables cradled in their arms. It's like bein' on a different world, another planet maybe, all of them shoutin' their special language and livin' a life ain't seen nowhere else I know of in the UFS.

Ahead, in that tall squat building, is the main operations of the Tivoli Clan and the manufacture of all the Flow this side of the country. There's other manufactories too, producin' Biff and Lang and Fist, but those are spread out across the Slumland. Even with the bakin' bread and roastin' meat in the marketplace, my body's tuned out those delicious smells of nutrients in favor of somethin' else. There's a toxic whiff comin' off the place makes my nerves jangle with anticipation. Smells like high. Smells like comin' up. Elenbar's words go itchin' like crotch fleas: *yer a shit junk-tard*. I ain't clapped a high since the Farm, but the power of my newly acquired sobriety fades in the face of this new opportunity.

"Ya square?" Elenbar squeezes my shoulder, hard.

"Keepers. In then out and gone we go." I'm lyin'. I'm already lyin'. The itchin' of her words are fadin' too. I *am* a shit junk-tard. Always gonna be. Nothin' gonna change that.

Puddin' touches my hand and offers a piggly-wiggly smile. It comes off nice before remindin' me why she's bein' so nice anyhow. Pity.

A few Tivoli loiter in front of the buildin', loungin' on the concrete steps. Each one shoulders a fully automatic Tik-Tik, the black gleamin' like fresh gear oil.

"Elenbar! Faggin' de whoop whoop 'round these parts!" a bald-headed stack of muscle shouts, barin' his white teeth. His brown face is streaked with sweat and somethin' that looks like white dust.

Elenbar smiles, tense, and they bump shoulders as we come up close. Then they see me.

"Yuh-yuh, de whoop with da wrong whoop 'round here." His smile is gone, and he grabs my arm.

Yah, this is gonna be a rottin' shit tit from start to end.

I'm dragged up the steps, and he ignores my stumblin' feet, half liftin' me by my arm, like he might wrench it off the joint just to make the point. I don't say nothin', my stomach rollickin' with anxiety and desire. The thought of huffin' some Flow is still at the back of my mind, the eternal junkie hope.

The double doors at the front are already held open by a couple of the others. They leer at me, and I see white teeth ain't the normal condition around here. Dull thuddin' music blares from somewhere deep inside.

"Hey-hey! Dat Tank 'round da *tasca*?" my cue-ball captor barks at another chalky-lookin' fagger standin' just inside. A point and shrug's all we get, and I'm dragged on. I crank my neck around and see Elenbar and Puddin' are followin' us. Elenbar's flexin' jaw is like a rod of rebar.

The main entryway splits off into a side hallway, and we follow it to a wide door. Muscle stack kicks the door open, and the music is suddenly full volume. Clinkin' glasses, the thud smack of pool balls, and... Smoke fingers the air, and I suck in a huge lungful. It's rife with Flow, and the metallic taste knots my guts up with desire.

Then I forget, just in that second, about Flow, about any kind of drugs at all. In the depths of a large squat armchair is Tank, and I remember why they call him that.

He rises to his feet, and his chair squeals with relief. He's without a shirt, his bare torso like a slab of knotty oak. But it's his head that's his namesake. The square bulk of his jaw is like the hull of a tank, thick and pivoted perfectly on a bulgin' neck of cabled tendons. They might manufacture Flow, but Tivoli got good rep for mainlinin' Biff until muscle overwhelms good sense. Tank's a prime showin' of it. He ain't a towerin' sort, but he's wide as tall, shoulders formin' sharp corners at his massive neck.

"Andi. Oh my. *Andi*." He coos my name and waggles his forked tongue at me. Did I mention that? Tivoli clip their tongues, splittin' them like snakes. Rite of entry or some such shit, but I've ridden more than one Tivoli tongue and it ain't as titillatin' as you might think.

I'm dropped from my shoulder grip and almost collapse to my knees. I stagger, and the rest of the smokin' starin' crowd bubbles with snarlin' laughter. They all know. Long-rottin' beef like between Tank and I gets known.

"Oh hey, Tank. You still bangin' around these parts?" I rub my shoulder and try to look like I ain't tricklin' a li'l pee down my leg.

Tank jerks his head in a pitbull nod.

Elenbar shouts too late.

A length of chain slips around my feet. I try to turn, try to strike at what's comin', but even as I do, gravity fails, and my feet are jerked from under me. My head smacks the tile as I'm lifted up by my ankles, Tank now inverted in my vision. I'm spinnin' and spinnin' at the end of a chain, world smudgin' as I go. Laughter's ringin' in my ears.

But all that stops when Tank slams his fist into my gut.

Payment & Punishment

MY WORLD SPINS, and there's no air. My lungs cramp around the pit of heat glowin' in my belly. Everythin's stunned and breathin' can't happen. Elenbar's shoutin', and there's a couple of Puddin' snorts, but it's all smudged beneath the wash of dizziness. The sledge of Tank's fist felt like it touched my bone stack through my gut sack, and I almost don't feel the second punch. Except I do because this one clips my spinnin' side, glancin' off a rib that creaks under the the force of impact.

Then, sudden as it stopped, air comes whoopin' back into my lungs. My lungs inflate like waterlogged balloons, and I gag with the force of it. Blood's poundin' in my ears as it backtracks into my brain.

"Stop, just stop this! There's bigger shit than squabbles over Andi's cocked-off idiocy!"

That's Elenbar, her words seethin' with...oh, that's mostly annoyance, actually. She even sighs, like this is all a giant theatrical inconvenience. My guts beg to differ.

"Dey dun doing to da Wall!"

Puddin' is still helpin'.

I'm tryin' to focus, even with the spinnin'. There's blurs that I think are probably them, because one looks like a meatball jammed on two short toothpicks.

Someone grabs me, and my world jerks to a halt. My eyeballs are swollen, like I been punched in them too. But that's the blood, and there's an awful lot of it wantin' to squeeze out my ears and eye sockets.

"And what's-the-what at the Wall? Why een rotting good force would yee go *there*?" Tank's voice is disbelievin'. I don't blame him. Goin' to the Wall is about the stupidest thing I've heard this year, and I run with a lot of stupid folk. I focus on suckin' in more Flow-flavored air, ignorin' the stitchin' throb of my ribs.

"They're doing sweeps. The Brigade is down. Maybe fer good. But it's more than that. They swept St. Aggie's. The network's breached, and our most recent contact said executions are going ta start again. Something's got the Society rattled, and they're starting extermination, smoking us all out of our hiding holes. And that might come ta include Tivoli."

I'm listenin' hard and hot in my teeth about it. This is straighter talk than I heard outta Elenbar since the Farm, and I'm less than pleased at hearin' it while my ass is kissin' heaven.

"Hmpf. Hardly. Tivoli serve a purpose. Society knows that. Yee know that. Wee have none tee fear from *el estado*."

"Really, Tank? Ya all tell the Society about yer own mites ya got stashed away? How's about they roll the snip-and-clip wagon up in here?"

The laughin' and quiet buzzin' of the room falls to complete silence.

"If yee know something, yee would speak it now." Tank's words are followed by the ominous click of cocked weaponry.

"Then let her down. Andi. I'll tell ya everything Tivoli needs ta hear because I need something from ya, too."

There's a ripple of laughter again.

"*Non.*"

"No? Did ya hear what I said? The Society is going—"

A spatter of boomin' gunfire silences Elenbar. I clap my hands over my ears, but the sound's gone. A tinny ringin' joins the rhythmic boom of the blood in my head. Elenbar's still standin'. Even my blurry upside-down vision can tell me that much. Tank lowers the barrel aimed over her head and brings it level. Puddin' squeals and covers her eyes.

"*La récompense* will bee made."

"What do ya want?" Elenbar doesn't move. She don't even sound afraid.

"Everyone knows Andi. What was done. What Andi done. Then, when time came calling, Andi ran. Hiding under Brigade skeerts. Yee didn't turn her back tee us. Yee done wrong. Andi must reap what Andi has *piantato*. As is said."

Gold teeth wink from inside his wide smile.

"Aye. All right. Payment. Punishment. That's what ya want?"

Tank nods.

"She'll issue a public sorry, go ta the higher-ups, and kiss their pooty-holes, too."

Laughter drowns Elenbar's words.

"Tradition says *uno* hand."

"One... Oh fer bucket-fucking sake. Ya going ta follow Temperance statute? Gonna string her up, too? How's she gonna help me through the Wall short a hand?"

My stomach squirms, which is bad considerin' I'm upside down and gravity'd be happy to oblige a squirt of vomit into my nose. But a hand? Cuttin' off my *hand*? I like my hands. I do a quick calculation. The right could go, maybe. Left's my wankin' hand, though.

"Perhaps wee finish the job the Society wants." His voice is oily with malice.

"Sounds like yer a big fan of rules. How many Transgressor mites ya got, anyway? Last I heard 'twas three. Outta the five. We chopping them, too?"

The metallic click again. Elenbar's gone too far. I can't breathe.

"Mee thinking not anyone of yee need to be walking out of here. Wall or not. Society or not."

"Then let's meet in the middle. Beat her. Whip her in the square. Draw the blood yer so desperate ta have. But let her go. Let this go. Bad blood'll run in the streets even when our business is done. The Society, Enforcers, even the brass *is* coming. You've got family ta move. As do we. Time is not on any side and certainly not on ours."

Silence. My teeth give a painful squeak because I'm grindin' them so hard. Don't wanna be whipped neither, but between hands and asses...well. Choice, that wily illusionist.

"*Oui.* The blood will run and cleanse this debt. Then wee bee finished."

There's a clink, and I fall, throwin' my hands out last minute, and it's about the only thing keeps me from snappin' my bone stack as I hit the hard tile. Blood rushes back to my feet, knives and needles prickin' deep in the flesh, but I'm immediately jerked to my feet, held up because I can't stand right myself. The rush of swishin' blood flow almost makes me gray out, but I hold it together. Because Tank's in my face, breathin' Flow and Biff sweetness against my mouth, a mere brush away from kissin' my lips.

"Andi. Oh my. Andi."

Blood Running

THE EVENING AIR is cold, and my nipples pebble in protest. Bein' shirtless don't help, and I try to block out the eyes on me, on my body. The whoopin' and growlin' crowd are gathered in a wide circle. I'm on my knees, of course. Tank always was the dramatic type. My wrists are chained together, slung around the flagpole they got in their market square. I'm still caked in dirt from collapsin' tunnel spew, and now seems a real poor time to be reflectin' on wide-eyed boys and Faline's scream ringin' in my ears—but my brain ain't ever listened to me. Ever.

"Wee all know of Andi and her crimes against the Tivoli. Against mee and the suppliers of our Flow. For this, she will receive thirty lashings of the leather. One for each gram stolen. Let blood pay this debt. Let *la equite* be had."

Didn't I say he's dramatic? The crowd cheers and whoops at Tank's words. Somethin' hits me in the side with a splat. Wet like a squishy tomato. Or maybe spit. I don't bother to look. Elenbar's in my side vision, lookin' anxious even though it's the deal she made. I'm grateful, I think. Okay, not extremely grateful—I'm still gettin' the whip, but it's a slight better than the other offers made. So I'm grateful for that. Next to her is Puddin', wide dark irises floatin' in the rheumy yellow of her eyes.

Thirty lashes don't seem too bad. Not great, but reasonable. I guess.

I hear the crack of the leather, brace for it, but there's nothin'. He's just testin' it, puttin' it on for the crowd, who loves it. The jeerin' amps about a thousand percent, and shackled hands won't let me cover my ears.

"One!" the crowd collectively shouts.

Oh, ain't this quaint?

The leather cracks again, loud and sinuous. It's less the slice of the whip than the heat it leaves behind, like a slap that burns, deep and spreadin'. *Okay. Thirty. Let's do this.*

"Two!" the crowd bellows.

Crack. Tank's playin' because this one hurts about ten times more than the last. The skin singes with the force of the lick. There's heat, but whether blood or just pain, I ain't sure.

"Three!"

Crack. I flinch, know it's comin', but the futility of it is clear. Tank's gettin' comfortable. This one lands across my right shoulder blade, a burnin' slick flayin' open the skin as it goes.

"Four!"

Crack. It lands firm behind the last one, widenin' the wound just made. A groan wrenches loose from my clenched teeth.

"Five!"

Crack. I actually cry out. I can't stop it. My whole back's a curtain of flame, scorchin' deep to the bone and inflamin' the tissue nestlin' around my beatin' heart. I glance at Elenbar. She's holdin' a hand over her mouth. Puddin' ain't there at all.

"Six!"

The lash peels open my back. Must have. Tears leave hot tracks down my face.

"Seven!"

I try to pull away, though it ain't no use, but my body tries anyhow. This one strikes lower. Feels like it nearly cuts me in half.

"Eight!"

Thirty. Thirty fuckin' lashes. I'm goin' gray, a pressure inside my head pushin' at my vision. Almost like bein' high. Almost.

"Nine!"

I sob against my arm, pressin' my forehead against the hot flesh.

"Ten!"

There's relief as I go, gray out, the world wobblin' in and then gone for a moment. The screams of the crowd throb in sync with the surge of my pulse. The voices become a rushin' howl, like a high wind, like the pound of waves on a pebbled shoreline. Like...like...

I'm hot all over, my body's burnin' up, and my arms drop to my sides. Elenbar shakes me. Then she slaps my face, both cheeks.

My tongue feels thick. "J—Jesus. What the faggin' waggin'? Is it done?"

Then the world snaps back, and wailin' sirens are floodin' the world with terrible sound. The darkenin' sky's lit up with blue, red, and white lights. They're close.

"Get up, Andi! Get up! Brass are here! Fuck, fuck!" Elenbar's mouth's a twisted smear of fear. They're very close. I stumble, tryin' to get up, but my knees are numb from kneelin' on the hard ground. My back is numb too. That's for the best.

"Eyyy! Eyy!" Puddin's bobbin' like a cork and wavin' her arms at us. She's pointin' to a vehicle, to one of Tivoli's mobbin' transport. They're all dark black tiger SUVs, white stripes painted across their hoods.

"Dis one got 'em keeeees! Keees!"

We run toward her. My muscles are wakin', and I'm more like a livin' person again. In the marketplace, between tents and shop stalls, I can see shadows movin'. Screams punch the air. Gunfire clatters, the chompin' rattle of the Tik-Tiks. I smell sulphur. Brass got laser weapons, and those only smell when they're searin' flesh and hair.

Somethin' whizzes by my ear, leavin' a stingin' path across the back of my neck. We duck low. My adrenaline's coursin' full, and I'm back in the world with both feet. We reach Puddin', and I wrench open the side door. Gleamin' keys hang in the ignition. Elenbar dives in and crawls to the driver seat.

"Dis go doom doom feeest outta 'ere!"

I open my mouth to speak, to pull her in—

Her head warps and explodes in a gush of blood and brain matter. Puddin' sprays into my mouth, into my eyes and nose. I drop back into the seat of the car, barely inside as Elenbar guns the engine. We squeal forward, gravel kickin' back against my legs still flailin' outside the door. My feet skitter against the quickenin' earth before I wrench myself farther in, the skin of my flayed back screamin' as it scrapes across the upholstery. The door slams as Elenbar jerks the wheel, weavin' through a couple parked Enforcers. Glass explodes across my body as the side window shatters, the laser blast liquefyin' the center into a spray of molten glass droplets. They pock across my bare chest and I scream, tearin' at the skin until they're mostly gone.

"Fuck! Oh my fuuuuuck!" I'm spittin' out bits of Puddin', the copper blood and twist of bitter innard fluids makin' me retch into the foot compartment of the seat.

"Stay down, just stay down!"

"Watch out!" I scream as the front tires bang over a curb. We slam back down on the main asphalt road. Elenbar's beelinin' to the bridge. If we make it over the Liberty, we're halfway clear. Sirens wail behind us, light reflectin' off the splintered windshield. They're followin' close.

The engine howls as Elenbar drops her foot to the metal floor. We fly over a bump in the road and my head slams against the roof. The back end fishtails, but she gets it under control. But lights flare in front of us, right in front of the Liberty Bridge.

They've blocked it. A full roadblock barricadin' our escape. The only way out.

"Ele! What do we do?"

"Hold on, ya fagger, just hold on!" Elenbar jerks the wheel, and we slam through one of the Tivoli pikes, the black flag sheetin' across our windshield before it's whipped away by the force of our acceleration. Then water, there's nothin' but water straight ahead of us. We sail off the edge of the embankment, a moment of silence as the tires leave ground.

We slam into the murky green water of the Anacostia River.

Junkie

THE RIVER SWALLOWS our tiger transport faster than I thought possible. We bob for a moment, then begin sinkin'. Water gushes through my shattered window and the force flushes me against Elenbar in the opposite seat.

"The water, I c—can't get out!" I splutter through a mouthful of river. It tastes like mold spores and dirty dishwater.

"Go ta the back, bust through the back!"

We scramble over the seats, the water sloshin' around our waists. We're almost underwater already, the cold river envelopin' us in the rushin' sound of the current and the gushin' water infiltratin' our temporary air bubble. We scramble over boxes in the back, but this ain't the way.

"Ele! We gotta let the car get full up!"

I can't see her face, but imagine its ghost whiteness. We ain't good swimmers. Almost drowned in the river by the Farm. It ain't good, and it's a mighty strong push to the surface because we're sinkin' fast. Maybe faster than lungs can hold air.

I hear a chokin' sob. Realize it's me. Water's sloshin' around my shoulders. Elenbar's bony cold hand is in mine, and I squeeze it, hard. The world shrinks like we're inside a leakin' balloon, our air gettin' smaller and tighter around us.

"Suck in that air! We're going topside! Together!" She digs her nails into my palm.

I fumble for the hatch handle at the back and turn it, suckin' hard at the last remnants of air. Water touches my earlobes. The handle isn't turnin'. I let go of Elenbar. Then my free hand touches the bag. The familiar feel and crinkle of a cellophane-sealed brick of Flow. Might be Biff. Or—

The air's gone, water swallows us up, and I kick at the back window. The whole pane pops out, obedient and whole. All's dark except faint light far above. Too far. Elenbar's foot slams my elbow as she shimmies past. My hand closes on, oh yah, it closes on the cellophane brick.

Because of course it does.

I tuck it in my pants. Then I'm kickin', swimmin', thrashin' my face toward where distant sky must be. My lungs're burnin' because I ain't a fish, this ain't my home. Ain't nothin' but death. My hand brushes Elenbar's kickin' foot. I'm right under her.

The light comes closer but then dims. River tide tugs at my body. Giddiness surges from the back of my mind. I could let go. I could stop. Just let it all go. I'm tired. So faggin' tired. The water thickens, and my arms slog through. Less and less, though. Less frantic. Air's bubblin' out my lips, can't hold it in no more. But there's a green glow; air's somewhere up there. Close. I think.

Everythin' gets bright like swimmin' in silvery silk. I almost breathe in, suck full lungs of water, because it's Ma. Slitherin' in the river, hair streamin' around her, robe ripplin' like translucent fins. The hollow ribs, even the saggy tits, like a holy angelfish. Come to take...me. Take me. To wherever we go after this world. I reach for Ma, reach for her hand. She's there, in front of me, reachin', but her gaze is filled with cobwebs, milky orbs unseein'. Because she's—she's—

I erupt through the surface in a great geyser. My lungs claw at air, heat scaldin' through me as I suck in whoopin' breaths, my vision splotchy with blackness and streamin' water. I look around, wildly, for Ma, but there's no white. No light at all except flashin' sirens far upriver because we're farther down than I thought.

"Ele! Where are you?!"

I hear a shrill series of twitterin' bird calls. Elenbar. *But from where?*

"Here! I'm here, ya twink!"

She's a few yards from me. My muscles are screamin' and the pull of the river rushes us farther away from the bridge. I look downstream and see the Wall, risin' ominous and still in the distance, marked by red blinkin' lights along the rim. Still far enough away. We got time.

"We gotta get outta the water!" I choke on a mouthful as I try to shout over the loud rush of the river.

"Nah, thought I'd ride it out, see what happens!"

We paddle hard towards the bank, but we ain't strong. The current's freezin' cold, but panic keeps a quickened heart warm. As I slam my palms through the choppy current, I feel the bulge at my waist. The brick of Flow. You know what else keeps you warm, other than panic? An upcomin' fix. I swim harder, my veins already itchin' as I imagine tearin' open the surprise parcel, seein' what's what.

My feet scrape bottom, and I slide for a bit until I find bigger rocks to anchor against. Elenbar's up a few paces from me and crawls out like a rat wearin' a soggy river diaper. My hand curls around the package. My teeth chatter with cold and my hands shake too, though that might be anticipation too. The riverbank butts up against the back alley of a few warehouse buildings. Maybe a manufactory, but probably just abandoned like most on this side of the Slumland. Plus there ain't no smell but the Anacostia shit water.

"Knockers! Shyte, fuckin' shyte!" Elenbar collapses beside me, slingin' her arm around my neck. I'm still suckin' air, but most the pain and dizziness is gone. Nothin' but cold and needlin' desire stabbin' my guts.

"Keepers. I'm freezin'." I look at the winkin' siren light in the distance. Faint sound ripples across to us, amplified on the coursin' water's surface. "What're we gonna do?"

"We keep going. Go ta the Wall. I half made that shyte up about Tivoli. I didn't really think Society would come ta them. Not like that. Not so fast." She's lookin' at the bridge too. I wonder if she's thinkin' about Puddin' like I am. The river's washed away the gore, but I swear I can still taste the buttery spatter of her blood and brains in my mouth.

"We've gotta stay focused, Andi. This is—this is bad. They're flushing us out, hunting us down. If we don't get out of here...no one will ever be the wiser. Won't be on any news report fer the public ta see. We'll just get disappeared, and it won't matter how many of us died or are dead. It'll be fer nothing. The Brigade will be stomped out. It's happening again."

She's said stuff like this before. Not that I ever half listened. But this ain't that time. I'm listenin' now. For a few minutes, there ain't no sound but the clatter of my teeth. She don't even seem cold. Siren light dazzles in the shiny pools of her green eyes.

"You said 'again.' What's happenin' again?" I rub my arms, and she looks at me like she just noticed I was here. I'm amazed she's still got her backsack, and she shrugs it off her shoulders, then opens the zipper.

"There's always been folk like us. Here, this is wet but it's something." She hands me a muddy gray T-shirt. "Transgressors living and walking the earth like anybody else, like any of the straights. I mean, we weren't called that back then. Everything was different. We were even seen as teachers, something special. As people of—well, people worth their ability. We sure didn't live on the streets. We lived in houses, right up next ta the straights. Even some straights weren't straights. Ya could love a woman or a man, could *be* a woman, man, or whoever ya are up here." She taps the side of her head, and I'm thinkin' about the doc. I'm also tryin' to ignore the brick of Flow pokin' my hip.

"Right. The doc, he said we were supposed to be natural women born. That bein' a Transgressor wasn't what was meant for us."

"Yah? What'd ya tell him?"

"I told him I ain't a woman. But..." I scrunch my nose, which is numb in the cold air. "I ain't a man neither. I mean, what are we really?"

"Well...what do ya feel?"

"I'm me. I'm just—I'm Andi. Whatever that means."

Elenbar rubs my arm, creatin' one spot of warmth on my freezin' skin. "Means a lot actually. There's a lot of words saying all sorts of things about what we are, what we're supposed ta be. Ya saw the Farm, they got all sorta thoughts about what a woman is, what a man should be. We carry the weight of those words."

"You said that once. That Transgressor don't mean what anyone thinks it means. That even the 'trans' is a word echoin' through time. A time when it meant somethin' to a lot of people."

She glances at me, surprised. "Didn't think ya ever listened proper ta any of my stuff."

"I listened some. Don't remember it all, you yam on so much."

She smiles and I do too, but my teeth start chatterin' again.

"We gotta get ta the Wall. We'll get what we get on the way. Scrounge some food, supplies if we can. We got less time than I thought," Elenbar says, reachin' for my hand.

I take it, and she yanks me to my feet. And the packaged brick of Flow slips right outta my damn pants.

It hits the ground with a soft thump, and I keep lookin' right at Elenbar, willin' her not to hear, not to see, not to know what a hump of shit I am.

"Andi." It's all she's gotta say.

"I jus'— I grabbed it. I was thinkin'—we could pinch it off, some rands to buy food maybe, or, you know, before we—"

The slap I expected but the punch I didn't. I hit the ground hard, flat on my back. Cold had dulled the roar of my painful back flesh, but the rash of gravel sears it anew. I scream and cover my face as Elenbar stands over me, expectin' her to kick at me, rememberin' her rage at Pint, and almost hopin' she does. Because I'm a junkie.

Piece of goddamn shit junkie-trash-belly-black-junkie-SHYTE.

But there's nothin', and after a moment, I lower my arm, ready to retreat again.

Elenbar just stares down at me. "It's done. That part, that life's done. It's gotta be. Ya wanna stay here, fiend it out, scram, and try ta make it? I'll let ya. But ya want ta come with me? Want ta make it through the Wall? Want ta do right by all of them that's gone down with the Brigade? Then I need ya with me. Yer head and body, knockers? It's done, Andi." Her face's a dead pail of serious milk.

I stare at the package, right next to my hand. The cellophane is all tight and neat and tucked. The huge amount of dry fluffy powder inside, nestled all safe and warm from the world.

Junkie. Fuckin' junkie. Can't stay off the juice long enough to do a run. Shit junk-tard. Fuckin' junk-tard. Trash. Tard. Junk. Fuck. Fucker. FUCK.

Words scratch at my skull, etched with the memory of Pint, Elenbar, the Sisters, Ma, the scream of a mite I can't save ever, the roar of slappin' ocean waves beyond where the dead sleep. The smell of vomit. Of pissin' myself. The chemical sweet of a come-down sweat. My mouth's waterin' and my hands shake. All I want's that package. All I want...want.

But it ain't. That *ain't* all I want. Bosco. The Brigade. To be somethin' else, anythin' else than what I am. *Junkie.* I don't think I got it in me, but I gotta try. With the way Elenbar's glarin' at me, the way this whole sewer slick world is turnin', I just gotta try. Somehow.

I look up at Elenbar and clench my jaw against the swell of gut juice sloshin' with desire. "Then help me. Help me up. Let's go. Before I change my mind and cock it all up."

She don't say nothin' but nods and drags me to my feet. I sway a li'l. I force myself not to look back at the package but to look ahead at the ominous silent sheet of Wall blottin' out the far horizon.

"I'm proud of ya. It isn't easy, probably won't ever be."

I hug my arms across my chest, feelin' small and empty. "Why's it always so easy for you? You've hit just as much as us. Dropped it twice as much, too."

Elenbar sighs and shrugs. "It isn't because I'm better. I just... Every time I want ta disappear in it, duck deep into the hole, I think about the Brigade. About ya, and Minnie, and P-Hat, and all the rest. How I'm gonna let y'all down if I don't get up and out."

"That...makes me feel worse."

"I'm sorry fer that. Let's just—let's go," Elenbar says.

"Do we just leave it? Sittin' here?"

"Someone'll find it. Hey, think about it—it's a fuckin' junkie Christmas fer someone real soon." Elenbar smiles and slugs me on the arm. It hurts, but I smile back. I kinda like that. The idea someone's gonna get a big surprise package. Though I still kinda wish it was me.

"All right, let's get the hell outta this shyte land."

Elenbar slinks her hand in mine, and I follow her.

I look back just once. Makin' sure it's still there.

Just in case.

The Wall

THE WALL RISES like somethin' from a dream or maybe my worst nightmare. It blocks the horizon and stretches higher than any buildin' but the cloudscrapers, higher than anythin' I've ever seen in my short life. The surface is a corrugated metal, like the sides of busted up shippin' crates, and it's sturdy. More than sturdy, you can sense the...the thickness just standin' by it. *How deep does it go? How big is this damn wall?* We all knew about it, we all talked about it—we grew up with stories about the evils in the Outer World the Wall kept at bay. So say the Society. Keeps out the chinks, pastels, pintos...chumsuckers, far as the Uppers knew. Not that they know anythin' about anythin'. But to see the Wall, to actually see it right here before me, is somethin' else entirely.

"Elenbar, I don't know if we can... I mean, how the bucket-fuckin' hell we gonna climb the sumabitch?"

"No. We're going right on through. There's tunnels all the way, access ports along the perimeter. Utility pockholes and the like. We gotta find the right one. Intel tells us it's marked somehow. Damn, we're running outta time, though." The sun's sunk behind the expanse of wall, and the streetlights are poppin' on in response to the encroachin' darkness.

I pull out an old watch with a busted face from my pocket. I pinched it off an Upper once in Hyde Square. Almost got snatched for it, too. The watch hands don't move, just frozen in place. Ain't a solar-charged one like most they make these days. It's a classic.

"Damn. Dead." I drop the copper case on the ground. Don't seem I'm gonna be findin' batteries anytime soon.

"No, bring it. We might be able ta trade it or use it fer something. Besides, we gotta keep our tracks clean. In case they come after us."

"You think they will?" I pick it back up and tuck it into my pocket again.

"I didn't think all that shit was going down, that Pint would turn it out and all the shit... I'm not sure, but we gotta go like we do. Like it's what's happening. Okay, now we gotta look fer the symbol. They said it would be marked, but not too well, nothing too obvious."

Pint. I wanna say somethin', wanna ask her if maybe it weren't that— maybe Pint was in the wrong place, wrong time sorta thing—but I remember the rage flickerin' in her glare, and the rise and fall of her furious steel fist. And 'cause I'm a lily-tit-twistin' coward, I don't say that. Instead I ask, "Who's they? And what's the marking supposed to be?"

"At the Farm. After ya went ahead, that brass bitch relayed a message ta me from the doc. That's how we coordinated getting out—she actually helped me, don't know why she bothered really. But they didn't tell me much. Not near enough, anyway." Elenbar adjusts the small backsack she snagged off the forty-two-line bus we took to get here. Least there weren't any fermentin' meat sacks on that one. We'd stopped at a shop and picked up a few flares and Nutri-Bricks, but we didn't have hardly any rands left, so it ain't much.

Elenbar's already walkin' along the Wall, and then she reaches out and touches it.

I realize I'm holdin' my breath. Nothin' happens, though, and Elenbar walks on, scannin' the height and length of the Wall. I follow her lead, tentatively touchin' the rough metal with my fingertips. I push against it, lightly, just to see. Of course, it don't budge, and again, there's that sense of, well, of massiveness. That the Wall contains entire cities or worlds inside. A chill passes over me, and I clench my fist against a tremor. I would kill for some Flow—or better, some Biff—but that's gotta be over. Like Elenbar said, that's gotta be in the past. Scorin' on the run ain't gonna be much of an option, and dryin' out on the run would be worse. Somehow I gotta keep it together, keep it all from fallin' apart. The thought scares the river shits right outta of me. *Faggin' junkie.*

"Hey! Ya with me?"

Elenbar stares at me, anger mixed with that glimmer of fear too. Ain't ever quite gone away since the Farm.

"Keepers, did they— Who the fuck are *they,* anyway? Who's the doc workin' with? And did the doc say what the symbol is, exactly? And how'd they know we're gonna go to the Wall, anyway?"

Elenbar don't answer, just lets me prattle on. So I'm assumin' that's a big fat *no* to all the above. Faggin' cucks, or *contacts,* or whoever feeds her the magical dose of condescension she waves around sometimes.

We're still walkin', and the Wall stretches ahead and curves, its true expanse and length hidden by the buildings and houses of the quarter and landscape it flanks.

I look up toward the top, at a crowd of crows squawkin' and scrabblin' along small outcroppings in the Wall. Some places where the giant plates of metal meet are peeled back slightly, warpin' maybe from weather, rain, or maybe people did it, tryin' to take the Wall down piece by piece. It's so high I can't imagine anyone would be able to climb it without fallin' to the most final sort of death.

"You'd think they work harder ta keep it clean," Elenbar grumbles, bein' irritable, but she's right. There's loads of trash and rubble at the base, and the wind kicks up and flicks the crumpled newspaper around. The wind is cold, and I pull my dumpster jacket around me tighter. It's like huggin' a piece of tissue paper. The tips of my ears are numb, and I wish we could duck inside somewhere. My mind wanders, dwellin' on the cold and how tall the Wall is. Then I trip, hard, and before I can throw my hands out, I've scuffed my face on the ground. The wind's knocked out of me and everythin' spins and I'm chokin'. My foot's a throbbin' hot prick of pain.

"Hey! Ya all right?" Elenbar shakes me. My guts unclench, and I suck in life-savin' air in big whooshin' gasps. There's tears and I'm cryin' and shakin', surprised by the suddenness of it all.

"Augh, my foot," I groan and clutch at my leg. Elenbar squeezes down my shin and foot, and I hear a clank of metal.

"Fuck, bunch of garbage and rubble. Think ya mighta busted yer toe?" She sounds worried so I shake my head, even though, really, my foot's throbbin' so hard I'm tryin' not to keep cryin' about it. Elenbar holds up the two metal hooks I've tripped over. They look like crowbars with handles at the ends of them. I bite my lip and struggle to my feet, one hand against the Wall to support myself. I look up and see...well, damn, I see the symbol, don't I? I point, and Elenbar spins around like I bit her in the ass.

"That's it, that's gotta be it!"

The symbol's a handprint, but only lookin' at it from straight down like I am. The paint is faded, old, but still visible even though it ain't all that big. Looks about the size of a real hand.

"Andi, you're a certifiable bookfucker!" Elenbar gives me a quick squeeze, then starts runnin' her hands along the Wall where we stand.

"But why's it all the way up there?" My lower lip's bleedin'.

The symbol is at least a two-person-length up the Wall, and ain't no way we could get at it from where we stand. I search for some sign of breach in a popped panel or somethin', but I don't see anythin'.

"Well, there's gotta be an entrance 'round here. They said there would be, and all else has been spot-on, hasn't it?" Elenbar runs her fingers along the metal, as though a hidden panel might exist, ready to pop open at just the right touch.

My foot's still throbbin', and I see Elenbar still holdin' those hooks in her hand, one in each like they're, well, like they're clunker arms welded to her fleshy frame.

"Oh, christ crackers. I think I know what we're supposed to do."

Elenbar looks at me, then at the hooks, and then we both look at the Wall. Yah, we can see it now. The small divots and outcroppings in the metal are actually hookholds, just big enough pockets to sink the ends into and haul yourself up. It's a damn job, and I'm not sure either of us got the strength for it.

"I'll do it," Elenbar says before I can. I'm grateful, though, I don't say it.

Elenbar glares at the hooks, thinkin' hard, then at the closest divots. She ain't quite tall enough to even reach the first ones.

"I'll haul you up," I say and give her an alley-oop with my crossed hands. She's light enough, and I brace against the wall so I ain't pushin' on my foot too hard. With the boost, she gets the hooks in almost right away, but I gotta push her up so she can get one hook up to the next one. Once she gets the first foothold, the rest seems easy, but it ain't. Pullin' your sack of guts and bones up a sheer wall, hangin' on to steel metal handles and tryin' to brace your crappy sneaks on the snags in the wall... I'm glad Elenbar is doin' it because I ain't so good with heights neither.

It takes a few minutes, but then she's at face level with the symbol.

"You see anything?" I yell up at her.

"No! I don't see anything!" Her voice's kinda muffled because her face is so close against the Wall. One of her legs quivers.

"Hey! Be careful, don't you come fallin' on my damn head!"

I hear her laugh, but it's high-pitched and scared soundin'. Then I worry she really is gonna fall, and I try to mentally prepare myself for havin' to catch her. She swings one hook to the right and manages to side crawl about six feet. I hear metal on metal and a loud squeal as a door opens. It's a hatch of some kind, and Elenbar scurries inside. A few seconds later she pokes her head out and looks down at me.

"Anythin' in there?"

"It's all dark. I can't see anything. Ya think ya can crawl up here if I throw down the hooks?"

I shake my head, my cheeks hot because I'm a hopscotch newt who can't even scuttle up a damn wall and my life might actually depend on it.

"Okay, just stay there a minute." Elenbar disappears back inside the hole.

The sun's slipped down farther, and it's almost proper night, light swallowed by the shadow of the Wall. The wind's still rustlin' the trash, and now that I can't see so good, it's eerie, like somethin's watchin' me. It's probably just the crawly creep of the darkness, though. I wish Elenbar would come back or say somethin' because the feelin' is gettin' worse as it's gettin' darker and colder.

Then I hear the growl.

It's bigger than a dog, but ain't no street dog ever sound so mean, ever sound so angry. I whirl around, lookin' for it, ready to kick at it. My heart's poundin' in rhythm with the pain in my foot, and for a moment, my body is one throbbin' organism, a quiverin' ball of flesh perfectly in sync with its own terror and pain. Ain't no one need a hit of Flow to feel that kind of fear.

"Elenbar! Ele! Are you up there?!" The growlin' comes again and continues, a throaty roar gettin' louder and closer. It's gotta be able to hear me, and I shouldn't yell, but I can't help it. I can't climb the damn wall without those hooks, and I can't climb it anyway without a leg up. I ain't no taller than Elenbar.

I see the eyes first. They gleam even in the darkness, as though lit up with an inner glowin' fire. That ain't natural, ain't no livin' thing got eyes like that. My mouth opens in silent screamin' because it's down a ways, down where we came to the fence, comin' off Winston Street. If I ever doubted they were comin', if I ever doubted they would follow, that doubt falls away right then. They are comin', they are followin', and they're here.

"Andi! Andi! Hurry!"

I look up and see Elenbar's face, only a faint shadow, lookin' down at me. Her wide eyes are pinholes compared to the wide gape of her mouth.

She drops somethin' over the edge. It ain't the claws, though. It's a rope. An actual ladder made of rope and I grab it and climb. I hear the creature scrabblin' in the dark, snufflin' and growlin' all the while it's comin' closer. Maybe it didn't hear us. It don't sound in a hurry, comin' along at a steady pace, and I don't look because I'm strugglin' with the loose rope, which ain't easy to climb, especially with a bum foot. The rope is scratchy and cuttin' my hands, and my legs tangle in the rungs. Panic almost overtakes my brain completely, but Elenbar's got her hand reachin' toward me, strainin'. So I climb and struggle, throwin' my hand out and graspin' hers. Our hands are sweaty, but fear drives me and I scrabble up and into the hole, bangin' my shin hard on the edge. Warm blood's poolin' already, slippin' down my leg, but I give zero fucks about such a flesh wound. Elenbar pulls the ladder back up, and we're both starin' down at the creature that's stalkin' the base of the Wall.

See, that's the power of fear, because it ain't a creature at all. It's some sort of clunker, a beasty-lookin' one, and the growlin' is actually the roar of high-powered fans rumblin' on either side of what might be the creature's spine. The eyes do glow, lighted by fuses and whatever powers the clunkers. It's rollin' by on four wheels, and as it goes, I see glass lenses on its top.

"Shyte." Elenbar pulls me back from the edge.

"What is it?"

"It's got cameras on it. Like at the banks and hospitals and stuff. It must be recording, lookin' fer us, or people like us. Seems to be some sort of nightly guard maybe. I bet it sees in the dark and signals the rest of the brass and clunkers. Did it see you?"

"I don't think so—well, I don't know, but I don't think so. Wasn't roarin' down on me. I thought it was. Hah, I thought it was a wolf or monster or somethin'."

Elenbar doesn't laugh, and I realize she must've thought it, too. I peer out the hole and see the creature rollin' past, fans roarin' and cameras swivelin' as it goes.

"Should we close the door?" I turn to the passageway leadin' from this entry point. The tunnel is rounded like maybe some kind of pipe for air or water. Don't look like the normal way people would enter.

"Let's wait a while. It'll be pitch as a witch once we close the door, and I gotta get my heart ta stop jittering first," Elenbar says. "Lucky they keep this rope here ta get in and out. Though it's bolted ta this edge. Huh. Ya would've been smoked."

I'm glad for it too. My heart's still doin' a skip, and my foot hurts much more now that we're safe up here. Scramblin' up the ladder meant not listenin' to the pain, but now I'm listenin' all right, and it's made friends with the pain in my banged-up shin. I pull my pant leg up and see it's already soaked in blood. There's a busted open cut on the front of my leg.

Elenbar looks grim as a syringe of anti-clap.

"It's fine, hardly even bleedin' anymore," I say.

"How's yer foot?"

"It's fine." It sounds like a faggin' lie as I say it, and it is, because it don't feel fine, don't feel fine at all. The pain overshadows everythin' else, and I'm suddenly tired, really dead-in-the-bones tired. We ain't really slept since the Farm, except for crouchin' in the alley for a couple hours in the witch-tit cold.

"Let's sleep. We'll leave the door open a crack, in case we need some light in a hurry. But this is as good as any." Elenbar must be in my head, and I'm so grateful for it. She opens her arms, and I crawl into them. The metal is cold, but exhaustion and agony win, and I immediately fall into a deep and heavy sleep.

Fox Holes

THE RUMBLE WAKES us both, rollin' from deep in the earth, under the Wall itself. Except it's much louder and echoes through the steel guts of the tunnel we're in.

"Holy horse fuckin'!" I grab Elenbar's arm, and we're both vibratin' slowly along the slick metal floor, the reverbs carryin' our weight like jumpin' beans.

"Hold on! It'll go!" We're both shoutin' over the bangin' roar of the earthquake and the groan of the Wall's attempts to stay upright.

But it does go, like it always does, and the sudden silence leaves a ringin' in my ears.

"Jesus prick-suckin'—you ever felt one like that? It's like it's right inside with us!" The back of my neck's damp with cold sweat.

Elenbar groans in reply, and I roll off her, my foot growlin' in protest as I do.

We're down the tunnel a few paces, submerged in darkness. The shakin' slammed the outer hatch shut, but I creep my fingertips along the floor until I reach it. I peek into the world outside, blinkin' hard in the contrastin' light. The risin' of the distant dawn's somethin' I've seen so many times comin' down off Flow benders, but it looks different with sobriety and my perma-surge of adrenaline. Elenbar places her chin on my shoulder, not sayin' anythin' as we watch the neighborhood startin' to wake. A gong of church bells sounds in the distance, and my gut clenches at the thought of St. Aggie's. Don't think their bells'll ring anytime soon. If ever again.

"Ya thinking about the Sisters?"

"They made it out. Sister Jordana anyway—she'll keep them safe." I'm thinkin' about the mites, wide eyes and empty heads. World blasted apart by things no one can rightly understand.

"Keepers, she'll keep them safe. And the others in the network will help. They ain't all going ta get scooped." Elenbar's tryin' to help, but it's makin' it worse somehow, talkin' about it.

We're quiet again, and I become aware, with a slow creepin' realization, of a tickin' sound comin' from deep inside the tunnel.

"Do you hear that?" My whisper sounds freakish loud, but I don't wanna lose the sound.

"Hear what?"

"Shh..."

It's a metallic clickin', like a piece of clockwork, tickin' away.

"Just the workings of the system inside. I think we should keep moving," Elenbar says, pullin' out a lighter.

"I wish we had a proper light. Ain't in love with the idea of crawlin' through the shit with nothin' but that li'l thing."

She grimaces. "Yah, well, time wasn't exactly on our side, was it? The Wall isn't that deep. We'll be out before the end of the day if we stay it straight and keep on it."

I don't say nothing. I grab the metal handle on the inside of the hatch door and pull it shut. The darkness is a new kind of frightenin'. I ain't ever been in dark like that kind of dark. I hold my hand in front of my face, but there ain't no outline even. I give up on seein' reality, and instead I see flickerin' streaks in my vision, though it ain't real light.

"We're in it now. No turning back," Elenbar says. Then she flicks the lighter, and the flame is bright and alive, castin' deep shadows around us. She gestures for me to follow. The tunnel is tall enough that we can almost walk at full height. We gotta stoop some, and as we shuffle along, my foot revives with a new and hot pain. I grit my teeth, resolvin' myself not to complain, not to worry Elenbar about it, but the sound of my unsteady gait draws her attention pretty quick.

"Yer foot gonna be all right?"

"No turnin' back," I say, and she nods.

There's a solemn mood as we creep forward and we hit an immediate left bend in the passageway. There's bends and forks in opposite directions. And suddenly nothin' seems to be takin' us forward, only sideways. I try to make a map in my mind, but I give up after six turns.

We're hittin' a stride, and it's somethin' like this:

Elenbar flicks on the lighter, and we look to see how far the tunnel stretches.

The lighter goes off, and we shuffle along in pitch blackness, steadyin' with one hand on the metal wall.

When we're gettin' close or sense we're gettin' close, because sensin' shit in the dark's a weird magical thing, the lighter snaps back on, and we check.

Repeat over and fuckin' over again.

We're stayin' mostly left, and there's bundles of cables runnin' along the ceiling of the tunnel. The clickin' sound gets louder, and we feel a breeze. We stop for several breaks, and I'm startin' to think it ain't gonna be just a one-day thing. Nothin's a straight walk through, and time's becomin' a blur in the depths of the Wall. We're above ground, but it's more like a cave, like we're deep inside the earth. All sound's a muffle, and there's rumblin' churnin' movement somewhere beyond our tunnel, like we're nestled in the womb of a giant clunker belly.

Elenbar flicks on the lighter, and it's snuffed in the breeze we're gettin'. She flicks it on again, usin' her body to block the rush as best she can. I peek around her and see a giant rotatin' fan.

"Shit stickers. I don't think we can go this way," I say.

Elenbar sighs. "We'll have ta backtrack, try another turn."

"I wouldn't recommend it." The male voice sends us both jumpin' so hard we crash into each other.

Elenbar holds the lighter out, but the tunnel behind us is mostly cloaked in darkness. "Shyte, ya fucking crawler bitch, come out here! Who are ya?"

"Easy, easy now." A man shuffles forward, his palms raised flat. His chin's a grizzled meadow of gray and brown stubble, cloakin' the otherwise skeletal hollow of his cheekbones.

"Stay back! Just stay there!" Elenbar's hand shakes, and the light shivers on the walls surroundin' us.

"Okay." The man squats and peers at us.. "Just thought you should know the other ways don't go anywhere, either. My wife is back there. We weren't sure who you were, so I came up ahead of her. Can I bring her to meet you?"

He don't seem a threat, as much as anyone can tell when you first meet someone. We look at each other in silent agreement. Ain't much else to do about it.

"Just go slow." Elenbar's tryin' to keep menace in her voice now that she ain't scared half outta her mind.

"Sure, sure. I'll be right back." The man shuffles back the way he came.

"What do you think?"

Elenbar gnaws on her fingernail. "Be careful. We don't know them. Could be spies fer all we know."

"Spies? In the Wall? He don't look so good. Maybe they're just tryin' to get through, too. Maybe they got supplies or found another way." I'm hopin' food, and like it's hearin' our conversation, my gut growls real loud. My thought process sounds good, sounds comfortin' even, but Elenbar's got the nerves too, the shakin' fear we've just met enemies in the dark. We ain't got no weapons, no food, nothin' but wits and grit on our side, and that ain't shit when you're a fox in a foxhole.

"Okay, we're coming closer now. Don't be afraid," the man says. He inches forward, enterin' the sphere of light and glances behind him, motionin' for her to come too.

When she emerges from the shadows, I gasp. I can't help it. The woman's face, her beautiful face, is half-gone. One side is red and shiny like the melted plastic of a doll. On her opposite cheek, a deep M has been carved into the flesh. The wounds ain't all fresh; they've scabbed with a thick crunch of crusty blood and healin' ooze. A Murder Maiden. You saw them on the news, but I ain't ever seen one up close before.

"I'm sorry," Elenbar says.

"It's okay, but you see why we're here," the man says.

The woman don't smile. Maybe she can't even smile with her face like it is. Her dark gaze is sunken, and she don't even look scared, just maybe dead inside or close to it. Beaten at the core where you carry the li'l light that's supposed to keep you alive. Sisters at St. Aggie's always had us singin' about that li'l light, and the woman? The li'l light ain't shinin' at all.

"Have ya...how long ya been in here?" Elenbar asks.

"It's been, what, four days now? Using my watch here." The man lifts his hand, shinin' a wrist timekeeper at us.

Elenbar lets the lighter flick off. Probably burnin' her fingers.

"Four days? You haven't found a way through at all?" My rumblin' stomach clenches at the thought of four whole days, stumblin' around in the dark.

"No. The other ways go to drop-offs, and we can't see beyond the bend. We've been talking about what to do,when we heard your voices and saw your light. Followed you a while, trying to make sure you weren't, well, a threat." The man's voice is filled with a silent apology for the same suspicions we had ourselves.

"Drop-offs? How far down does it go?" Elenbar asks.

"Not sure. Our flashlight died...well, we guess yesterday. We couldn't check them all, but maybe, with you here, we can find a way."

Elenbar flicks the lighter back on, and my chest blazes with a surge of hope. Together seems awfully better than muckin' through alone, lost in the growin' maze.

Elenbar looks less convinced. "So you came into the tunnels, looking fer a way through? How'd ya find a way in? What are ya going ta do when ya get ta the other side?"

"We had to. They threatened to... They threatened to kill her." He glances at his wife, but she don't seem to notice. She ain't lookin' at any of us, really. "I couldn't let that happen." His voice drops to a whisper. "I mean, she would have died having the baby. The baby, too. The doctors all said it, and I couldn't part with her, not like that." He presses a hand to his mouth and tears shine in his eyes. "So I paid a lot of money and found out about these tunnels. They say once you're on the other side, you can find help, or others who are making a new life. Better than watching your wife on trial for doing the only thing she could. To save her own damn life."

"What happens if there ain't nothing on the other side?"

The man looks at me, and his eyebrows tighten. "Well, what are *you* going to do if there isn't? We're lookin' at the same thing, aren't we? Baby killer, and— Well, I know what you two are. I'm in no place to judge, but we're all stuck in the same damn hole together, *ain't* we?"

I like him. Elenbar lets the light die again.

"He's right, Elenbar. Let's just— Hey, let's just check out these drop-offs. See what we've gotta see. Unless we've got tools, ain't none of us gonna to be able to get through there." I gesture to the fan behind us, before forgettin' no one can see me anyway.

Elenbar flicks the light back on.

"All right, let's go then. Show us." It's a command, not a request, but the man just nods and turns away from us, one arm slung around his wife's shoulders. They shuffle ahead, still stayin' within the sphere of light as we bring up the rear. Then Elenbar flicks off the light, and we plant our hands on the tunnel wall for guidance.

"Don't like it," Elenbar whispers as she pulls close behind me.

"What? Why? They're ain't no harm to anyone. Look at them. Damn near dead themselves."

"Say we help them find a tunnel and keep going, who's ta say they won't beat us down and take the lighter fer themselves? Leave us in the dark after all."

It don't seem a likely thing, but Elenbar's in a mood so I don't say nothin'. We follow them for a while, and then we hit the previous junction.

"This is where we hid when we heard you pass by. We didn't have a light so this one we should check out. We checked most of the others, though it's hard to tell with all the turns we made along the way. Could be more back there," the man says. He leans against the wall, makin' a small space for Elenbar to creep by. She slinks by him, glarin' like he's gonna make a move, but he don't and she leads the way, movin' slowly in case a drop-off comes. For a while, there ain't, so we just keep shufflin' along. We take another turn, and we're hittin' straightaways again. Elenbar's flickin' off the light like before. It's colder, and the breeze is pickin' up again. I got a bad feeling we're gonna be encounterin' another—

"Fan," Elenbar says, stoppin' short and flickin' on the light.

I peek over her shoulder and see that it ain't a fan pointin' at us like the last one. It's a fan in a drop-off hole, with the tunnel continuin' ahead on the other side of it. We cluster closer to the edge and peer down. It's a long drop, and it would be a bitter end to fall into it, what with whirlin' blades at the bottom. The wind it's pushin' is colder than the other one.

"This is probably part of the cooling system," the man says. "Keeps the tunnels from collecting too much heat. The other fan is probably just part of the ventilation system, circulating the air. We must be getting closer to the machinery that runs, well, whatever's inside this Wall."

"What makes you think there's anythin' inside?"

The man stares at me funny. "Well, they couldn't have cannons and a defensive perimeter without machinery, could they?"

I feel stupid because I ain't sure what the faggin' hell he's talkin' about, but curiosity overpowers ego. "There's all sorts of stories about the Wall. Most it from scumsuckers who don't know shit from tit."

The man arches his eyebrows and looks at Elenbar, who don't say anythin' either. I figure Elenbar probably knows more than I do, because she listens and has friends higher-up who tell her stuff, tell her more than a cock-knocker like me is gonna know. Least that's how she always comes across.

"The Wall is the defensive perimeter surrounding the United Free States of Liberty, protecting it against foreign invaders."

"No faggin' shit, you douche nozzle. I got that, but what do you mean cannons and stuff?"

"The cannons are what protect us from the foreign invaders, so say the Society. The Wall is fortified with giant cannons and targeting systems in case they try to send planes overhead."

"Cannons? Like real gun cannons? Pirate-ship kinda cannons?" My mind's reelin' but doubtin' a lot of the garbage flowin' from this pussbag's mouth. "And they just sit inside here waitin' for invaders? The Free States haven't had invaders in, well, forever."

Surprise flares in my chest as Elenbar speaks. "Wasn't as long ago as you think. There were attacks during the Third World War. They tried to storm our borders, and I think that's what really made them beef up the walls. Didn't know they got cannons in it, though."

"Yeah, the cannons and defensive perimeters started getting built up after that. We lost so many soldiers in the War. Congress, the group before the Society, declared measures to save human lives. That's how clunkers ended up running the streets in the Slum—I mean, the lower quarters." The man looks embarrassed. "Though that's all ancient history. Hardly anyone knows all of that except what they teach in early schooling." The man stops, uncomfortable again like he just realized Elenbar or I ain't ever been in proper "schooling."

"Well, knowin' it ain't helpin' us here, so it ain't of any use to me." My cheeks are hot.

"You're right. We're just as lost as you," the man says.

Still like him okay. He don't seem so bad as other Upper cubi-squares.

"So, we can either figure a way over this or backtrack and hope ta tit we find another tunnel back the way we came." The cold wind snuffs the light, and I shiver, pickle flesh growin' all over my arms and legs.

"No guarantee there's another one back that way, and even if there is, we might just run across more of these," the man says.

"Why don't we just go back home?" The wife speaks for the first time, and her voice's shriller than I woulda thought, what with her dead-lookin' eyes and everythin'.

"There isn't any going back. I already told you that," the man whispers in a hiss.

"But you could go back, you could still go back to work. You haven't even missed a day yet. They don't even have any idea you're gone, not really gone. You're just on vacation. I could just, just, go on ahead. By myself. You could still have a *life*, David."

David. The name lodges in my brain.

"Not an option. Just stop it. I'm not leaving you, not ever, so we're going ahead together. It isn't a life without you."

She cries wet breathy sobs, and I'm glad for the darkness because it don't feel like a conversation we should be allowed to see. Too personal and all.

None of us talk for a while, and eventually she stops cryin'.

Only then does Elenbar flick the light back on. She inspects the metal gratin' of the tunnel and where it connects with the drop-off. Maybe thinkin' maybe we can link arms or somethin', if just one of us can get across.

"All right, this is gonna sound crazy, but hear it all the way." I don't like when Elenbar starts sentences like that. "David, I think ya should throw Andi across." She jerks her thumb at me, indicatin' I'm the sack of shit she's talkin' about.

"What? Throw her across?" He's blank at first, then scowls. "Throw her across *that*? That's absurd. There's got to be a better option than that. What if I drop her?" He's annoyed, but nowhere near the horror I got about this sewer swill of an operation.

"Andi's the lightest, and she can hop across without a problem. Once on the other side, maybe we can link hands and make a human bridge...or something."

I raise my hand. "Can the one gettin' chucked have a say in gettin' chucked?" Everyone stares at me, and much as I faggin' hate the truth, I ain't got nothin' better. Now is one of those moments I really need somethin' better.

"We could..." I peter off because my brain's a traitor, refusin' to provide solutions, and I wanna rip it right outta my ear pocket and stomp it beneath my shitkicker heel.

"Uhm, I'm not sure it will work anyway," David says. "Once she's across, I mean. Even if you could link hands, there's nothing to stabilize each person on either side. You could end up pulling each other down, and I don't think you could reach across anyway. Seems wider than that."

"Well, do ya have any glorious sun-in-yer-ass ideas then?" Elenbar's bristlin' with a special kind of rage, laser pointed on David, though I can't suss out why she seems to hate him so much.

"Maybe. I'm not sure if it'll work, and it didn't seem worth mentioning. Until now."

Elenbar's ears turn bright red.

"Okay, what is it, then?" I say, tryin' to buffer whatever storm of maggoty shit's about to explode between these two. The tunnel's startin' to feel mighty small.

"I noticed, as we were walking the tunnels, that there are markings at certain points. Utility panels or maybe crawl spaces to allow people to get in and repair certain connective points. They'd be a lot smaller than this tunnel, but if we can get inside of one, we might be able to crawl past this point and come out the other side. And no one would have to be tossed." David smiles at me like he's doin' me a holy-hole favor.

Elenbar snaps the light off. It's lookin' quite intentional, and I'm embarrassed she's actin' this way. Like a bratty mite, instead of the leader of the faggin' Brigade.

"Thanks, cuck," I say. David don't say nothin' at his new nickname. "We should give it a shot anyway." I'm tryin' to ignore Elenbar, even as she's elbowin' me in the dark. All my nerves are gettin' pinched. "But let's sleep first. I'm ripe and ready to catch some hours before we go muckin' about inside walls." The irony isn't lost on me, but it don't seem worth the laugh.

"Yes, let's sleep. We could all use it, I'm sure," David says.

Elenbar keeps the light off, so I'm assume she's signalin' some sort of agreement.

We all just sink down where we're at, and I resist the wantin' meanness to pinch Elenbar's tit for bein' such a miserable cunt instead of the leader I need her to be. She don't make any motion to huddle together, and though I'm glad, anger don't keep you warm for long. Within minutes, I'm shiverin', and my foot's also achin' real bad again, throbbin' with the cold and walkin' up and down the tunnels all day. Or night. Or whatever time it is. I hear David and his wife whisperin' quiet-like, and I can't hear what they're sayin'. I'm glad about that too because everythin' is too damn much right now. Piled high on top is the horrible crampin' hunger in my gut.

Yah, I'm mighty miserable, and about ready to chuck my own damn self across that faggin' drop-off. Or maybe down it.

Good Omens & Bad Solutions

WHEN I WAKE up, Elenbar's got the light on and stands at the edge of the drop-off.

"What is it?" I stagger to my feet, my foot snivelin' like a botched root canal, cramped from bein' huddled on the cold metal.

"We should leave them."

I glance back at where David and his wife are huddled in the shadow beyond our halo. Now it ain't hunger crampin' my stomach; it's a nauseous unease.

"Elenbar, why are you bein' like this? You've been a right twat since we fell in with them, and they ain't done nothin' to us except doin' same thing we're doin'. Tryin' to survive."

She whirls to face me, tears shinin' and lips twisted in an angry sneer. I step back, surprised and a li'l afraid.

"Because they ain't us. They ain't *us*. We're here fer one reason: the Brigade. We've lost everything. I don't even know if P-Hat or any of the others are even alive. Pint, burn that fuckin' traitor—he brought it all down because I was too stupid, too *fool* ta see what was what. He wasn't *us* neither, and he dropped us right into the lap of the Society. Offer gets too good, any of *them* will do the same."

I realize then what Elenbar's on about, what's really got her riled to the point of belligerence.

"You're pissed they ain't *s/he*?" I say the word in a whisper, like a swear, because it is. "Like us?"

Elenbar crosses her arms across her chest. "I ain't pissed about it, but it's the way it is. They got no idea about the gutter, don't have any idea what it means to really survive. She got all cut up because she got a baby sucked out her twat, and that's the real hardship, isn't it? She wouldn't even be killed if they left the Upper Side moved to the Slumland. Just hide out like all the rest do. But no, better ta crawl through the tunnel, burrow through the Wall ta god-knows-fuckin'-what, better that than squat in the gutter with us punky garbage. Andi, they ain't us, and they ain't ever gonna be. The worst thing the Brigade ever did was align ourselves with those who don't know what it is ta be us."

I hadn't really thought on it like that. Some of it makes sense in its fucked-up way, but it ain't right. A pinch in my gut tells me that. I don't like it. Don't like it at all.

"You told me once the Brigade's supposed to represent all people...not just the pretty and the righteous type. Ain't that what it's all about, anyhow? They ain't any more responsible for what's happened to us than the mites gettin' dumped at St. Aggie's. They're stuck in it, too. Same system wantin' us all gone, all assigned and proper—well, it's the same gone and fucked up her face and almost killed her, ain't it?"

Elenbar scowls but doesn't say nothin' so I roll on, my brain churnin' as fast as I can speak.

"Movin' to the gutter with us wouldn't change any of that, would it? They'd still be under the same boot. They lookin' for freedom same as any Transgressor breathin' on this earth. Maybe more even, because they've least had some of what it's gotta taste like. Least the illusion of it." I'm surprised by my thinkin', and I forgive my brain for bein' a wad of blowie sludge last night. It sounds pretty good, sounds like somethin' Elenbar herself might've said before all this.

But she just glares at me, and the pinch in my gut becomes a punch because I see it, see a small glimmer of that same deadness. Same as the cold pock of ash in the eyes of David's walkin' dead wife. "Still. We should go."

"Like leavin' Bosco? Because he ain't us, neither." There's a knot in my throat. "I ain't gonna do it, Ele." The name spills out my mouth before I can reel it back in. That baby St. Aggie's name, but it sounds like truth right now, because maybe none of us ever left the mite we were at the cathedral, and I'm hopin' Ele's in there somewhere, hearin' me. "I can't do it. Makes me feel sick just thinkin' it. What if they were we? Ain't no one better than anyone when you're six feet in the hole."

"Feeling sorry's a mistake, and mistakes are gonna get us killed."

"Well, we ain't dead yet."

"Yet's a mighty close place to now."

We hear them stirrin' then, like they're wakin' up, and I'm glad because it means we don't gotta sneak off, but I watch Ele closely. Somehow can't shake the name now that it's rolled off my tongue a couple times. She's stranger than ever, and I wonder if she ever left the Farm, or if only a mutated shadow of her former self did.

"Hey, so, we have a little food," David says in a proper mornin' whisper.

Even though my stomach's sick instead of hungry, I still manage a lick of joy at the thought of eatin'. Seems like a good—oh, what's that word, um, oh yah, like a good omen.

David extends a small snack bar toward me, and I clench my fist to still the tremble before takin' it from him. We'd eaten the few Nutri-Bricks we'd bought on the first day, and it was a drop of water in a mighty dry and hungry bucket.

David extends a small bar towards me. It's wrapped in bright silver cellophane and has a cheery logo on the front of a smilin' monkey. None of our Nutri-Bricks ever got monkeys on them. I clench my fist to still the tremble before takin' it from him.

"We got only two left. But I figure if you two split that one, we'll split ours, and it'll keep us going a little while longer anyway." David shrugs.

"Thank you." I wanna call him a cuck, but might be sloppy manners to insult the hand bringin' food. "This here's a feast, you know, considerin'." I open the bar's wrappin' and break it in half. I bring it to Elenbar, but she shakes her head.

"Come on, don't be such a hard ass. You need it just as much as I do," I say, but she ain't hearin' me. I wait a tick, but she really ain't gonna take it, so I eat the whole thing, angry about havin' to do it and angry she's makin' me feel like a damn traitor for doin' it.

"Are we ready to try this?" David and his wife are on their feet. She gazes down the dark tunnel from where we came.

I'm scared Elenbar's gonna tell them off right there, make a scene, but she just looks at them and nods, stiff like a slab of frozen pond scum.

"All right then, last place I saw one of those utility panels is back here a ways," David says. We retrace a few feet, and he shows us what he's seen. It's a square panel of gray, not real obvious like it's anything but part of the Wall. Unless you really knew what it's for, might just be a shadow or a little different color is all. He motions for Elenbar to come closer with the light, and she frowns as she does, which makes me wanna smack her same she does to me when I'm bein' a twat about somethin'.

"Here, just along here," he says, runnin' his fingers along the edges of the panel. "Ahh, yeah, there's some screw heads at the corners. Just need something that can fit inside them and we can unscrew them off. Then we can get in. Maybe."

"And what do we do about the panel at the other side? Screws only go one way," Elenbar says, soundin' smug as a preacher's mug.

"Well, might have to deal with it when we get to that side. I think we could bash the panel outwards, but I won't be sure until we see the backside of it. If it doesn't work, tossing Andi is still an option." He smiles, but Elenbar don't, so I smile for her and I'm lookin' like a snivelin' moron, but I don't know what else to do. The tension's buggin' me. David's wife still stares off down the tunnel, like she's gonna make a run for it. I might join her.

"All right." It's that commandin' tone like Elenbar, somewhere, got crowned Queen of the Faggin' Death-Trap-Tunnels, an infuriatin' iciness sendin' the royal message that he's lucky she's stoopin' to the idea at all.

David riffles through his pockets. He reveals a shiny quarter rand, the large eagle emblem gleamin' in the flickerin' light. He crouches by the panel and sinks the coin edge into the crosshatch head of the screw. Everythin's quiet, and Elenbar flicks off the light again. The dark and creakin' sound of the twistin' coin makes my skin do a shimmy.

"After the War, they changed all the screws," David says, and I'm glad he's fillin' the heavy silence. "Severing the international trade meant producing them all inland, and they decided to abandon any remanants of the metric system completely. Pure chaos for a while, but the building of the Wall meant a lot of new jobs and once they figured how they wanted to do it, everything seemed to fall into place. This Wall...man, people were excited about it. Supposed to solve our problems." David's sayin' all this as he continues unscrewin'.

"Gee whiz, cuck, this what proper schoolin' gets you?" I cross my arms, a li'l in awe and a li'l annoyed at his brain bein' filled with all sorts of neatness.

David cocks a brow at the nickname, like he's wonderin' what it's all about. Then he shrugs. "Well, I'm not sure about that. My father was a history teacher. Suffered through more than a reasonable share of practice lessons and just his general obsession with the War. He was a soldier in it."

Elenbar clicks her tongue, and I glare at her.

"So what was gonna happen with the Wall anyway, once the War stopped?"

"I don't think they ever intended to take down the Wall. It wasn't about peace. Not really. I think they were just getting people to be scared about everything outside the Free States. But all we did was close up all the problems we had inside from getting out. Honestly, I wonder what the world out there is like. If it's any better since we stopped interfering in it all," David says as he keeps twistin'. It's slow, tedious work, and Elenbar flicks on the lighter again and sighs. Loudly. He ain't even finished with the first one.

"Hey, cuck, you got another one of them?" I ask, wantin' to kick Elenbar in the head.

David riffles through his pockets and hands one to me. I crouch, followin' his example with the bottom screw. It starts slowly emergin' from its metallic cocoon. Elenbar flicks off the light.

"So why'd the Wall seem such a good idea, anyway?" Talkin' passes the time, and I'm curious, bein' all clean and clearheaded. He don't talk like anyone I know in the Slumland. Some of the stuff sounds like what Elenbar's flapped her lips about sometimes, but his is smoother, like outta a book I ain't read.

"Well, long ago, even before my dad... They had a big problem with everybody wanting to come in. Least, they felt like it was a big problem. I don't know how big because people don't talk about that part so much. This is just what I've been thinking to myself, but I think the War was just an excuse to do what they had always wanted to do anyways. Though this time they got to use the bombings and danger of the 'Outer World' as the excuse, instead of just admitting they didn't like, uh, certain people coming in."

"Were they right, though? I mean, if people were attackin' us and stuff." My foot aches from bein' crouched on it like I am.

"No. I mean the War *was* terrible and millions of people died everywhere. They still aren't sure exactly how many did. But look at how bad things are even still. We got the, uh, well, the gutters and people are just as poor and beaten down as they ever were. And politically, things have just gotten worse and worse. What was always about freedom suddenly became about control. About what people could and couldn't do. A lot of people say it's after they took the guns away, but I think it was long before that."

"Only guns I know are the Tik-Tiks Tivoli got in the compound." I abandon the screw and stagger upright, a cramp radiatin' into my foot.

Elenbar flicks on the lighter, lookin' like she's gonna turn my ass inside out, but she sees my face and sticks out her other hand instead. "Hey, give me that." I let her take the rand from me, and I take the lighter. She sinks down beside David and continues where I left off.

The screws are tight and very long. Each twist jerks the wrist, and Elenbar and David wrenchin' arms pump in odd synchrony as they battle the threads.

"Tsh. And who do you think lets Tivoli keep those precious guns?" Elenbar suddenly says, and David arches his eyebrows, surprised. "Society decides who gets what, and Tivoli been flooding the Slumland with the Flow fer decades. Think they been running without permission?" Elenbar snorts. "It weren't the guns. Guns don't work against clunkers anyhow, and once they started rolling them out, a lot of people just gave them up. But it was slow, not fast. Little changes so people don't notice the ground eroding out from under their feet. Except fer Charlie's Resistance. The real trouble was the Temperance movement, taking our bodies from us." Elenbar's jerkin' twists suddenly get angrier, harder, faster than David's. I flick off the light. "Just look at yer wife... Just trying to save her own damn life, but because of some convoluted moral clause, she can't even do that. And look at us. Bein' born a certain way and fer some reason it's the wrong way, decided by someone who's never breathed a single breath of compassion in their life."

"And stuff like the PERMIT program," David says.

I snort a laugh. "Hey, cuck, anatomy lesson: down in the Slumland, you ride enough pricks, you gonna get one, want it or not."

David chuckles, and it sounds real. "Huh. Well, in the Uppers, we get the fancy birth regulation chips implanted. If you're somehow unlucky enough to get pregnant anyway, well, there's a lot of bad things that can happen."

My brain's hummin' with excitement. This is all more than I've ever known of the Uppers. Most of it don't matter to the peeps in the gutter anyhow, because we don't really do what the Society says we're supposed to anyways. "You gotta get the PERMIT thingy."

"Yeah, it means Parental Education and Restructuring Marital Integrity Training," David says, like he's readin' a fancy pamphlet.

"Population control became a huge problem along with everything else, especially since no one is allowed to leave. Plus they became paranoid about the, well, about you guys, and the effect it was having on the 'traditional marriage.'" He pauses and I wanna flick on the lighter so I can see his face, but I don't have to because he says, "Which, frankly, is fucking bullshit."

I'm grinnin', somehow glad and relieved to hear him finally say it out loud. Because it's such a *monumental* pile of bullshit it's hard to understand why everyone ain't usin' their brains.

David continues. "So, to have kids, you have to complete the PERMIT program. Convince them you'll toe the line and have the baby in the hospital so they can get assigned if they need to. So many of the babies do now."

I flick on the light just to see how it's goin', and I see Elenbar's hand shakin' a li'l.

"But what do they make you do?" I ask, tryin' to ignore her warnin' signs.

"Oh, it's mostly boring stuff on how to be good parents, how to discipline and raise children the right way. But the Marital Integrity stuff is just creepy. They divide up all the men and women, and you have to take gender seminars on the roles within marriages and how to be proper husbands and wives. Melissa and I compared notes when we met up afterwards," he says, and nods at Melissa. *Ah, finally her name.* "It was a big joke to us at the time. A stupid government loophole to get through. We were in love, and we didn't even care about all the other stuff it really meant. That Melissa would belong to the Society once she ever got pregnant. Lord, the medical tests alone were hugely stressful, and if you tried to duck out of them, they sent Enforcers to your house. Still, even with all that, I thought once they discovered that having the baby would likely kill Melissa, and the baby too, that they'd let us leave the program. Let us save Melissa's life."

"Ain't ever so simple," I say.

Melissa's still starin' off down the tunnel.

"No. Well, and you see what happened," David says.

I do see, and I force myself to stop starin' at her. She probably don't need people with bug eyes starin' at her scorched-up face all the time.

David's screw falls out of the hole, and I let out a squeak of delight. Elenbar wrinkles her nose in disgust, and I quiet. Hers comes out a moment later, and they start on the next two. They work in silence for a while.

My mind's spinnin' about the PERMIT program and everythin' that's happened to David and Melissa. Elenbar's wrong. They were *us,* maybe not in the same sufferin'-for-our-crotch-parts way, but they had troubles and maybe fightin' the same kind of fight we were. I mean, the stuff the Brigade's fightin' against is the same—all that body control and sayin' what's what for everyone in the UFS. Then I think about Pint, about how things went so wrong. How did my gutter buddy go from my side-to-hip ally to turnin' traitor on all of us? If he even really did. Elenbar losin' her mind like that... I wonder if he's dead. Maybe—well, it could be the drugs, that hot source of Biff he was floatin' on when we found him, but scorin' ain't that hard long as you're willin' to turn ass for it, and we'd all done that. What could've made him betray us, betray his family? Because that's what we were. We were family, the only family most of us had anyway.

There's a ping-ping as two more screws hit the metal floor. I expect the panel to pop off, but it takes both David and Elenbar pryin' the edges up with the rounded rim of the rands to get it loose. The jarrin' squeal and bang of the heavy metal panel reverberates throughout the tunnel, the echo engulfin' us as it spreads away, repeatin' down faraway corridors. My blood ticks in my throat, though I ain't sure why. With how deep we've come inside the Wall, no one on the outside's gonna hear. It's like we've been entombed—like mummy monsters on the old black-and-white vid shows I've seen. Buried alive maybe, and I try not to think about what's going to happen if we do get stuck, because even if we make it past this li'l patch of nothin', there could be worse later on, worse than we can even imagine. The worst is often far more fucked up than my mind can conjure, and that almost scares the piss right into my panties. Not that I'm wearin' any under my jeans.

"A'ight. Andi, think yer still the best ta do it," Elenbar says, peerin' into the pocket behind the missin' panel. "Tighter than a locked-up virgin twat, but ya ain't nothing but all bones anyhow."

I can't even be real offended. "I'd like to thank the tunnel diet for all I've accomplished." My heart's poundin', makin' it hard to breathe against the rattle it's makin' in my chest. I peer into the opening, behind the panel where this crawl space is supposed to be.

"Are you on the faggin' juice? How the jesus-cocksuckin'-hell am I supposed to get through there?"

There, wadded up like a canopy of snakes, is the greatest jumble of cables, gears, and computer parts I'm ever gonna see in my shit-junkie life. I got no idea what half this stuff could be doin', but it's all coiled up like a living jungle, waitin' to throttle me once I get inside.

"Scared, ya twat?"

"You don't have to do it, Andi. I can try. Or, Elenbar, you might try yourself. We don't have to make anyone do anything. I'm sure there's another way we can go about this," David sounds so reasonable, it really fuckin' pisses me off.

I hand the lighter to David. "No, shut it, you cuck. Fuck it, I'm goin', you pissin' twats." And before I can change my psychotic tiltin' mind, I wedge myself in behind the wall. There's about a foot that ain't all cocked up with the inner workin's, and I wiggle my body in as far as it can go.

To say I'm squished ain't givin' the right idea. I'm *fuckin'* squished. It's hard to breathe, and it all smells like burnin' oil and sludge, so that's makin' it all worse, and my gut's swirlin' and my old friend, blind-seething-panic's, settin' in too. Yah, and terror's also feedin' my belly fire. I'm trapped behind this fuckin' wall, wigglin' to christ-cracker-heaven on the hopes, somehow, I can get to the other side and break my way through. I squeeze my eyes shut and suck in breaths bigger than the space I'm wedged in.

"Hey, take these," Elenbar says, and I manage to look back at her. She's handin' me the rands, and I reach out my hand to grab them. I flinch as she lets go, and I butter-fuck it, droppin' them down, down, down into the inner bullshit clutterin' the wiggle-way.

"Ya fucking shitting me? Gawd, fucking damn this fucking cock-fuckery wall-suckery," Elenbar grumbles and hisses, squattin' down and gropin' into the darkness, her fingertips searchin'. She surfaces with *one* coin and she extends it to me, eyes blazing. "Ya fuckin' drop it and I'mma come in there and kick yer queer twisted ass."

I carefully take it like it's made of moonbeams and theoretical virginity. I don't even breathe until it's safely in my pocket. Seems like everythin's determined to get lubed up and puckerfucked on this trip.

Then it's just me behind the wall again. They've shut off the light. At my back are the tightly coiled conduits and electrical boxes with painful pointed edges, but somewhere, deeper beyond all that, I can hear a faint thumpin'—like a drum embedded in the wall is reverberatin' a message to me, echoed by the drummin' of my own heart. It's almost comfortin', like there's a bigger heartbeat than my own. and I'm swallowed up by the heat and pressure of bein' squeezed in here. For the first time in a long time, I feel kinda safe.

The lighter flicks back on, a distant glow at the end. "Ya stuck?" Elenbar pokes her head back in the hole, glowerin' at me like I'm gettin' a pop-off without her knowin'.

"No, I got it." The light snaps off, and I wiggle again, though it's pointless at first. Then slowly, ever so slowly, my limbs are inchin' farther along the passageway. I suck a hiss of air as I bang my tailbone on a square corner, but the pain gives me a little more rage fuel so I use that to push myself farther, deeper, harder against the force of the tunnel's wall and the strange machinery at my back. It's also dark as an alley fuck in here, and I don't have no light and I wouldn't be able to spare my hand anyway, it's so busy grabbin', pushin', and guidin' stuff out of my way. It's all by feel, and after a while, I realize my eyes are shut anyways. I'm really movin' now. Soon my hand claws at air, and I realize I've reached a fairly open pocket of space. I squeeze into it and take a deep tummy breath that was impossible in the earlier small confines. Might be at the front of the panel, so I knock on the metal.

Elenbar pops her head back in, the light now a real small distant glow that illuminates her face. She's ghastly in the shadows, and I shudder.

"Go down a few more feet, then yer there," she says.

I run my fingers along the outer wall, and my index pricks against the sharp point of what must be one of the screws. I swear under my breath and stick my finger in my mouth. It tastes like blood and oil.

"How am I supposed to open it?" I call back down the corridor. David pokes his head in, and Elenbar glares at him because he's mighty close to her, probably touchin' her, to see where I'm at.

"Can you can use your knee or leverage your leg up to push outwards against it?" David gives me a thumbs-up, and I wanna call him a faggin' cuck idiot because there ain't no way I'm gonna be able to lift my leg enough to push outward against it, but I don't have any other ideas so I kinda do what he says, slidin' my knee as high up as it can go, makin' the bone smart against the hard, unforgivin' metal. I push, but it ain't gonna. It ain't gonna go.

"Ya need me ta come down there, hold yer hand?" Elenbar calls to me.

I grit my teeth, makin' my jaw hurt and I try again. The metal bows a li'l, but the screws hold it real faggin' tight. I imagine those screws on the other side, long and deep, snug in the metal they're meant to stay in.

"Run! Oh god, run!" That's Melissa, and I'd nearly forgotten the sound of her voice. Now it's all terror.

"Oh slippery shit! *Fuck*! Andi, don't breathe, if ya can—don't breathe at all!" Elenbar's face disappears, and there's bangin' footsteps. They're runnin', runnin' *away* from me. Somethin's happenin', and I catch a tiny whiff of somethin', somethin' bad, and I gulp air and hold it.

The light's gone, and it's just me, holdin' my breath, alone in the dark.

Breathin' for Two

ANDREA. DEAR ANDREA...

Don't think ya'll understand. No, that ain't how I wanna start it...

Look, world's a fucked-up place, k? I wanna tell ya it's different, somehow it'll be different for ya. But it maybe won't be. Might never be. I'll tell ya proper, though, ya can decide it for yerself. The Sistas at St. Aggies...they're good ladies and they'll care for ya. Like they did me. As for the s/he thing...I'm sorry. Maybe I shoulda ended it for ya, maybe should've never brought ya into such a shit place. But I couldn't do it. Couldn't be a murd...murdier...well, whatever. Since yer first kick to ma bladder, I loved ya. So, member that more than the rest of this. I loved ya. Now live, damn it. Live a better one than me.

Yer Ma.

"Andi! *Andi!* Wake up, ya fucking wanky twat, wake up!"

I come back to it in a spasm of pain and I'm heavin' my guts up before I even open my eyes. When I do, I'm half-blind, bleary with tears, and half in Elenbar's lap, vomit smeared across her flat tummy. For a minute, a horrible wrenchin' minute, I think we're back at the Farm, back in that room, back—but no. There's no table. And Elenbar's cryin' a whole lot.

"That's it, get it all out. You're going to be okay, Andi." There's David's voice, calm and low, more peaceful than Elenbar's barkin' sobs ringin' in my ears. I try to speak, but my voice is a croak and my lungs are on fire, burnin' on the inside like they've become the ember tip of a synth stick.

"Ma..."

"Don't talk. Ya shut yer mawhole," Elenbar says, her voice ebbin' with relief, though I still hear the sobs in it. My vision's still all gummed up, like I'm lookin' at the world through the bottom of a vodka bottle.

"My...eyes."

"It's the gas. Probably burned you pretty good, but the fact you regained consciousness at all is a good sign. Here, drink this. I'll wash your eyes too."

The lip of somethin', a bottle, gets pressed to my lips, and I drink, though it hurts to swallow. The water's warm and stale. I long for the cold quench of rainwater. Even the shit flow of the Anacostia, that freezin' rush of sewer swill, sounds like the best parts of biblical heaven right now.

My head's gently tilted back, and water splashes my face. I cringe, because it burns, but it's gotta be for the best. The gas, or whatever the hell, needs to fuck right off my face because I happen to like my face, and it definitely needs to get outta my faggin' eyes before I go blind.

"Okay, there we go. I'm sorry, Andi. Fuck." David swearin' gives me a surge of inexplicable satisfaction. "This was all a terrible idea."

"Cuck. How—" But my throat seizes. This has gotta be be near the hundredth time I've been knocked out, poisoned, beaten, and almost dead. All within a matter of days.

Fuck this month.

Fuck this year.

Oh yah, fuck this life while we're at it.

"Melissa crawled after ya when we got back. We were down the tunnel a ways, plastered against the ground, suckin' air through a vent in the floor. But we all got a bit of the burning, none so bad as ya, though." Sounds like there's an apology tucked in Elenbar's voice somewhere, but I don't care for it. I look over at the mucousy shadow I think is Melissa and flick fingers at her. Hope it looks grateful or somethin'.

"I knew the gasses might be a risk. They pump the tunnels full of it to kill, well, people like us trying to get through and pests that might hole up inside here. But now we're really on a clock. The next phase will be sweeps, cleaning out the bodies left behind. Not sure what that entails, but I don't think it'll be good for us in any form." David says this matter-of-fact, like it somehow wasn't fuckin' important before.

"Thanks fer the public bulletin before stuffing Andi in behind a wall. Ya wanking straight, fucking cock pumper." Elenbar's yellin', which is good because I can't.

David's shoutin' too, but I just shut my eyes and will it all to stop. My gut's real sour, especially bein' pitiful empty, but anger don't fill it up none.

"Fucking poisonous gas and now tit-twisting brass gonna come crawling through here?" There's Elenbar, pissed—but also scared. "We just need to keep moving. You hear that, Andi? We'll be looking at the ocean from a balcony window soon enough."

"David." Melissa speakin'. "We need to hurry."

With her words, a sudden reverberatin' clang sounds somewhere in the distance. No one speaks except my guts, threatenin' to release an epic purge with the adrenaline and the poison gas turnin' my guts to sewer.

"Let's go," Elenbar hisses, and she pulls me up onto my feet. David's got the lighter at full flame, but everythin's just a blur of faint light. I stagger and lean heavy on Elenbar, but she takes the weight and don't say nothin' about it, and we all move forward in shufflin' silence. The clang in the distance repeats, and it sounds a bit far off, but I ain't got any idea what the hell's in here, whether faggin' brass or deployed clunkers.

"Just keep moving," David whispers.

A bit fuckin' unnecessary since we're all movin' just about as fast as we can go without makin' a huge racket about it.

Then we hear it. The low rumblin' growl. Like outside the wall.

Elenbar stares straight ahead, her jaw flexin' as the muscles grind teeth. It's one of them guard thingies. Beast but machine all the same. And it's in here, breathin' loud like an asthmatic Fist Queen. Like Ma. I clamp down on that shit train of thought. Ain't no thinkin'-about-Ma time. It's run-your-faggin'-tits-off time, and we do, best we can, considerin' I'm a sack of decomposin' road smear. Even with our best tryin', we're slow, even with fear jackin' my head and bowels, even with my vision gettin' clearer. I can see better the details of everyone's faces comin' back, and I'm mighty relieved, though it's lost beneath, you know, fuckin' terror at bein' swept up and killed in this goddamn tunnel.

"We need ta stop. Andi can't go on and on like. We need ta breathe," Elenbar hisses.

"I'm fine, just keep pumpin' on."

"Andi—"

"Just fuckin' *go!*" My voice's too loud, much too loud, and it clatters like a marble down the metal hallways. They all stare at me, and if there were a cliff nearby, I would've dove head off it. No one breathes. Don't think a single blink is made. But the huffin' and growlin' don't sound louder, nor urgent. Just maintains its grumblin' in the distant tunnels.

"Sick or not, I will cut yer dip-sticking squeaker box ya do that again." Elenbar's expression ain't light. It ain't nothin' but dead serious. I nod.

"Let's duck down here. For a minute." David says.

We all step off the main, well, whatever. This all seems to be a kind of a main artery tunnel or somethin'. A smaller tunnel divides away from it and dead-ends a few paces down.

David points. "This is where we bunked down when we first saw you two. Easy to just roll on by and not even see long as we keep quiet."

"Great. We just backtracked all this way ta pin ourselves in a dead-end spot where they can scoop us up right quick. Great idea," Elenbar says.

"They'll find us anyway." Melissa offers this extremely helpful information, and I wanna slap the teeth outta her faggin' face.

"They're not going to find us, sweet bird." David slings an arm around Melissa and draws her close, but it's like she ain't even there. She's lookin' far off, like she's glimpsin' some ominous shit in our near future. But you gotta be whacked to know shit like that.

The growlin' revs, sudden and loud, and fuckin' *close*. Like it's right around the corner. Oxygen's a joke, ain't needed, ain't a fuckin' option. No one breathes. David's shoulder presses against my chest as we huddle against the back wall of the dead-end trap. Up ahead there's a faint glow of light. Glowin' red mad-dog eyes. My hands are slick with sweat, but I grope for Elenbar's hand anyhow. We slime our fingers together.

Then it appears, and it takes all I got not to cry out. It's huge. Its mass almost fills the tunnel itself, and the glow is piercing light in the otherwise complete darkness. The growl that was so far off in the distance is now a bellowin' snarl, the steel plates of the wall hummin' with its throaty vibration. This one's a li'l different than the one I saw outside, but just as I'm sussin' it out, it just rolls by, not even slowin'. The roarin' growl recedes, a tidal wave of sound suckin' back out to sea. Or hell. Or wherever the faggin' source of demon robot monsters be.

"It just kept going." Elenbar sucks in a breath.

"So, we have some idea. It might circle back, check out these dead ends later. But for now…" David don't finish.

I let out my breath in a sudden whoosh, louder than I thought, and my head pounds from holdin' it in so long. "We gotta follow it."

David's resparked the flame, and they're all starin' at me like I'm a pink lady doin' pirouettes.

"Just…" I wave my hand. Ain't time to explain.

I stagger to my feet and struggle toward the main passage, pausin' just a moment to peek around the corner. All's dark, but the growl is far off ahead, sound bouncin' back at us. It's a risk, but I got an itch about somethin'. About where it's goin' and more importantly, *how* it's goin'.

"Come on." I step out, and David's at my back, the small halo of light surroundin' us. My heart's hitchin' in my throat, the thought of comin' face-to-face with the snarlin' growlin' baddie don't make my nethers happy none. The growlin' gets louder, steadily, like we're gainin' on it. We've turned another corner, and suddenly, the torchlight shows its back end, square and bulk up ahead a few paces. David snaps the light off.

But the beast ain't got any idea we're behind it. The roarin' sound is still fuckin' terrifyin', makin' my head spin, but it's stopped and we wait near the corner, ready to run. The glow of its eyes provides just enough light that we can see its outline and reflection off the steel walls. Then there's a whirrin' sound as some sort of arm detaches from the side of its body. It's got a screw thing at the end, and it inserts it into the wall.

David elbows me in the back, and his lips are at my ear. "This is the drop-off. It's gonna cross it."

"Wow, cuck, thanks for catchin' up, because of course it is. How these rollers get around these tunnels with drop-offs all over? They gotta have some way to cross."

A clunk sounds, and the beast moves forward with a jerk, the growl revvin' loud again. As it crosses, we see there's a floor over the shaft. Whatever the key is, whatever it inserted, it's the answer. It's how we get across.

I look at Elenbar, then at David, then to Melissa. "That baddie? It's goin' the fuck down."

Belly Fires

"THIS IS A terrible idea. Andi. Are ya listening, ya twat?" Elenbar's hissin' in my ear.

"There ain't no way forward. You wanna go back?"

That quiets her for a minute.

"Look, we can't be sure how it's going to react, what it will do or even if this will fool it. It might be much smarter than we think." David's eyebrows almost touch with the force of his frown. I don't appreciate his negativity right now.

"Yah, cuck, but ain't no other way forward. We ain't gonna get ahead of the pits unless we nab that screw-key thingy it's got. You know it, I know it. Unless we're all agreein' to head back?"

Everyone's quiet, but I'm strong and certain. I also feel like I got worms in my anus, a squirmin' of fear and general bad hygiene. How long we been in the Wall ain't for certain, but our smell's signalin' days. My stomach stopped growlin' long ago, and my throat still burns like I'm swallowin' flame. We got problems.

"All right, let's go over it again." David places a hand on the sheet of metal propped against the wall of the tunnel. We'd passed it a while back, but it was just another piece of refuse, another scrap of junk. Now it's the whole of our plan.

"Okay, David and Elenbar, you'll drag the plate out when you hear me comin' and slide it over the pit."

"It won't stay for long. It isn't long enough to cover the whole thing." David crosses his arms.

"I got it, but balance it like, on the edge, as far as it'll go without fallin'. Hope to hope we can get it to roll ahead, trick it for just a moment, and its own weight will send it topplin' down into the fan."

"What if it falls through the fan?" Melissa's eyes are wide shimmerin' pools in Elenbar's flickerin' light.

"Doubt it. Fan's got wide blades. It'll likely wedge in and cock it up for sure. It's just gotta be busted up enough for us to snatch the key." Again, my words sound sure, confident.

"I don't like it," Elenbar says.

"Me neither." David nods at Elenbar.

Least they agree on somethin'.

"Fuckin' hell, do you have a better plan? Any idea? Anythin' at all? 'Cause my throat's piss sore and I don't think any of us got longer than another few days." Rage makes me bold. Desperate.

They don't say nothin', but Elenbar snaps off the lighter in silent protest.

"All right, let's do it," I say. "First, I gotta climb back behind that wall and get to the other side."

"Right. That went so fucking well last time." I can hear her sneer even in the darkness, and I can't help but agree.

THE HUMMIN' ROAR reverberates through the steel beneath my feet, makin' my toes tingle like my shitkickers are too tight. Creepin' along in the dark's the worst part of it all. Elenbar's got the torch way back, and it's just me here. The clunker beast made a couple passes, scoopin' up trash and bits of paper, shovelin' it all into a fire-belly incinerator it's got in its guts. The ultimate janitorial staff.

Now it's directly ahead, its lighted glare and fiery belly the only glow in the dark. My words that sounded so strong, so sure, now seem like a cuck's wet dream, wet like the droplet of pee in my briefs. Ain't got water to spare for a right pissin', though, so I creep closer, closer than I ever dreamed or imagined in worst nightmares. The growlin' is so loud the air's vibratin'. The beast's still rollin' along, methodical-like, stoppin' every few feet to assess and scoop up more bits of trash. It scoops up some sorta furry animal, dead from the gassin', and shovels it in. A horrible stench emanates from its belly, and it's all I can do to keep from retchin' out loud. I been followin' it for a few paces, tryin' to jack up my courage, but I gotta do somethin' and soon. We're gettin' farther from the others, and I'm losin' conviction. This all seems like a horrible faggin' idea now we get down to it.

Fuck it. "Hey! Hey, you overgrown toaster!"

The words sound stupid, but the beast whips around with such speed every hair on my body stands on end. I suddenly wish I hadn't stood so close, because with a bellowin' roar, it comes for me. I spring back, almost lose my footin' as I spin and start to run.

Fuck. It's fast. Too fast. Oh my jesus-lickin' christ, so fast! A sharp stabbin' pain punches through my back as it hits me with somethin'. I lose my footin' and hit the ground hard. The air woofs out of my chest. I can't gasp, and time stretches as I wait to be crushed beneath its rollin' tires, waitin' to be scooped up and shoveled into that roarin' fiery—

"Hey, asshole! Yeah, right here!"

I lift my head, and the faint glow of the beast behind me illuminates a shape, a body. It's Melissa, her eyes flarin' with that li'l light I thought was gone for good. My head's spinnin' from lack of breathin', and I almost get decapitated as the beast rolls forward, its underbelly smackin' me on the dome. It does the trick, though, and I take a whoopin' suckin' breath in, ready to vomit from pain and the black spots swarmin' my vision. The recedin' glow and roar tells me she's leadin' the chase. Ain't part of the plan, but I'm grateful all the same. I stagger to my feet and force myself to run, to follow them.

I turn the corner to see Elenbar and David lit up in the red light of a flare, one of only two we got. They're holdin' the edge of the plate over the shaft, standin' on the edge of it to keep it out as far as it'll go. Melissa's only a step ahead, her hair ripplin' behind her, ends singein' in the heat comin' off the fucker. Then she jumps. I scream because she's gonna fall, she's gonna plunge down that pit with the beast right behind, right fuckin' on top of her. But she makes the narrow gap, hittin' the plate and scramblin' forward. David grabs her hand just as the beast hits the edge of the drop-off.

There's a moment, frozen like a snapshot, burned into the deep places of my mind, where horror and nightmares live: Melissa's scramblin' across the plate, David's got her hand. They're lit in the ominous red glow of the beast's burnin' belly and flamin' eyes. I think she's gonna make it. I really do.

Time snaps forward. The beast hits the edge of the drop-off, tippin' forward and the top of its head clips the end of the plate. The side they're standin' on snaps up, almost takin' them with it, and Melissa's wrist gets caught on the vertical edge. Her hand, held by David, and her body weight draggin' down the other side, breaks the bone, the splintery edge shredding through the skin at her wrist joint. David releases her hand, then screams and tries to grab it again, but Elenbar's got him around the waist, keepin' him from fallin' in too. The plate snaps all the way up, then slides down the side of the shaft, Melissa fallin' with the plate and the beast right on top of her.

I can't breathe. It's a moment, only a flash, and then the boom drowns out the screams and plunges the whole tunnel into one continuous echo. There's a flare of light, so bright it hurts, then it snuffs out like a candle. Everythin' smells of sulphur and smoke, and I can't hear nothin' but the ringin' in my ears.

Grief

DAVID'S SCREAMS RICOCHET through the tunnel, and though I expected it, the yowl of horror still rocks me back like a physical shove. Elenbar's flare's dyin' down, almost extinguished, and David's twisted face flickers in the sputterin' red light. I pray the light dies quick. He's writhin' against Elenbar, and she finally lets go because he's about to pull them both over the edge with his flailin'. The last thing I see, before it all goes dark, is David crouchin' at the edge of the shaft, reachin' down, reachin' and screamin' Melissa's name.

It goes on for a time. I crumple to the ground, shiverin' with cold, hunger, thirst, despair. *It should've been me. Supposed to be me.* Darkness can't blot out that last snapshot, Melissa's wrist, the splinter of bone...

Eventually David's screams edge off, fading into a wailin' moan. Elenbar hasn't said nothin' this whole time, but now that it's quieter, I hear a faint whisper. She's whisperin', I'm guessin' to David, and I wonder what she's sayin', hopin' it's helpin' in some way. Though what can possibly help that kind of hurt, I got no idea. My own face is a puffed-up fleshy bag of tears, my eyes swollen from cryin' so hard. I think about P-Hat, Bosco, Tandy, Puddin', and even Pint, but it makes me cry all the more, so I try to stop. Then it's Ma. And the boat. And the crashin' ocean waves and shriekin' wind.

Shriekin'.

I jerk awake. I've nodded off at some point. The tunnel is quiet and still dark.

"Andi? Can ya hear me over there?"

"Keepers."

"Shyte, thought ya maybe kicked off in yer sleep. Ya all right?"

"Yah. Where's David?"

"I'm here." The voice that belongs to David is a raspin' growl, and I shudder at the sound. Don't sound human.

"Shit. I'm sorry. I'm so fuckin' sorry."

No one says nothin'. My tongue is thick in my mouth. I need water. The disorienting darkness makes it hard to tell if I'm spinnin' or if it's just a wash of dizziness from wanderin' these tunnels so long.

"We need that key." It's David speakin' again.

"We could wait. We don't gotta do anythin'—"

"We'll die if we don't get out of here soon." His voice is final.

"All right. Okay, then. What do we do?"

"We only got one more flare. We can't go wasting it unless we gotta," Elenbar says. She flicks on her lighter, but it's a mere pinprick from where I'm sittin'. "Can ya see enough with this?"

I scoot closer to the edge of the shaft and peer into the black yawn below. I can smell scorched oil and somethin' that smells like burnin' hair. I try to block it out, but it comes, an ugly warped mental image of Melissa, crumpled and crushed beneath the beast. A single tear squeezes outta my scratchy red eye. I knuckle it away.

"Can't see a tit for tit down there. We gotta use a flare or somethin'."

"Here."

We look over at David, and he's pullin' his outer jacket off and the sweater underneath. Then he pulls the jacket back on. He stands and walks down the tunnel, swallowed up in the darkness beyond the sphere of the lighter. Elenbar lets the light go out, and we wait.

"What's he thinkin'?"

"He's gonna make a torch," Elenbar says, and she sparks the lighter again. Sure enough, David emerges with a piece of a steel rod, kinked in the middle, and without sayin' anythin', he wraps his sweater around it.

"It won't last long. When you get down there, you might find some oil or something from the machine that you can use to dip the torch in, make it last longer maybe." The growl in his voice is mostly gone, and it's flat now, a dull strummin' of vocal cords too raw to do much else.

"Right. You keep it lit from your side. I'm thinkin' I'm gonna need both my hands for this suicidal shit." I regret the words as soon as I say them, but David don't even flinch.

I think Elenbar's glarin' at me, though it's hard to say until she lights the torch and, yep, her eyes are borin' hateful holes into my head. I'm glad I'm on this side of the pit. She comes to the edge and kneels, extendin' the torch as far as she can without topplin' over. The light don't extend far, and I can tell it must be hot. Elenbar's suppressin' a grimace of pain.

Below, the top of the beast is visible. The twisted metal looks evil and ominous in the flickerin' shadows. The glarin' bulbs, once red with hardwired hate, are now just blackened sockets. I don't say it out loud, because I might vomit if I do, but below the curve of its monstrous bulk...it's Melissa's hand. The shadows make it hard to see, but the shape, soft in the sea of twisted metal and angular destruction, can only be human. I swallow back a mouthful of spit and sour stomach juices. I wonder if Elenbar sees it too, but if she do, she don't say it.

"Knockers. I think it's stopped for good. I'm gonna have to...well, hop down, I guess." My voice shakes. I don't wanna jump down no hole. The height and crumpled mess of the beast means it's only a bit of a drop, and it's covered the fan. But I don't wanna jump into a yawnin' abyss of circuits, sharp metal, and mangled flesh. Down there with Melissa.

"Ya keep it tight. Don't go busting an ankle or yer goddamn head or something. I'm not coming after ya."

"Your sentiment's makin' my crotch tingle." I flip Elenbar a one-fingered salute, and before I can change my mind, I jump.

I hit softer than I expected, but my foot still simpers at the impact. There's an unsettlin' give to the whole mass and then a loud screech as the whole thing drops a couple feet. The whole tangled mess of circuits ain't jammed tight enough. We're beginnin' to slide down the shaft.

"Andi! Move yer ass!" Elenbar's voice sounds far away. The light barely reaches down here at all, and my stomach knots. I got no idea where to look. Can't see anythin'.

"Watch yer head!"

I dodge the fallin' torch, which whizzes by and thunks against the metal slab of the beast's belly. I snatch it, liftin' it up so it don't snuff out. A sudden loud, wrenchin' squeal comes from below me and we drop again, another foot maybe. The weight of the plate, the beast, and Melissa must've broken through the fan grate entirely. My legs are icicles, but I gotta move.

"There, on the left side, Andi! Remember? Look for the arm!" David's yellin' down at me.

I focus on the left side, swingin' the light over the folded creases of metal where its arm once was. *No.* My stomach's a pit of squirmin' maggots. The small hinge of the key arm is wedged against the wall of the shaft. There's no way I can reach it. Ain't nothin' we got can move this beast, nor force the crumpled side open.

"Get me outta here! It's fucked! Ain't gonna go!" I'm starin' up at Elenbar and David's faces, glowin' in red light. She's lit the last flare.

"What? Yah, hold on ta yer ass! Don't go anywhere!" Elenbar strips and so does David. I can't see what they're doin', but my heart's slammin' against the slivery bones of my ribs. They're really far away. How far have we dropped? As though it heard me, there's a rumble in the shaft and the squeal of metal grindin' against metal. We're movin' again. Just a li'l before it jerks to a stop. I force myself to breathe.

Then a long rope slides over the edge. They've tied their fuckin' clothes together, a Peter Pan escape plan. It's comin' down, faster. I reach up, stretchin' to grab it.

Another squeal cuts the air, and Elenbar's shirt brushes my fingertips. The ground vanishes beneath my feet.

I'm fallin'.

Lost & Found

"FUCK." I GROAN, NOT knowin' what's what. I might've gone gray for a minute, passin' in and out. I wiggle my toes, then my fingers, half cringin' against pain I'm sure will come. Then it does and I don't bother stiflin' the scream. The sound reverberates louder and louder, the echo bouncin' back at me from a hundred directions until my ears are ringin'. Everythin' is blackness, can't see a tit shit.

I focus instead on the pain. The initial rush has edged off and spreads mostly from my back. But I can move. Don't seem I'm dead. Don't seem I'm a gummy potato sack like those faggers I've seen on the vids, breathin' through tubes and blinkin' Morse code at teary-eyed nurses. But I feel pain. It's hot as I try to move. Something's stuck in my back. As in, a piece of something, probably a piece of the beast, is jammed into the flesh near my spine. The heat's mingled with the hot wetness I know is blood. Don't need to see it to know it. I can't even see my own fingers in my face. Almost poke my own faggin' eyeball out.

"Why do you hate me? The fuck I ever do..." I try to ease over onto my side, but I'm caught, and pain meets pressure. Whatever it is, I'm hooked like a faggin' river trout and pullin' to the side feels like it's rippin' my spine outta my body. And I don't want my spine outta my body. Needs to stay right where it fuckin' is.

I groan and stop movin'. Exhaustion sweeps over me.

And everything's hot too. Like I've dropped out of the circulation of the venting system. There's no movin' air, and I feel like a wet cat in a wool sock. Might be the room itself, wherever the fuck I am, or my own body tryin' to immolate itself in protest of havin' to live this shitty shithole life. The air's wet and humid.

I focus on breathin'. Let my eyes close for a while. Just keep breathin'.

A clickin' sound wakes me up like flippin' on a light switch. My whole body shakes and shivers, even though I'm crotch-sweat warm. Ain't a good sign. I try to keep my teeth from chatterin', but the traitorous molars stammer on. The clickin' sounds echo from all around me, and I ain't sure if it's comin' or goin'. It's like holdin' a buckin' power line; every one of my hairs stands prick up. I'm waitin' for the roar of another beast, the shout of brass, or maybe some of those furry things I saw dead in the tunnel. Maybe gonna crawl over here. Chew my face off. Like rats gnawin' on a washed-up hand on the river shore. Seen that more than once.

What I don't expect is the sound of singin'.

The voice sounds like a wet broom, a raspin' swish against the otherwise silence of the place. Sounds almost pleasant. My gut twists. Might be brass. Don't think brass sing, but could be a jovial fagger hidin' down here. But my throbbin' back reminds me...well, it reminds me I might die. Not even might. Fact is, I *am* gonna die here. *Sometimes choice is the greatest illusion of all.* Tandy said that. *Ain't it a bitch?*

"Hey. Hey!" I test my voice, and it's strong. The singin' stops. The clickin' does too. "Hey! Who's there?"

No answer.

"Hey, please! I'm...I'm stuck here." The dark presses in on me. I wish the singin' would start again, even the clickin'. Somethin'. Anythin'. I feel...alone. "Are you there?"

The silence stretches on, and my eyes are burnin'. Got no idea why I'm faggin' cryin'. Except I'm alone. In this pit. Impaled on a spike, and I don't wanna die. Ain't ready to die. Not like this anyway. Without Elenbar. Without...anyone. The tears become a sob, and my throat bulges with the swell of caught-up sadness, like a wad of cotton balls I'm tryin' to swallow dry.

Suddenly the clickin' starts up, and it's right next to my faggin' head.

"Hey! No, wait, hey!" My sob becomes a choke of surprise. A sudden flare of light blinds me.

"Oy! Aya oin' own, 'ere, ya slop?"

I squint into the light. At the bottom of the heaped-up wreckage of the beast's body is a man-lookin'...person, I guess, with the shaggiest beard I've ever seen on a livin' thing. It looks like matted steel wool.

"I'm—I'm stuck."

"'hy?" He glowers at me and comes closer, shinin' his hand torch directly in my face.

"Hey, you dick duck! You're scaldin' my sockets."

"Ay yuh." He doesn't move, and he doesn't stop shinin' the light.

"Look, I'm—there's something stuck in my back. I fell. From up there." I point. "Can you help me up?"

He looks, shinin' the light toward where "up there" must be. The light illuminates a small square shaft far overhead. Very far overhead. Melissa's crushed body and the beast were probably the only things that kept me from snappin' my bone stack.

"Oh yuh? Mmm, ay yuh." His voice is thick with a strange accent, like his tongue's half stickin' to the roof of his mouth. Can hardly understand the twat, but I don't care.

"Come on, come on. Do you understand me?" My teeth chatter so hard I can barely get the words out. "I need help. Help?" I wonder if he's daft, loopy-like. Singin' down here in the tunnels, lookin' like a puff of gutter trash. Gotta be daft.

He scowls and puts the hand torch on the ground. The beam of light cuts across his body.

"Holy christ crackers, what the actual fuckin' fuck?!" I can't help it. I'm screamin'.

From the waist down, this wild transient—well, he's a clunker, ain't he? But somethin' even worse than that.

He jumps back, scared by my shriekin'. He glances around like somethin' gonna jump at us. The clickin' sound comes from a set of insect legs he's usin' to walk on, made of the same hummin' gears and circuits the clunkers got. Half flesh, half machine. Like Elenbar's arm but so much fuckin' worse.

I take a shudderin' suckin' breath and force myself to shut my mawhole. He's inchin' away from me, pickin' up the hand torch as he goes. I'm losin' my chance, my one and only chance to get outta here alive.

"Wait! No, wait, no, I'm sorry! I just... Fuck, I just... Are you, okay? Your legs."

He stops movin' away, still lookin' afraid and suspicious of me. I motion for him to come back, to come closer, my heart yammerin' and my head shriekin' that I'm a goddamn fool.

"Yuh 'urt. Yuh 'uck."

"Yes. Please. I need your help. I'm... I'm a good..." But a good what, I ain't sure. Don't think I'm a very good person. Especially not right now. But my head's fuzzy, and I'm seein' blinkin' black spots in my vision. The echoes of my screams are gone, but there's still a ringin' in my ears, constant. The pain in my back snakes around the front of my rib cage, makin' it hard to breathe.

He clicks closer to me, those legs movin' in disturbin' coordination. Like a human spider. My gut shudders as he gets close, but I force myself to keep a neutral expression, to clamp down on that jerk of horror wantin' to explode all over my face.

"'Oy 'elp ya up. Yuh yuh." He creeps up the mound of the beast's body, legs carefully pickin' their way up the twisted metal remains. The heap creaks, and I worry he's gonna fall himself, cock it all up, but he gets right up next to me, a frightenin' mutt monstrosity. But he's my only chance.

"Ya 'ome up, ya 'et up 'ow, ay." He extends his grubby hands toward me.

I reach up and clasp my hands in his. The skin is rough like gravel, grimy, and coated in dirt and what looks and feels like oil. He steps over me with four of his spider legs until he's straddlin' my body. I'm shakin' hard, bracin' myself for the pull, bracin' myself for the pain, but nothin' coulda prepared me.

"'Ere 'e o-o-go." He pulls up, and I'm surprised by his strength. Flesh rips away from my body, like shearin' a sheep's wool. I'm screamin', but I don't even hear it. My vision explodes in a white-hot cataclysm of pain, snakin' up into the base of my skull, and I wonder if I'm done. If I weren't a potato sack before, I might sure as shit be one now, but I'm up and off the spike. I collapse to my knees, sobbin' and shakin' with the agony. A gush of fluid runs down my back.

"Yuh 'leedin' all 'ver."

He's lookin' at me with concern maybe. Or curiosity.

My throat's burning like a colony of red ants have made their home there. "Do you, do you have water? Something to drink?"

He stares at me blankly. I simulate drinkin' from a bottle. Comprehension comes like a beam of sunlight, and he slings a backsack around to his front. He brings out a bottle, might be his collection of piss swill, I don't care. I snatch it from his hand and rip the top off. The bottle is crusted with dirt, and it flakes as I chug the contents. It tastes odd and metallic, but it's water. It's fuckin' water. I drink hard and fast.

Then I stop and vomit. The slurry of water and blood splashes the ground, gut crampin' like the liquid squirts you get drinkin' river water. I'm shakin' and heavin', though it's just blood after the first surge of water. My back spasms with sudden horrible pain. Think I'm—think I'm grayin' out.

"'Elp. 'eed 'elp." He grabs my arms and jerks me to my feet. Then he takes my hand with an odd tenderness and tugs me along. I stagger, followin' the spider man as he leads me out of the cavern. His torchlight reveals machinery and large square shafts along the walls. Fans hum in the distance. But I can't—too weak to go anymore. I sink to my knees.

"Stop. I can't... Fuck." I'm shiverin' and shakin', fever seepin' through my bones. My whole body aches. My tongue is swollen and thick.

The spider man don't say nothin' else, just scoops me up into his arms like a sack of rotten apples. I let him and surrender to the throb that is my world. The womb of the tunnel presses in on me, and the warm arms encasin' me make me feel fetal, withdrawn, more inside myself than I've been, maybe, ever in my life. But maybe that's just fever. Blossoms of color obscure my vision, and for a while, I'm adrift, back on that boat with Ma, the waves smudges of cotton and the sun shinin' hot and stark in a purple sky.

Bird Man

I HEAR BIRDS. Twitterin' and singin'. The rustle of tiny wings. I can imagine them, even with my eyes closed to the world they're livin' in. I think of the cotton sea, a bushy-faced wizard starin' into my face, but it's fadin' like dreams do. The harder I try, the more they leave me. As they all leave me. Then there's nothing but the birds. I smell them too, a fetid odor of shit, but not human-ape shit. It's got an exotic stank you ain't sniffin' on the regular.

I try to open my eyes, and my eyelids flutter in meek protest, not ready for the light's assault. I ain't sure I'm ready for the world outside my own brain, and the light is real, it's powerful, it's—

"The ocean." My voice's a croak, but what I couldn't smell beneath the layer of piddlin' bird smear is the smell of the ocean, the salt. Least what stories tell it like. Somehow it's the wet of the air, the wet touchin' my face through a, yes, it's an open window, and it faces out on a sheetin' canvas of sky blue. I wanna get up—wanna go to it, but my arm, it's heavy, so heavy. There's a shackle around my wrist. Steel. Locked. I lift my leg, and it's shackled too. The bright light, the surreal floatin' of the world streaks with my mind with splotchy black and red.

"Hey. Hey! Who's out there? Can you hear me? Let me up outta this shit!" The words scrape out of my charred throat. My body is wakin' for real, adrenaline givin' me strength. The room is stacked stone, a door at the far end. Three bird cages sit along the wall, filled with the winged rat-lookin' things you see scroungin' bread and shittin' on tourist trouts. They're the cooin' undertone, purrin' like they're plumb tickled with their fancy caged digs, but I ain't a bird and I ain't tickled not a faggin' bit. Another cage contains brightly colored li'l fliers, in flashy neon sign colors. They're the ones twitterin' like mad, lashin' against the walls like they're ready for the door to spring open any minute. Yah, those are my peeps right there.

I shake the shackles, but they're very heavy, and the rough metal chafes. Then I see the water. Right next to me, a glass of shimmerin'—well, maybe not *shimmerin'*, but it might as well've been holy water milked from the swingin' scrote of an angel. It's in my reach, and I snatch it, bringin' it to my mouth. I crane my head and feel a strange pullin' and vague heat in my back. All these sensations I ignore, though, suckin' the cold water in thick swallows. My guts rollick, and I slow, because I'm just gonna spew it all out again if I don't. I breathe deep, close my eyes, and take another small sip. Then another. Sip. Sip. Sip. Soon the water's gone, and I drop the metal cup. It clatters on the stone ground.

The heavy wooden door opens, scrapin' loud against the flagstone, like on cue.

"Yes, oh yes, I thought you might be waking this evening."

To say this man's old ain't even the half truth of it. This man's ancient, a relic, like the old plates in the rectory the Sisters kept for special guests who never came to supper. Even his skin's dusty with the accumulatin' filth of the ages, creasin' deep into his forehead and along his cheeks. His gray scrub beard mighta been white once, but it's grimed with thick black tar and flecks of metal bits. Though it's hard to say, I think he's the wizard from my dream. Ain't dressed in no robe, though, just a tattered button-down and patched coat.

"Let me outta here." Don't think I need to scream it.

"Yes, yes, of course. I will do just that. But—but I do have to ask who you are. What are you doing here? Not many make it this far through the Wall. It's been a long time since anyone's made it." He wrings his hands and peers at me. When I don't say nothin', he sighs and draws a stool over nearer to my bed. His knees creak and let out an ominous pop as he sits down. "I am not going to hurt you."

I swallow down meanness and try for—what's that word...oh, diplomacy. "I'm Andi." *Sounds stupid.* "We're— I'm tryin' to get to...get outta the Free States. For good." That sounds even worse, and I nibble on the tip of my tongue. The pain in my back is gettin' worse, and heat radiates up into my neck.

His mothball eyebrows arch high, and disappear into the mop of hair across his forehead. That's grimed whitish too. "You don't travel alone. I have seen the others you came with. Though I fear they may be gone from this world by now."

I'm numb. Can't breathe.

"What do you mean? What's happened to them? Can you see them?" My voice's thick, my eyes swollen with tears, perched hot and heavy at the rims.

"They've gone beyond the lens. Perhaps that means they made it. Though…" He twirls one long wisp of his mustache between long fingers. "Well, it gets harder and harder. People lose hope, you know. Without hope, it is truly hopeless."

"But—but they were all right? Before they—before you couldn't see them anymore?"

"After you fell, they waited for a long while. Perhaps too long, then moved on."

My throat is slick with a surge of stomach acid and flarin' anger. "No. They'll make it. Elenbar'll make it. She won't give up. Never has, never will."

The words feel true, but he just stares at me, placid as a sewer toad.

"Perhaps you're right. But, now then. Where were you hoping to go? Once you breached the perimeter and made it beyond the Wall? After all, what can anyone do once they're in the Detachment Zone?"

Elenbar had said we'd call for help, find that radio tower. Maybe reach those contacts sittin' in the blockade ships on the ocean, but I don't know this puff of crotch dust. Might well be brass, or workin' for the brass, though it don't look that way.

"Well, who are *you?* How can I trust you? And where's that…the…" I don't got any idea what to call him. "Clunker freak" sounds too rude to speak aloud. Considerin', freak or not, it saved my shitty ungrateful life, maybe.

"Oh, you mean Boy? He's doing his sweeps. Didn't finish them, as he found you in such a state."

"Boy? What kind of name is Boy?" I'm almost offended on his behalf.

"Mm. It's not a very good name, true. I didn't expect him to survive more than the night he came to me. I—didn't want to belabor false hope and so I called him Boy for simplicity. But as each day went on, he kept living and then the name stayed. And so did he."

"What's wrong with his, you know, his legs?"

The man stands to his full height and squeezes his lower back like he's got a pin in it. "He too had an accident. Not all different from yourself, though it severed his spinal column and his lower limbs were crushed beyond saving. Amputation saved his life, but it didn't seem right for him to be confined to a bed for the years he would continue to live. So I did what I could."

"You built those, um, tinker-tinks for him. So he could walk. He tryin' to get through the Wall too?"

The man sighs like I'm exhaustin'. "This is all for another time. I feel supper will do us all well. Can I have your word you will not do us harm? Boy and I?"

I gape at him. "If I was gonna, would I tell you?"

He smiles and shrugs. "I still believe in people, I suppose. I still have hope, foolish as that is." He produces a small key and unlocks my shackles.

I sit up, and the vague pullin' in my back nearly snaps me in two. Prongs of pain scald around my rib cage, all the way into my fingertips.

"Holy horse fuckin'," I hiss and fall back on the bed.

"Go slow. Your injuries were severe. I placed two rods in your back, and they will need to heal, or you will sustain further damage."

"You put what into my back?" Rage mingles with the pain. "What the hell you thinkin', this ain't no hospital!"

"Rods. Metal rods to stabilize the spine." He looks like he's gonna come over and examine me. I stagger to my feet. Almost fall over, but I don't take the arm he extends to me.

"I'm fine. It's fine. I just—arrgh. You a doc?"

"No. An engineer. Most I've learned about the human body has been by necessity. Most who come through need some measure of help, though most do not survive unfortunately."

"How long has it been?" My head's swimmin', but I'm also rememberin' some other stuff, other than the cotton sea and wizard. Bright lights and the whir of a saw. There's pain in the memory too, though I stomp down on that part.

"You didn't—you didn't do nothin'—" I grab my crotch, lookin' for Mister. But he's there and nothin' seems moved around or nothin'.

"Oh, no, my dear. I have far more important things to attend to than the moral mongering of the Society. Nature designed you as intended." His words are like a warm bath, and I let myself sink in a li'l, a rush of relief at not bein' snipped and somehow bein' alive enough to stand.

A feathery technicolored head pokes outta the man's shirt and squawks, "Moral nature, moral nature!" It reaches up with clawed feet and begins to scale the length of his matted beard.

"The hell's that?" The fluorescent color of the bird's thin feathers looks like pictures I seen in animal books. Ancient history-of-the-species kind of stuff. But I ain't ever seen nothin' so bright livin' outside a drag club.

"This here's Oliver. Found him half-drowned on the shoreline—he's a long way from home as you might imagine," the man says, his voice still all warm and smilin'. He affectionately scratches the top of the bird's head.

Oliver whistles, then chortles, "One is two! One is two!"

"Who are *you* anyway?"

The man winks one of his ancient blue eyes. "They call me the Bird Man."

The Ocean

SUPPER SMELLS LIKE the biblical jesus-feasts of heaven. I got no idea what they could possibly be eatin', but it smells better than the egg foo yung a-la-dumpster I ate with Elenbar. Bird Man ladles a bowl full of steamin' soup and places it in front of me. The feathered streak of strobe light called Oliver is munchin' on a pile of fruit things. His beak's stained red with the juice.

We're in a kitchen of sorts, cloistered on the outside of the Wall. One large window faces out on the ocean, the roar of the waves a continuous sheet of distant sound. Boy hasn't come back yet, and Bird Man seats himself across the small wooden slab table from me. I spoon the soup into my mouth and almost weep like a newborn fetus.

It tastes better than anythin' in my life. Better than a Flow-jacked fuckin'. Better than the hug of the Sisters. Better than... Well, nothin's as good as this.

"Be cautious. You haven't eaten in a long time. You will be ill." He's probably sayin' this because I'm nearly chokin' on the huge mouthfuls I'm suckin' down. But unlike the water that made my gut swim, this soup's a magical elixir. My body sighs and opens to it, welcomin' the heavy volume like its mother's milk.

"What is this?" I murmur between mouthfuls.

"Fish from the ocean."

I gag and cough, splutterin' a mawful back into the bowl. "What the hell?! You tryin' to kill me?"

Fish are poisonous. They're swoll with the toxins of the shit we pour into the river, marinated in chems and decay. Hardly any fish left at all, and the ones still livin', we ain't allowed to eat. Not even starvin' gutter flies do that.

He gazes at me calmly. "You've nothing to fear," he says.

"The fish are faggin' sewer! Don't you know that? How're you so old and don't even know that?"

"The ocean fish are not poisonous. They're nutritious and filled with vital minerals your body desperately needs. Don't fear. I wouldn't feed a guest a toxic meal." He sounds so sure, so calm, I believe him.

"How are the fish in the ocean not poisonous?"

He smiles and takes a small sip of his soup before answerin'. "The ocean is vast. Larger than the United Free States all combined. Any toxins that do spill in are heavily diluted by currents and shifting tides. There are certain times of year we don't fish, but we monitor conditions closely. We couldn't survive without the fish and without the eggs. Oh, yes, there are eggs in the soup, which we collect from the seabirds who nest on this side of the Wall."

I stare into the bowl, really lookin' at what's swirlin' around in there. There's strands of white I'm guessin' must be egg. Kinda like Chinese slop soup I've seen.

"It's really not...?"

"It's really not. Please, eat." He motions to my bowl and then continues eatin' his silently.

I take another slurp. It's so good. Toxic or not, I eat the whole damn thing.

Boy enters through the back door, his steel joints squeakin' as they flex. That door leads back into the tunnels, and there's two other doors I ain't been through. They're just slabs of rough wood shoved in doorframes, but they stay shut anyway.

"Why's he go out there?" I lick the bottom of the bowl.

"Why don't you ask him yourself?" Bird Man don't gotta say I'm a twat to know I am one.

"Uh, yah. Hey, Boy—uh..." *Why's it so hard to talk at him?* "Why do you go out there? Wander around when you can go down to the water or somethin'?"

Boy blinks black eyes at me and holds up his armful of—well, it's stuff, ain't it? No one's gotta tell me where it's from. Thinkin' about that gas, the beast... Lots of good and bad ways to die inside the Wall. There's somethin' looks like a sweater and some sparklin' bits catch the light. Boy lays his discoveries on the table, rands, brass medallions, clips, and other personal effects thunkin' against the wood. Seems like bad fortune to be touchin' the shit belongin' to the dead, but dead's dead, as they say—no one ain't got any use for it except the livin'.

Bird Man stretches, all his joints poppin' in a visceral cooperation of age.

"'Ime. 'Ere's 'ime." Boy holds up a gold and gleamin' pocket watch. My stomach quivers at the sight of somethin' so pretty in such an ugly time and place.

Bird Man takes it from him and smoothes his fingers over the scratched surface. Even scratched, it's still gleamin' all fancy-like. The type of thing I'd pinch off an Uppers tourist trout while he's ridin' a wank. Strange lookin' back on it now. Like it's another life, another world, but it ain't been all that long really. Seein' my ma, escapin' the Farm...everythin' that's come since.

"A beautiful timekeeper. I do love keeping the time, knowing its comings and goings. Though it becomes less important with age." Bird Man smiles like it's a private joke I ain't supposed to get.

I try not to eyeball it like I am, but my palms are already itchin'. I want it. Don't even know why I really want it, except my old busted one's burnin' a useless hole in my pocket, and I ain't ever had anythin' so fine. Not without pinchin' it off for a vial of Flow.

"Here, Boy. Keep it, won't you?" Bird Man tries to hand it to him, but Boy grunts and skitters back, like he's not sure if it's gonna bite him.

"'O, 'eed 'o 'ime. 'Ime's in 'ere." Boy knocks the side of his head with a knuckle. The metallic rap tells me there's more than bone holdin' his dome together.

Bird Man nods, and walks over to the shelves linin' the far wall. The shelves are bustin' over with books, papers, and weird bits of bones, from li'l creatures that creep in the darkness—he places the timekeeper next to a bleached-white skull.

"Mm, time's a great and wondrous thing, except when you have none." Bird Man hobbles toward the kitchen.

I force myself to not look at the watch's perch. I force myself to think about somethin' other than what I'm already decidin' to do.

AFTER SUPPER, I'M ready to slip back into a comatose undreaming world, but the thought of what Bird Man said, about Elenbar, those words "gone from this world" are echoin' in my head, and I gotta know what's happened.

"You said you saw them. A lens? How?"

Bird Man turns to me from the small sink where he's washed our bowls. "I will show you."

"I have to go help them. Elenbar—we've got a mission."

Bird Man nods once and doesn't say anythin'. He leads me through one of the other back doors, leadin' deeper into the Wall. I follow, stiff and achin' pain radiatin' from my back. Sleep's tuggin' at me now I'm filled up with food, but I gotta see for myself.

We step a large cathedral-lookin' room, ceilin' high and domed, like part of a church got slapped down here on the coast. A doorway continues on the opposite side, goin' farther still into the Wall.

"Well, knock the cock." My voice echoes. It's like the cavern where I fell, but here it's cool, not stiflin' heat and sweat. "What is this place?"

"It's the monitoring hub." Bird Man hobbles over to the far wall and touches it. A screen lights up and chirps. Then, in the middle of the domed ceiling, a giant picture flickers, and becomes clear.

I'm starin' at a tunnel. The giant vid screen makes everything near life-sized, and the dark maw is illuminated in green glow. This tunnel looks like maybe one we went through, though they all look the same. Then the picture's flickerin' to another tunnel, and another. Some are in bright color, fully lit by harsh light. The rest are darkness. The pictures shuffle by in slow progression. Ain't nothin' in any of them, until—

"Wait!" But it's a dead tunnel rat. Not a dead Elenbar. My gurglin' sack of soup relaxes a li'l. A few of the other tunnels show more furry dead rats. Then one that's smeared with blood. Bright red blood.

I'm shakin'. "What—what's that?"

"It is not your friends. But another wandering soul who did not have the means to survive. The gas likely ruptured their insides, and they threw themselves down a shaft. It happens quite often." Bird Man's voice is flat and unsurprised.

"Bucket-fuckin' hell. That's...that's what Boy goes out into the tunnels for, ain't it? For bodies."

Bird Man nods. "Yes, we do our best to keep the lower level clean. The smell can become quite unbearable with the humidity and heat."

I shudder, imaginin' the types of smear Boy gets to clean up. "Why do you live down here?"

The pictures keep shiftin', and for a while, we don't say nothin' at all, just watch the pictures changin'. We still ain't circled back to the tunnel spattered with blood.

"I designed the Wall."

Bird Man still watchin' the tunnel pictures, his face serene, calm, and unmolested.

My mind reels. "Y—you designed it? Then you came to live in it? But why?"

"It was never meant to be this way. The Wall was initially designed to power the cities." His forehead creases, and I realize it's a smile. Least what I can see of it. Might be a grimace too. "The Wall capped the rivers, creating some of the largest hydro plants in the world. Green energy was supposed to change everything. After the pipelines failed, it was supposed to save us, make our world a better place."

"Then they came."

He looks at me, surprised. "Yes, they came. The Day of the Black Blood. The Daesh Eye attack changed everything. People were afraid and enraged. All they needed was a leader to tell them it was okay to be angry and afraid. That there was a clear solution, one that would certainly stop any future attacks and protect against corruptive Outside influence."

"But they were wrong! The Wall didn't solve anythin'. Not a tit-shit thing." My voice squeaks.

"Oh, of course it didn't, and my creation became a monster. When they put the laser cannons inside of it...I tried to stop it. Tried to destroy it from the inside. But my design was, well, it was quite well executed." He bows his head. "I failed. Again and again. Security hounded me. Then age and infirmary did." He heaves a sigh and the weight of it makes me feel like I'm drownin'.

"So, then what? The fuckers win. Like they always have."

The picture flickers, but it's not a tunnel. It's the ocean. The shimmerin' deep blue water spreads farther than my eyes can follow. It's beautiful. Then the picture flickers, and it's more ocean, even a small slip of coastline bein' pounded by huge frothy waves.

"Is that where the blockade ships are? Out there?"

"Ships?" Bird Man stares at me, hard. "Andi. There haven't been any blockade ships in nearly a decade."

Truth Hurts

"WHAT? WHATDYA MEAN there's no blockade ships? It's the reason we can't get nowhere. Why the Free States is bricked up like it is."

Bird Man watches me gravely, like a child spoiled with high fever.

"Answer me! We're supposed to—to—" But what we're supposed to do fails me. Like it has all along. Elenbar knew what to do. She knew where we were goin', who we're supposed to talk to. *I got contacts from a long time ago. Remember the blockade sitting in that ocean out there? I got contacts who can get us help.* She'd said that—help was there on the Outside. Maybe it was once, but long ago was way too faggin' long. I dig my fists against my temples, hard until black stars swim in my vision. "Is there—is there anything at all there?"

Bird Man spins away without speakin' and turns off the illuminated screen before headin' toward the exit. I follow him outta the monitoring hub, now pit dark with the vid off. Back in the small kitchen, it's like the inside of a teacup. I slump back onto the creakin' stool, confusion, rage, and despair makin' a swampy sewer of my mind. He busies himself makin' tea. He's made tea at least seven times today, and sets a cup in front of me. I don't protest, don't got spit enough to do it, and besides, tea don't seem the worst thing.

"It's been a long time since the Free States actually needed a wall." Bird Man fills my chipped cup with steamin' tea water. Smells like grass and ash.

"But the Daesh Eye. The attacks..." I take a sip. Dribble it back into the cup. Tastes like it smells.

"It's also been a long time since the teachings of history resembled anything true. Do you think the Society wants anyone to have any sort of truth?" He arches his furry white eyebrows.

My head hurts because he don't make any nip of fruitin' sense. "So what...it's all a faggin' lie then? The Society figured how to dupe a whole country?"

He shakes his head. "Not the whole country. They didn't need to. They just needed to make the lie look better than the truth. Then the country would, as you say, dupe itself. The truth is, Andi, the world Outside has gone on. The War is over, has been for a long time. But the Society owns the airwaves. All the information presented on those government-issued com pads is vetted and designed by them. Defectors and differing opinions are dealt with permanently."

"But people would want to know!" I push my cup of tea away, my mouth a pucker of sour. "You can't say people would just—would just *not* know. That they'd wanna believe some sack of sewer shit the Society wants to feed them. No one would choose that!"

"Maybe they didn't realize there was ever a choice. Such is the nature of the subconscious." He sips his tea and regards me with obnoxiously serene eyes.

"That's the shittiest shit in the shit." My stomach's squirmin' at the thought of P-Hat, of Pint, of Minnie, and Puddin' and all the rest of the faggin' Brigade, dead or scooped. And here Society's been suckerin' us like toothless babies swingin' from a milky tit. Like there ain't nothing we know that they don't. "Then it's done. It's all just done like that. We got no idea about anything real and everything we came here to do... Look, I gotta find her. Find David. Everything Elenbar said we was gonna do—"

"Ah, but it isn't done. Not at all. There's more to be known and more to understand. Because, you see, the people may be blind, but the Society is blinder still." He rises to his feet and digs at his back with gnarled old-man fingers.

I think of something. "But what about the radio? You sayin' the Outside World never tried to contact any of us? How'd the Society keep it all from comin' through?"

"Though there's no nefarious military waiting to kill us outside the magnificent Wall, the communication block ensures all information stays under their control." His eyes glimmer, and there's that bushy smile. "Well, not all information. There are primitive means of communication that still prove to be quite effective."

My stomach rollicks again.

My ma's got a shop. I can hang it there fer a while. I wonder if Minnie ever made it. Or...it hurts to think it, to even let the mind wander near the barbed wire fuckery of imaginin' dead faces, because ain't no one made it. It's churnin' cement in my guts and in my head. No one except maybe Pint, and I try not to think about his face either, all busted up and bleedin' all over the floor of the Brick. Whether he lived to breathe another day, whether he ran back to the Society, or whoever made him think peehole-fuckin' the Brigade was a good thing to be doin'.

"Are you all right?"

I flinch and see Bird Man starin' at me, his wide forehead rippled with wrinkled skin.

I shrug and knuckle a traitorous tear away. "It's jus—what's it all for, anyhow? Why are you even here on the Wall? Hangin' day to day watchin' Boy sweep up skags, waitin' for nothin', then?" There's another slip of tear, but I leave it. Ain't no point.

Bird Man leans forward against the edge of the table. "Because it isn't nothing. It's a far greater something than you can imagine. But do try, try to imagine it now. Has all hope been truly snuffed out behind this infernal Wall? Has the Society truly stomped it out of you forever? I think not, because here you are. Did hope not bring you here, too? And perhaps it is the answer to your final question: I am here because I have hope."

"And what? What're you hopin'll happen?"

"You. You are my hope, one I thought would never come." He's smilin', but I don't understand how he can or why.

"I ain't no hope. I ain't anythin' but—" The words catch like a fishhook in my throat. *A junkie.*

"There are many things you don't yet understand because you're young in a world now terrible and old. But youth is your greatest gift. I want to give you something."

I'm blinkin' back tears as I watch him shuffle through stacks of papers, lookin' at a few books before settlin' on a li'l brown plain one. He brings it to me. It fits perfect in my hands, the outside worn and soft like the downy skin of fresh plucked pussy.

"I don't write."

"It isn't to write in, though there are pages towards the back should you ever have the desire." He motions for me to open it.

Inside's some of the prissiest wrist flappin' I've ever seen. The swirl and tangle of pretty letters that might've been a piece of artwork on an Upper's living room wall. "This—who wrote this?"

"My wife."

I can't hide the gawp, and he chuckles, probably ain't surprised at what a twat I am.

"It's all right. Youth rarely remembers the *amore* of the old. My wife was a glorious writer, and she wrote many beautiful things. Most of all, she wrote about hope. Maybe someday you'll read them. And maybe they will come to be very important to you, as they have been to me all these many years."

I swallow hard against another fishhook of feelin' because I realize exactly who I'd give this to. In an instant, Bird Man's wife or not. Bosco would love this. Would've loved it. He always liked old stuff like this, always showin' me one dumb collection or another. If it was real good, he wouldn't even sell it, would just stash it to look at sometimes. I pinched an old book from him once, sold it for a couple vials of Flow. He must've had an idea, but he never said nothin' about it and I never did say I was sorry. But this here, well, it's a whole universe better than the old tattered book I pinched off him so long ago—the best sort of sorry is one worth more than the gum flappin' of empty words. This book's the perfect kind of sorry.

"You shouldn't give it to me. I ain't a reader, ain't a writer. I hardly got nowhere to take it anyhow. I'll just ruin it." I try to hand it back, but he steps away like he ain't seen me do it.

"Well, tuck it away. Maybe someday you'll be trapped on a desert island somewhere and need something to pass the time." He winks at me, though I ain't got any idea what half the shit he's sayin' means. Ain't no desert islands around here, and I sure ain't plannin' on gettin' stuck on one. But I nod all the same.

"Well, yah, thanks then."

Bird Man putts around like an old train, makin' more tea, whistlin' under his breath as he pours some out for himself and one for Boy, who's snoozin' by the open window. The whole scene is so...unreal and weird, like a place dropped outta the rush of time, like nothin' bad ever happened, no Society ever reached hands inside this quiet cozy place by the sea.

And all this coziness...all this *rightness*, well, it twists at me. A surge of rage boils in my guts because thinkin' about this nice quiet place gets me thinkin' about Elenbar and that gets me thinkin' about the Brigade. And Bosco and all the rest of all the dead people who ain't ever gonna know quiet or peace or goddamn tea with goddamn Bird Man, and there's all this shit I'm supposed to be doin', but I ain't because I'm sittin' in this goddamn room with this goddamn—

"I gotta get the fuck outta here!" I slam the cup on the counter, lukewarm tea sloshin' over my fist. Boy's head snaps up, and he stares at me. "Look, I don't mean to be a twat, so thanks, but I gotta find Elenbar. I gotta get outta here. There's—there's shit we gotta do."

He nods like he's been waitin' for me to say somethin' about it, but he don't meet my eyes and it makes my stomach do a nervous flip-flop.

"Yes, you do. And I know exactly where they are."

Bigger than Friendship

MY HEART'S IN my throat like a wadded-up wank rubber. "Where? Where are they?"

Boy gazes at me, his eyes black pinholes in the sea of his scrubby face. Then to Bird Man who gives a small shake, like I can't see when shit's not right.

"You've known all this time, didn't tell me, just left them in there! Well, where the bucket-fuckin' hell are they?" I jerk toward Bird Man, and the rods in my back become stabbin' scaffolds of fire. I crumple at the knees, staggerin' against the wooden table that squeals like newly robbed virginity. Bird Man don't move. Don't look real concerned at all.

"Drink your tea. The anesthetic will help you with the pain and help with the sleep you need. You are still not well," he says.

"Look, get fucked. I'm leavin', gettin' outta here—" I suck a slip of air as another spasm rocks my core, flickin' through my gnawed-up nerve endings.

"There's more than friendship you need. You need information." Bird Man turns away, and I see him rifflin' through a waverin' stack of papers with curled edges. I can see some sort of drawin' scrawled on the surface. "There's a far greater danger that will mean the death of more than just the Transgressors. More than just the Brigade." He looks at me. "I'm sorry. But the danger is more real than that."

I slide back onto my seat, pain fannin' down my spinal synapses. "I don't faggin' care about whatever the fuck you're getting' up to. I gotta get back to her. To Elenbar."

"And you will, because you'll need her, too. You'll need all the help that can be brought within reach. You'll be reunited soon, but first I have to tell you—"

"Did you not hear? I don't give a *fuck*." My voice is loud, punchin' back off the walls like gunfire, but it ain't a shout really. The words crawled up from where my guts meet my spine, feelin' like truth.

Because I don't. I don't care about nothin' but seein' Elenbar. Seein' her alive. Seein' her as somethin' other than a face at the top of a collapsin' shaft.

"But you do. You care so much it might destroy you. May destroy us all." Bird Man stares at a piece of paper clutched between his knobby bone fingers. "Will you listen? Just a while more?"

"I'm goin' to Elenbar. I am."

"I would never presume to stop you, but she'll need this, too. Drink your tea."

She'll need this. It's this more than anything givin' me pause. I ain't done nothing but cock it all up. I drink my tea. Anesthetic or not, still tastes like dusty crotch. My mind's whirrin'. I ain't done nothin' but get nowhere, except here. And here I could do somethin'. Get intel for Elenbar, give it to her. Actually make myself a use beyond a huffin' hole for Flow.

Fuckin' junk-tard.

"Yah, right, what then? The faggin' hell is it?"

Bird Man places the page in front of me. It's a schematic. Elenbar showed me how to read them kinda, when I joined up with the Brigade. Came in big use when we scouted joints for poppin' or made big trouble in the public squares. The lines show the shapes of things from different angles so you can see them in your head and get a real picture of where you're gonna go. Where you're supposed to be. Though I ain't got all the schoolin' on the details, it's definitely a picture of the Wall and a machine inside it. Gears and squares and stuff lookin' like the maintenance shaft we'd been shufflin' through in the dark. Fans.

"'His 'ere's yuh 'oom. B-boom-boom." I'd forgot Boy was there. He clicks two of his pincer legs together with a clack-clack.

Boom-boom ain't ever a good thing.

"Yes, Andi, there's a bomb inside the Wall." Bird Man places a finger on the center of a square thing, between a mass of fans and cable lines.

"A...bomb?" It don't look like much. A square and scribbly mechanical mess. My chest clamps down on the hot pulse of fear palpatin' under my sternum. "Faggin' hell, it's the Daesh Eye. They've rotted into the Wall. Like they always said was gonna happen. Jesus H. Christ crackers." I got a sock of vinegar where my guts oughta be.

"Daesh Eye." Bird Man sighs. "Listen, Andi, we have nothing to fear from Daesh Eye. Not anymore."

"'Hey 'one on 'way 'ow." Boy picks his way over to the table and knots his hands around the cup of tea served by Bird Man. The skin of his fingers look like melted brown crayons, muddled where it oughta be tight. He takes the cup and disappears through the door toward the monitoring hub.

I'm strugglin' to focus on the situation. My pain's ebbed some but so has my mind. Faggin' anesthetic—sweet numbin' drugs, but I don't want it now. I gotta focus. "Nothing to fear? They scorched the coast! The Day of Black Blood, remember? You so old you forgettin' that?"

"And there's an armada of ships blockading the Wall?"

I don't say nothin'. It's all pigeon-toe shit, history bein' turned inward and wrong.

"There is nothing to fear from Daesh Eye because they are no more. Like the armada and the blockade and whatever other nonsense the Society would have you hear. Lies to cover up the sins of their own father."

"Their...father?" That vinegar sock's seepin' into my body like a toxic adrenaline, fightin' against the damp of the drugs. "Then the bomb? Is somethin' else comin'? Comin' to attack us again?"

"It's the same as it always was. The same true enemy we've fought for decades. The only true enemy of the United Free States of Liberty." His blue eyes are like burnin' pricks of righteous light.

"Tell me. Tell me all of it."

"I told you I engineered the Wall. Well, one of many who helped in the effort, but I led the design. The Wall wasn't meant to be as it is now. I told you that, as well."

My brain's sloggin'. Tea's still workin'. Don't want it to, but it is.

"It was designed for producing power, to create green jobs and new opportunities." Bird Man seats himself beside me and begins scrawlin' on a scrap of paper. I can't read it because my vision's whomped into two. "Well, they turned it into...what it is now. I told them it wouldn't work. Not forever. The shaking of the earth, those little earthquakes cropping up more and more? There are serious problems. Problems the Society cannot ignore any longer."

My head's really swimmin', and I'm tryin' to make like a turd and float.

Bird Man stops writin' and rolls the scrap up into a little scroll before goin' into the bedroom and returnin' with one of the cooin' rats. My brain puddles with confusion as Bird Man ties the scroll to the scaly foot of the bird.

"Dat's—" I clear my throat. "That's why they call you that."

Bird Man don't say nothin' but scoops the bird into his hands and walks to the window facin' the ocean. He presses the bird to his mouth, kissin' it like a small feathery child, before hurlin' it forward. The bird bounces and bounds on wings meant for great flight. A gray blip, then it's gone into the yonder.

He turns back toward me. "Are you ready to hear?"

Blurry, drippy, smeary as I am, I nod. Because I am. Ready to understand it all as it truly is, the real state of the world I been livin' in.

The door creaks, and I turn to look, though the world bleeds and streaks when I do. Boy skitters out of the monitoring hub on his arachnid quarters, starin' at us.

"'Hey're 'ere," he mumbles through a mouth that don't work quite as it should.

Bird Man straightens, and the air in the room's a sudden boil, his concentrated stare glintin' with anger and, yah, there's fear in them too. "Who's here, Boy?"

The back of my neck prickles with sweat.

Boy shifts his weight, clickin' back and forth on his mechanical foundation. "S-s-society. 'Hey 'oming 'ow."

Emergency

I'M SEEIN' IT, but I don't wanna see it.

The vid screen of the hub's shufflin' through the different feeds, but Bird Man keeps scrollin' back over three of them. Three different angles of Enforcers. Brass. It ain't a lot of them, in the sense they'd only need half to kick my teeth all the way through my asshole. But there, marchin' through the maintenance tunnel, one of the very same we'd walked through, looks like the whole faggin' army's come to have Sunday supper. Harsh light's poppin' on in the tunnel as they walk, and as they near a big shaft, like the one I fell down, the lead brass pickle dick pulls out a key fob. Just like the clunker beast had, the one we'd failed to get. The butter-fucked plan that got Melissa stomped under a whole heap of clunk-a-junk.

"Then it is true." Oliver's tuggin' on a strand of his long chin sweeper, and Bird Man swats at the feathery twit. "I wondered, but the flair for the dramatic has always been the Society's preferred taste."

My pulse mainlines a surge of adrenaline. "What? What the faggin' hell you talkin' about?"

"The anniversary of the first bomb of the Great War—the Quiet—is upon us. Andi, I have something very important to tell you, and I need you to remain calm."

Best way to make sure someone ain't gonna be calm is by tellin' them to be. My palms itch.

"That bomb in the Wall? They're coming to detonate it."

"Bomb! Boom, bomb!" Oliver screeches helpfully.

Sound drops, my ears mufflin' the world because my brain's overheatin'. I unstick my tongue from the roof of my mouth. "Detonate...the bomb?" I step back. Because the exit's that way. The door leadin' to the ocean, a door leadin' to somewhere, anywhere, except bein' trapped inside a Wall with a fuckin' *bomb* about to go off.

Bird Man's still starin' at the vid screens. "Remember what I said about staying calm? This is that moment."

Boy shuffles behind us, his metal feet clickin' like scissor shears against the flagstone.

"I mean, that's real great because I was startin' to think I might wanna live here, it bein' a real nice safe neighborhood and all." Apparently fear likes sarcasm, too. "Can we please get the rottin' fuck outta here?"

"We can't do that. What I said, about you bein' my hope—that's all true." He turns to me, tall and straight, a muscle flexin' near his right ear, and lookin' like he's a right-hand angel bent on vengeful justice. But I ain't sure I'm all that vengeful. Nor all that concerned about justice, either.

"I need you now, Andi. We all do."

"I ain't sure what you're yammin' on about, but we can discuss this after we get outta here!"

"I know you don't understand yet. I realize you're frightened. But this bomb—"

"If the Daesh Eye or *whoever* planted it, then let the Society stop it! Detonate it? That's insane! They're comin' to disarm it—they've done it before! They stopped the bomb in Yorktown! A—and in Corning! They can stop this one, toowe just gotta get clear of it. Let them handle it." But my throat's slick and sweat's tricklin' down my chest because that don't make sense. None of this makes sense.

Bird Man looks, well, he looks disappointed. Like I'm poppin' a squat and shittin' on the rug.

I'm too terrified to be offended. I take another step back and nearly trip over one of Boy's long jointed legs. He catches my arm and peers into my face, wide black eyes borin' right into me like they can see all the goods and bads muckin' together in my head, like he can see what a faggin' junkie *coward* I am.

"'Ait. 'Lease, 'ait," he says.

If Boy weren't holdin' me, I'd probably dribble into a weepin' mess because I got no idea what to do, what Elenbar would want me to do, but every nerve and gut and shitkickin' part of myself is tellin' me to run and keep runnin' until all ain't nothin' but memory.

"What are we supposed to do?" I cry instead.

"We're going to stop them. We're going to stop them from detonating the bomb."

"But w—why would they detonate it?" My throat's raw. I been near killed in every possible way, and now I'm gonna die inside this Wall, without Elenbar, without anyone, and it's more than my poor ticker can stand.

"The—" And then somehow I know. Don't I just fuckin' know? "The Society. It's their—oh faggin' hell, it's *their* bomb, ain't it?" I don't gotta wait for his nod.

"Yes, they are the ones who put it there. Now listen to me. There's much you don't understand, but understand this: If we don't stop them from detonating it, not only will it decimate the Grayland Quarter—*your* quarter of the Slumland—but it will create the catalyst for the greatest War the world has ever seen. Greater than the Day of Black Blood and greater than all the atrocities that came before. It will be the end of the Brigade, the end of all hope of freedom, and perhaps the end of mankind upon this earth." Bird Man's voice don't shake, it don't quiver, it don't give any sign it speaks anythin' other than holy biblical kind of truth, except real.

"But I still don't understand." I push off of Boy, forcin' myself to stand, forcin' myself to swallow back another wave of cryin'. "Why? Why would they do this?"

"Because the Wall is going to fall anyway. The Wall has been ready to for a long time. And it's close, closer than ever, and if they cannot stop the Wall from falling, they must create the conditions giving them the greatest advantage."

My head's spinnin' because the more he talks, the less I understand, the less I comprehend about the shitbowl world I been born into. "Why would it fall? How could the greatest wall on earth just fall the fuck down?"

Then Bird Man—I swear he does—hidden beneath that wool jungle of face mop, the fagger smiles. "Because I designed it that way."

Best-Made Plans

BIRD MAN MADE me sit, and there's a cup of tea steamin' in front of me, but I ain't ever wanted sustenance less in my life. My gut's a swirl of bile and fear and confusion.

"I worried. Perhaps I knew what they planned to use the Wall for. In my obsession for clean energy and salvation, I didn't want to believe anyone would truly use the Wall in such a way. But just in case, just on the chance they did, I built in a failsafe. A structural weakness that, unless corrected over time, would lead to the eventual collapse of certain segments of the Wall. My only regret is I didn't make it weaker. How many have died as I've prayed and waited for my monster to fall?" Bird Man sips his tea, but his fist is a clenched knot of sinew and bone.

"Then they proved you right." My head's like a bowling ball on a sapling. I can hardly lift it. Everythin' in the world seems to have echoed into madness, and all I can think about is Elenbar. What she would say, what she would be shoutin' at this puff of shit. But I ain't got the strength to do it myself.

"Yes. My worst fears were valid. They closed the borders, and once they realized what I had done, what I was trying to still do, they pursued me, and I disappeared into the Wall as I said. This tower—once meant to be a secret hideaway for the writing of my memoirs, alas—has become my own tower of isolation. It appears on no schematic." Bird Man swallows the rest of his tea in one gulp.

"Then what? How are you supposed to stop it?" I don't even want the answer, my lips numb, but I gotta, just to know how far crazed shithouse rats burrow.

"With you, we can stop them. I know where they house the bomb, and though they placed it for maximum structural impact, they failed to consider its other weaknesses." He springs to his feet, age suddenly just a construct of imagination, and riffles through stacks of papers.

I heave a sigh too big for my lungs and pinch my nose hard. It's all too much for my brain, for any brain, except maybe for this mad fagger here. Boy's been pensive and quiet, and I'd say that's odd, except he's always like that. "I don't even wanna ask. Really, I don't. Even if you could, what are you supposed to do about the bomb? You built the faggin' Wall, but you got bomb knowin', too?"

"No, no, no. The bomb is far more complex than any of us can contend with. But that's not what's important right now. We need to stop them from accessing the bomb, buy more time." Bird Man unrolls a blue gridded map on the kitchen table, dumpin' my mug off as he does. The cup clatters against the floor, but he don't seem to notice or care.

I lean over the map, tryin' to see as he does, tryin' to understand and feel something other than just misery, other than complete sureness we ain't gonna be able to do tit shit about any of this. The grid makes my head spin, though, makin' the Wall look about ten times more confusin' than just bein' in it.

"Look, look, here." He's skimmin' his knobby fish-bone fingers over some lines at a funny-lookin' spot on the map. "This is a structural scaffolding holding up part of the ventilation system there. You can collapse the access points here and here. The rest in between will collapse under its own weight."

"Wait, no, no, no. Back up. You said 'you.' I ain't goin' back in the Wall again. No. Not with a faggin' bomb and a whole fistful of Enforcers ready to gum fuck my faceholes. I ain't doin' it."

"Oh, dear, well, yes. Boy will go with you, prime the explosives I've been assembling these last few months. So you won't be alone, really." Bird Man don't even glance at me.

Oliver pops outta his pocket and squawks, "Boy! Boy! Boy!" He flaps over to one of Boy's hinged legs where he perches, and cleans his fruity feathers like he ain't got no cares in all the world.

"No. I'm serious. You lookin' at me? Look into my buggy eyes when I say this. N. O. Ain't no green on this earth gonna make me go back in there. *You* do it. You know what you're doin'you got this locked down. I can— Look, just—just tell me where the radio tower is. Elenbar said there's one here and we can send a signal, for help. To the Outer World." I'm panickin' because I ain't goin' back in, I just ain't gonna do it.

"Radio tower?" Bird Man stares at me, contractin' his beetle brows. "My dear Andi, this *is* the radio tower. This tower, my tower, is the point of all communication with the Outer World."

"Then why the faggin' hell ain't you called for help yet?" My head's about to spin through the goddamn roof.

"They would never get here in time, and besides, the coordinated efforts aren't ready yet."

"If you don't start talkin' sense, I'm walkin' outta here. Right down to the damn ocean, and I'll swim if I gotta. What are you talkin' about?"

Bird Man sighs, and plants both hands on the map as he stares at me. "When the Wall fails, the Enclave—that's the military faction of the Union forces on the Canadian border—are planning a coup to decapitate the government and retake the UFS. But it's not ready *yet*. So I could send a call and no one would be able to come, to stop this bomb from going off and ruining all plans of this united front attack. It may be too late already. And excuse me, but you very well *are* going into that damn Wall. Understand?"

I—well, I ain't sure what to say right then. My gears are chompin' on his words. Except for one thing. "And just what makes you think I'm gonna do a goddamn puckerfuckin' thing like that?"

He storms away from me, headin' back to the monitoring hub, and I follow because I'm about to blow gaskets at this crotchety fagger tellin' me what's what about what I'm goin' to do—

But there's Elenbar. Right on the vid, large as life-size can be on screen. The greenish glow of the night camera shows they're in full darkness. There's two angles, pointed right at Elenbar and David. At least, I think the huddled mass of shudderin' knockin' bones and skin is Ele. A few feet away from her, David's got his head restin' on top of his folded knees. Like children. Alone in the dark.

"Damn it, you're going back in there because how else are you going to get *them* out too? They have wandered back into our view, so they haven't reached the other side and are lost. You think we're the only ones facing obliteration if that bomb goes off? So are they. So is everyone from back home, your home. Isn't there anyone you care about but yourself?" He's angry, pensive thoughtful Bird Man eroded away by my stupid selfish—

Because of course there is. There's lots of people I care about. Elenbar, sure. David, yah. But then there's... My heart's hurtin'thinkin' about it, but there's Bosco. And the Sisters. All the li'l mites hidden somewhere in the Slumland, not knowin' shit about shit. And yah, they're all probably *dead*, but if they ain't, if one of them still lives and breathes—if Elenbar is livin' and breathin'—then there ain't anythin' else to say about it.

"Goddamn it, cocksuckin' christ crackers."

Well, except that.

The Return

FUCK THIS.

I'mma say those words too, right to Elenbar's faggin' face when I see her. Ain't never gonna tell me I ain't done nothin' for her. For the *Brigade*.

The smell of the tunnels is worse than I remember. Though half that's my own pit sweat and the stink of fear. But also smells like dead festerin' shit—maybe one of those fuzzy rat things. Rottin' somewhere. Really wish I ain't thinkin' about that, because it's bad enough I'm stuck in this Wall without thinkin' about rat things. I'm scared too, wedged in this ventilation shaft runnin' parallel to where the brass are gonna come out. Wedged in here with a bomb big enough to bring down this whole section of the Wall. I'm tryin' to keep my mind wrapped around the picture Bird Man showed me on the schematics. Least I got a hand torch that works proper.

Back behind me, circlin' around the other end, is Boy. He's gonna prime the home-cooked boom sticks of dynamite Bird Man mixed up. Line them up so we can collapse it all right on top of the heads of the brass comin' to set off the big bomb.

And we're supposed to be doin' all this without settin' off that big bomb ourselves.

While Boy's doin' all that, I'm squirmin' toward where Elenbar and David are. They've gotten themselves into a dead end. Not sure how they've made it as far as they have. But Elenbar don't look good, huddled over like a sack of gutter trash. I gotta get to her. I don't think it, don't let it in. The thought that she could be, might be—

Faggin' shit stickers, it really does reek something awful in here.

I'm crouch crawlin' through this shaft, and though it's hurtin' my bent back and makin' the rods feel like mighty big-ass splinters, I'm makin' good progress. But then, of course, because ain't nothing in my life ever easy, I see the reason it smells so bad. And why this ain't gonna be an easy jaunt.

I really wish I ain't got light to see what I'm seein'.

A few paces ahead of me, curled up and wedged in the narrowin' junction between segments of the shaft, is a body. A bloated discolored body of a person.

My gut lurches thinkin' it's Elenbar or David, but I see quick it ain't. The face is pointed right at me, one arm extended like it's askin' me to pull it on through. I seen enough dead gutter flies to know what seasons do to a body, though this one's mighty well preserved, bein' all tucked inside the Wall. But ain't no resistin' time, and it does funny things to flesh. The faggin' smell of loose guts and festerin' wet spots never gets easy.

The bigger problem is this guy/body/thingy is blockin' my way. Which means I gotta touch it, and my gut don't like it when I touch dead things. Fact, it's stagin' a protest right now, and I ain't even come close to touchin' the purple puffy skin bits yet. Wish I had a stick. Though pokin' dead things never goes well, and I'm tryin' to block out a certain memory of a certain puffy thing that popped in a certain disgustin' *boom* sorta way.

Lessons livin' on the street teaches you: don't poke dead things with sticks.

I reach out and press on the forehead, testin' stages of rigor. Lucky for me, in that not-so-lucky way, the body ain't stiff, so it gives a li'l. But again, in that not-so-lucky way, the skin deflates and I retch at the smell. I wriggle around so my feet are against it because I want my face as far away from the putrefyin' mess as I can. Boy, bein' the tinkertot he is, couldn't get in here, so I imagine there's probably lots of skeletons holed up in little hidey spots like this. A whole Wall filled with them. I shudder and shove against the body's head with both feet.

There's more squish than slide. My feet collapse in on the shoulders. We ain't moved, though, more the body just cavin' in on itself. The smell's even worse, like an ass maggot's crawled up my nose and died. I retch again, a stream of fish stew streakin' the tunnel, splashin' my hands. Which makes me retch even more.

"You hearing this?"

I freeze. My foot's halfway inside the chest cavity of this body, decayin' ooze threatenin' to engulf my leg, and someone's talkin' in the tunnel beneath where I'm holed up.

"Something's in there. But it might be those tunnel rats they were talking about. Don't let your head get all spooked. That shit's contagious. Don't need everyone climbing the walls. Bad enough with that effing awful smell."

Men's voices. One sounds like a squeakin' nut stain, while the other's got a throat of gravel. But it don't matter. They're both standin' right under me, and I ain't gotta see the vids to know they're brass.

My foot sinks farther into the mess of human remains, and I jerk it back, not thinkin'. There's a suckin' squelch as my foot pops loose.

"There! It's up there!"

Sweat's burnin' my eyes like a squirt of misplaced cum. I can't breathe, know I can't, because they're lookin' right up at me waitin' for sound, any sound. But my arm's crampin', my gut's bubblin', and any second my lungs are gonna collapse needin' air so bad.

"Screw it. Hand me that tazer. Rat or not, we'll toast the sucker good."

Goddamn faggin'—

I slam my feet against the skull of the body, ignorin' the poppin' sound as it compresses down into its own guts.

"It's moving! Get it! Right there!"

I kick again. Gawd, there's so much of it, and the body keeps masticatin' under my feet. There's a loud buzz of the chargin' tazer, and the body liquefies, the last resistance givin' way with a gush. I turn and begin rakin' my way through the mess, fingers clawin' at the bony mass, shovin' the sturdy bits aside so I can shimmy through.

It's like swimmin' through a soup of regurgitated afterbirth.

"God, it's a big one! Turn it up!"

The pop of the tazer booms against the shaft and the metal shivers before deliverin' the blast of current, makin' every hair on my body stand on end. The second delay is gone, and my arms and legs seize with the shock of the blast. Flesh smokes and the liquidy bits of the corpse sack vaporizes, fillin' the whole shaft with the stench of cookin' guts and rot.

But I'm alive. The metal deadens the shock, and though the heat sears my palms and knees, it ain't enough to stop me. I claw through the tail end of the corpse sludge, slidin' on pulverized membrane and goo. I throw myself around the next bend, a sharp left that's gonna take me outta their reach, take me beyond the tazer.

"It's still moving! Holy shit, I think it's a scag! That ain't a rat. Go back and get them!"

The metal sears hot again, and my limbs jerk with the second seize, but I've already moved past the direct hit. I throw myself forward, floppin' like an air-drowned fish. The voices are shoutin' and carryin' down the tunnel, away from me, but toward where the rest of the group must be. I'm gaspin' as I crawl faster, my hands and knees burnin' from the scald of the metal. Skin's already sloughin' off, leavin' a slick of ooze and blood behind me. Though some of that's the body-sack sludge I'm covered in. The stink of it festers, and the sour tang in my mouth's from the bits I sucked in durin' my desperate dash to freedom.

But I ain't thinkin' about that because I'm hearin' the poundin' of footsteps from somewhere close inside. The sound of brass and Enforcers and more tazers. They know I'm in here, they know I'm slidin' around inside these vented shafts, and there ain't time to get to Elenbar before they find me or find Boy.

Or before we gotta blow the dynamite.

Coo & a Call

I'M LOST. MY mad rush to put distance between me and the rest of those stompin' boots has turned the schematics all upside down in my head. I'm lookin' at it in the light of the torch, but I can't stop my hand shakin' and none of the squiggled lines are makin' sense. I got no idea where I am and worse, no idea where Elenbar and David are.

I can still hear shoutin' and scufflin', but they're far off now, deeper in the bowels of the tunnels crisscrossing away from me. But just like I don't know where I am, where Elenbar is, I also can't tell where my shaft is gonna cross back over the main tunnel where they are. Timin' is everythin', but so is position.

I'm supposed to be scootin' over to where Boy is, check in with him, before goin' to extract Elenbar and David. But I ain't sure where I'm gonna come out. The bends I've taken in my mad dash might've taken me just about anywhere. Somehow I've gotta backtrack, but I ain't got the time to do that, neither. Tears are burnin' my eyes, and the gridded schematic is gettin' smeared with the ooze and blood of my scalded hands. I can't stop shakin', and my throat's wrapped around a sob so big it's chokin' me.

Goddamn shit junkie-trash-belly-black-junkie. Elenbar's voice whispers to me in the dark of my mind. And she's right. Can't lock it down, can't do a single run, not a goddamn singular mission without fuckin' it up. A cock-up always ready to let down.

Can't even straighten it out for a goddamn clip through the Lane. Bosco's voice is a hiss followin' close as I slide forward on my ass, shinin' the light around the next bend. More metal and another straightaway that ends in a T-junction. *It'll eat you alive, and all's left is bones.*

The sob wrenches free, and I grab at my throat. It hurts the very glands with the force. The sob echoes, but I don't care. Because it don't matter. I'm stuck in here. I'm lost. How am I gonna get out before Boy's gotta blow it? Elenbar's gonna die. David's gonna die. I'm gonna die, all because I can't fly it straight, can't use a single goddamn cell in my brain to push through when shit goes down. All my life, I've gone from one cock-up to another, and Elenbar's the only one who's kept me goin', kept me alive even as I've worked so hard to blow it all up time and again.

Junkie. Fuckin' junkie. Can't stay off the juice long enough to do a run. Shit junk-tard. Faggin' junk-tard. Trash. Tard. Junk. Fuck. Fucker. FUCK.

I curl myself up around my charred knees, my sobs rockin' back and washin' over me, amplified and repeated by the metal walls of my eventual tomb. Because it's where I'm gonna die. Ain't no more beyond it. I'll be another stopped-up bloated corpse—though I won't, because soon I'll be lit up in the flare of a detonation. Either by Boy or by marchin' brass. The Wall will fall, and everyone I've known and loved will die anyhow. Whether by the comin' War or the war that's been fought against us since we slid free of a ma's womb, our only true comfort in this fucked-up sewer bowl of life.

I've cried my last, the sob drained outta me. But a last echo pops back at me, a barkin' wail that don't hardly sound like me at all.

Because it ain't.

I knuckle my swollen sockets and sit up a little, strainin' to hear. Might be brass again, and I brace for an oncoming assault. But ain't no sound.

Then the cry comes again. But it ain't a wail like I thought. The blur of my cryin' melded with the call of somethin', somethin' familiar to me like the whiff of Flow, the chemical sweat of a high. My skin prickles with recognition.

It's the Brigade. True to tit, it's Elenbar. Cooin' and chirpin' from somewhere in the mess of these steel guts. The bird calls we used to signal each other. To call to one another. The chirp of my partner as I tag a shithouse wall. The chirpin' call to signal me in a sloshin' river. Somewhere. Maybe close, could be real close, or maybe not. The distortion of distance is a real thing, but there's a flutter in my chest. That li'l light, the li'l light the Sisters always had us singin' about, is flarin', it's hopin'. Because somewhere Elenbar's alive and she's callin' for me.

I smooth the crumpled schematic and stare at it. Force myself to really look at it. Still ain't sure where I'm at, but I gotta try. If I go back...

I crawl, my hands and knees radiatin' pain with every foot I manage, but I try to focus. Count the bends. I've made a right turn, then down a long straightaway before a T-junction. I check the schematic again.

Crawl back to the beginning of where I was, then search for a right, straightaway, and then a T-junction. There's several of them, but think, Andi, *think*. How far could I have really gone? Bein' scared and rushin' makes distance all wonky, but how far could I really have scooted along on all knees and hands? I trace the shafts with a scorched fingertip.

It's gotta be—well, no, it's *probably* here. Right here.

The cooin' call comes again, and I cup my hands around my mouth and envelope the air through tight lips. The answerin' call.

At first there ain't no sound, ain't no reply, and clearly I've just gone mad, gone wonky. Just dropped all my eggs bein' here in this tunnel alone. But then it comes and it's louder, excited maybe, like it's recognized me and is beckonin' me with hands I can't see, only hear. I keep movin'.

At first I don't think I'm gettin' closer, but the directions of the shaft seem to be linin' up with the schematic. The chirpin' call still sounds distant, but I chirp back again. My gut clenches because the brass might hear me, might hear Elenbar, bringin' them all on top of us, but none of that matters if I can't get to her first. If I can't get outta here, then none of that matters anyhow. And I have hope.

I turn onto a straightaway, and the coo that comes is so close it almost frightens me. Blood's rushin' through my anemic junkie veins as I scoot down the final stretch.

They're right under me.

"Elenbar? Elenbar! It's me, I'm here. Right here, there's a vent cover, unscrew it. Hurry!"

I hear scratchin' on the metal underneath me and the squeal of a screw. My heart's like one of Bird Man's sparrows, twitterin' against the prison of my rib cage.

The panel screeches as it's pulled away, my torchlight bouncin' as I aim it with shaky hands.

David's face stares up at me, wide eyes lookin' like dead mice in a pail of milk. "Oh god, Andi, it's actually you."

"Come on, you cuck, get me down." I reach for him, and he grips me tight as I slide through the small openin'.

"We gotta get outta here, we gotta move fast. Where's Elenbar?"

His face, already sheet white in the glare of the torch, turns to bleached bone.

"Andi, I'm sorry. I think she might be... I think she might be dead."

Sacrifices

"NO. NO, WHERE is she? Where the fuck is she?" I grab David's shirt, his stained ripped shirt, and nearly tear it off his body.

"She's over here. She was hardly breathing, and I just couldn't... I couldn't bring myself to check again. The sound, it was awful."

I shine the light in his face, fear minglin' with rage. "You left her? By herself? Where is she?!"

He don't say anythin', just points down the corridor. I run.

The corridor hits a dead end and splits off in either direction. I step in and shine the light to the right, then to the—

"Ele!" I throw myself down beside her, droppin' the torch as I claw at her shoulders and shake her. "I'm here, right here, don't go, I made it! I'm here!"

Ain't nothin' but terrible silence, her body limp, and then she mumbles. I can't hear it, but it's there, a croak of sound carried on the terrible wheeze of her lungs tryin' to draw air. I lift her chin, and the glow of the torch shimmers in her bloodshot green eyes.

"Yah, yah, it's me. Your residential fuckup, here. I'm right here."

Her pupils focus and take me in like she's really seein' me now. Her arms lift and drape around my shoulders, heavy and weary like they've carried mountains.

"I got you, I've got you. I know you're down, but we gotta go. We gotta move you. Here." I pull a pouch of water outta my backsack and angle it between her chapped lips. "David!"

She swallows, then coughs hard, a rattlin' wet slap inside her chest cavity. David appears around the corner and reaches for her. I glare at him.

"How'd she call for me, bein' like this?"

"That was me. She... Before, when you fell down that shaft. She was calling to you with those bird sounds. When I heard you, crying, I thought maybe you might hear them. I wasn't sure, but then you called back. I'm sorry. I couldn't... I thought we were...you were..." David's voice shakes, but his face is earnest and real and sorry.

"Faggin' cuck, just help me get her up."

He grabs her clunker arm and I grab the torch before slingin' her human one around my neck, tryin' not to think about how hot her skin is, how she's practically aflame with the heat radiatin' off her damp flesh.

"We gotta hurry. This whole place is gonna go boom real soon. We need to get to Boy."

"Boy? Who?" David gasps. Elenbar's barely able to prop her own weight up.

"Jus— Later." I struggle with the schematic and the torch, tryin' to see and hold Elenbar at the same time. "Here, this way, go this way."

We half carry Elenbar down the next corridor. Boy's down another straightaway where the dynamite's hopefully been primed, hopefully ready to blow. And then, because like everythin' else, plans are made for gettin' fucked up—

"Hey! Hey, you stop! Right there!"

The shout comes at our backs. I glance back and see two peckerheads at the far end of the straightaway, shinin' torches at us. They're decked in full uniforms, but their clean baby-butt faces make me think they're newly spawned tadpoles.

"Fuckin' hell, run!" But I didn't need to say it. We yank Elenbar off her feet, carryin' her in the fastest sprint shuffle we can manage.

"Boy! Boy! Run!" I'm screamin' because it don't matter now if the whole place hears us. We're outta time, been outta time. I shoot another desperate look behind us, but only one's comin'. The other's split off somewhere, probably roundin' up the rest of the brass fuckers who came on their field trip.

We skid around the bend, stumblin' into the wide-open room of one of the pump houses. Boy stares up at us. Coiled in tight bundles along the overhead beams are packages of the dynamite. In his hand is a small black switch.

"We gotta go! Go!" I scream.

But Boy don't run. He rises up and skitters toward us. David shrieks and drops Elenbar completely, steppin' back in horror at the half-clunker spider man that Boy is.

"David!" I collapse under Elenbar's saggin' weight.

Boy scoops Elenbar up like she don't weigh nothin' at all and hands me the black switch. David's standin' there, his mouth slack and eyes nearly buggin' out of his small sockets.

"*Move*, you twat bag!" I punch him in the head, and he stumbles, seemin' to come back to himself. Boy's already on the move, and I drop the schematic because this part I've memorized, the mad dash back to the tower.

David and I run together, feet poundin' in perfect sync as we enter the straightaway leadin' away from the pump housin'.

"Stop! I will shoot you down. Stop now!"

The peckerwood's burst into the corridor behind us, face bright red and glowin' with the chase.

I don't even hear the charge of the tazer, only feel the current as it slams into my spine like the domed front of a bullet train.

My teeth snap hard as my chin slams against the ground. The world's gone streaky and bright, and ahead of me I see David's waverin' runnin' body. He ain't seen me fall yet. Ahead of him is Boy, metal gears churnin' as he pumps all eight legs, Elenbar's head lollin' over one of his arms.

The brass peckerwood's nearly on top of me, his face contorted with rage as he levels the tazer at me again.

I feel the heavy metal casing of the switch in my hand.

Junkie. Ain't nothin' but a junkie.

And like a real junkie, ready to blow it all up again and again, I flick the switch and blow up my life, prayin' Elenbar and everyone else is far enough away to escape it.

Buying Time

THE CUP OF tea is scaldin' hot, though the heat is blunted through the thick swath of bandages coverin' both my hands. My ears are still ringin'.

In the other room, Bird Man's settlin' Elenbar on a soft bed. David's starin' out the tower window, into the night now smotherin' the view of ocean, though the faint roar of the continuous waves signal its invisible presence.

"My God. I can't believe you made it all this way, that you survived the blast. I can't believe you did it." His voice is a distant muffle through the ringin' sound of my ruptured ears. David turns to me, but I can't meet his gaze.

Because I can't believe it, either. I threw the switch and died. Except I didn't. Dried blood still crusts my arms, the splatter of brain smear still clotted in my hair. The peckerwood waffled in and exploded outward with the force of the blast, fallin' upon me and coatin' me with the remnants of his mortal self. The blood dryin' in both my ears tells me my hearin' might never be the same. But I'm alive, somehow. Even cockin' it all up time and again, I'm alive.

"How's your head?" David rests a hand on my shoulder, and I wince. My whole body aches and burns and creaks.

"It's shit. Think I'm goin' for a new model, next time."

He manages a whimper of a smile and returns to his cup of tea, sittin' beside me. "What is this place? Who are they?"

"This is the tower. The radio tower Elenbar told us about. This is it. And in there's Bird Man. Spider guy is Boy. They helped me after I fell, been explainin' a lot to me about what's been goin' on in the Wall."

"And the bomb?"

I nod. I'd already told him about the tickin' inevitable hidden inside the Wall. About how the Society's rigged it to take out all remnants of sanity, to stage terror and justify more war. Like me, he didn't wanna believe that either.

"He's the reason I got to you all. Was able to get you out."

"You came back for us. I'm not sure I'd have done it. Come back, I mean." David's gazin' deep into his teacup, like it's got the secrets of courage hidden inside.

"I had to. Elenbar. She's always come back for me. Even when I don't deserve it, she's always shone sun in my ass and made it right."

"Well, she's lucky to have you. That you have each other."

I'm sure he's thinkin' about Melissa, and I clamp down on it, close my eyes to it, because my mind's already too full of sad. Ain't room for any more.

"She is strong. The infection would kill weaker creatures," Bird Man says as he enters the room.

My heart quickens. "Is she gonna be all right?"

"Perhaps. She is very ill, has been for a while. I've given her medicine and something for the pain so she will sleep soundly. But her body will need every ounce of strength to recover. Unfortunately, there isn't time for the long period of rest her body so truly needs." Bird Man crosses over to the teakettle and prepares a cup.

"What do you mean? She's restin' right now. She can have all the rest she wants."

He glances up at me, solemn and stern. "Not yet. You did an incredibly brave and reckless thing, throwing the switch as you did. You ensured none of the explosives could be dismantled, and so most, though rudimentary, detonated as we designed. The blast brought down most of the corridors surrounding the bomb."

"Most? Only most?" My stomach squirms.

"We could not prevent all access without causing serious damage to the Wall's integrity."

"What about the rest of the brass? Will they come here? Will they find you?" My eyes are hot again, and the ringin' in my ears makes my head ache.

"The rest of the forces retreated out of the tunnels before they collapsed, though many were indeed likely killed in the blast. They will regroup and send back word—eventually yes, they will return, and yes, they will find me. But, Andi, you have bought us precious time. It will take returning forces considerable effort to work around the damage we've caused. But eventually they will reach the bomb. And yes, they will detonate it. Though they will likely be more cautious now that they know enemies live within the Wall. More will come, and we cannot hope to stop them. Not alone." Bird Man sips his tea.

I squeeze my eyes shut. "Then what? What do we do?"

"You run. You go to the Enclave and tell them all you've seen, all the intel you've gathered. Their plans to intervene will need to accelerate. They may still be able to prevent this tragedy or change the course of what is to come."

David clears his throat, and I force myself to look at him.

"When will they come for us?" David asks.

"Soon. I have sent word to the Enclave to send transport. To get you all out of here. They can also help Elenbar, if she can stand the struggle until then. You did well, Andi." Bird Man lifts his cup toward me, toastin' me, his blue eyes shimmerin' with—

Heat rushes to my face, and I slide off my chair. Without lookin' at Bird Man, I go to Elenbar's room. I close the door behind me and sink down beside her. She's covered in thick blankets, and her face is ashen. It's no wonder David thought her dead because lookin' at her now, even in the gentle flicker of lamplight, she really looks it. Like every next rattlin' breath is her last.

I grab her bony human hand and squeeze it hard, but ain't no response, just another rattlin' wheeze.

"Ele? Can you hear me? We're gettin' outta here. Actually gettin' outta here. Just like you said, and help comin'. They're gonna take down the Society. Everythin's gonna change, it really is." My words get pinched in a sob. I need her to glare at me, to say somethin', to yell at me, to tell me what a fuckup I am. But she don't say nothin'.

"Just keep breathin' then. That's all you gotta do, keep breathin'. You do your part, and I'll try to keep from cockin' it up, knockers?"

"AND THERE WAS little that could have been done about that, anyway. The War had already begun, so far as the Society was concerned." Bird Man sips his tea.

I take a sip of mine. Tastes less and lesslike crotch ash, and it does help with the pain. Bird Man took the rods out yesterday, and though it's stiff as a clunker prick, I'm movin' better each day.

David looks up, a smear of ink on his nose and a growin' stack of pages beneath his scribblin' pen. "See, that's interesting. In primary, they told us Daesh Eye had almost won the War entirely. That the Wall and cannon grid was the only thing that brought it to an end. After they dropped the big bomb, of course." Bird Man's got David started on the real version of history, and he's been writin' it down like a feverish fuck fly ever since.

"Well, they would say that. The Wall stopped the Union's involvement in the War. Dropping the bomb was in violation of almost every international treaty of the time. The explosion and fallout destroyed the Daesh Eye and obliterated most of the Central East entirely. The Wall—and the bombs—stopped the rest of the world from punishing the Society for what they had done. And continue to do, as you well know. The Transgressors and Murder Maidens." Bird Man grimaces, a flicker of rage in his otherwise placid gaze. "It all serves the fear machine, and the Society needs that to stay in control. Why, if people weren't so afraid, imagine what they might accomplish."

Bird Man nods, and David keeps scribblin'.

Most of this, I don't got any idea about, though it's hard to care about it all happenin' so long before now, and I'm thinkin' about Elenbar anyway. My guts full of wigglin' worry worms thinkin' about her. Pale, shaky, half in the world and half out already. I been tryin' to pull her back to the land of the livin', but it's like she left somethin' behind in the Wall, and I ain't entirely sure it's gonna come back.

"Andi?" David's voice brings me back in the room. "You all right?"

We're alone. Bird Man and Boy are gone, probably to bed. Outside the window, the ocean's a sheet of black, though you can still smell it and know it's always there. I love that.

"Yah. Just thinkin' about friends. From back before." I pick at one of my fingernails. They've grown longer than I can remember.

"Ahh. I'm sorry." David puts his pen down and closes his eyes. I realize he's smellin' the air, smellin' the salt. Guess he loves it, too.

"What do you think's gonna happen? After we hear back from them up north?"

"Happen? I have no idea. Never thought we'd make it this far. Never thought I'd make it without...well, without Melissa." David's lookin' at me, but I can't look at him. Not right now, like this, in this quiet warm room, with salt air waftin' in as he talks about his dead wife. While I'm rememberin' old friends. Rememberin' Bosco.

We're quiet for a while.

Then David clears his throat. "The question is, what's going to happen to Elenbar?"

Somehow I'd managed to forget her, just in the moment, though lately all I do is think about what's going to happen to her. If she's gonna make it. If she's strong enough when the time comes to go.

"Nothin's gonna happen to her. Because she's gonna be fine. She's gonna live."

Ain't nothin' more to say after that.

Days

THE SOUND OF propellers.

I launch myself at the window. David pushes in beside me, and together we crane our necks, gazin' out at the clear blue sky.

It's a small thing. Ain't much of nothing, could be a bird if you didn't have an idea what to look or listen for.

"They've made excellent time. How fortunate." Bird Man's come in from the Monitorin' Hub, and he don't crowd us but stands back, hands folded as though in silent expectation.

"How they gonna land? Ain't nowhere to land!" The Wall, the ocean, the everythin' beyond—ain't no way a plane's comin' down, except by crashin'.

"No, look, it's a seaplane." David touches my hand, and points. I ain't sure what a seaplane is, but I nod like I do.

Then the bedroom door opens, and my head almost pops off as I jerk around to see her. It's Elenbar. Actual Elenbar, holdin' the doorframe like it's life support. I throw myself at her, and almost knock her to the ground, but I can't help it. My heart swells, and—between the promise of escape the plane's brought and Elenbar bein' alive, really alive— today's like the best damn day of my whole shitty junkie life.

Elenbar squeezes me, though it's weak, and she's smilin' for the first time since... Yah.

"'Lane. P-d-'lane. ''Oin' land 'here." Boy's joined us, and the room's pulsatin' with hot emotions as we all watch the plane make a lazy circle around the distant buoy.

A bright red flare shoots up into the sky and pops with a brilliant flash. The smudge of smoke's like a stroke of paint against the blue canvas of the sky. The nose of the plane tips as it begins to descend.

"We need to go. They may already be under surveillance. Time is short," Bird Man says.

"What? Now? But—"

Bird Man nods. I run into the room and pick up my one change of clothes, stuff it into the tattered backsack I been draggin' since the Brick. Ain't got nothin' else, really. Oh, except Bird Man's...no, gonna be *Bosco's* book. I tuck that carefully between my rags. Just in case there's ever a Bosco to give it to.

I'm breathin' hard, though it's all nerves.

"Be careful on the stairs. They are not in good condition," Bird Man says. He opens the far door, the one facin' the ocean, and a high-spirited wind slams through, nearly shovin' him back inside. Payin' no mind, like the wind's just a wisp of gauze, Bird Man ducks his head against it and leads the way.

Elenbar and David follow, but I stop. Now's the time. If ever there was gonna be a time—I look back at the watch. The gleamin' gold watch sittin' on Bird Man's shelf. He don't need it. None of them need it. It's already in my hand, heavy and cold, and I'm tuckin' it into my pocket before I get up the sack to really think about what I'm doin'. Seems it's the least I oughta faggin' get, squirmin' through the Wall, and blowin' myself up doin' it.

I whirl around. Boy's starin' at me from the depths of his jungle-scrub face. My gut squirms with cold shame, like swallowin' slivers of ice. He reaches out a hand, and I flinch, thinkin' it's comin' for my face, my throat, my—he lays the puckered callused hand on my shoulder.

"'Or yuh. 'Ake wi' ya 'o fa'way."

"I'm sorry." Words are out before I can reel them back in. I go to pull out the watch, to shove it back at him, cold shame becomin' a surge of molten hatred of my goddamn *junkie* piece-of-shit self. But he wraps his hand over mine and squeezes it. Shakes his head.

My throat's hard like I swallowed a sack of rand coins.

"Hey, Boy. Thank you. For helpin' me. For helpin' with...well, with everythin'. You didn't have to do it, and you saved me. Really, you did. You know that, right?"

He nods once, a tight nod like it hurts some.

"You and Bird Man gonna be okay?" It's the first time I've given a faggin' thought to it. About what's gonna happen to Boy. To Bird Man. Guilt's a stabbin' thing, like steppin' on a nail.

He nods that tight nod again and don't know why, but I throw my arms around his bushy neck. Everythin' of him smells like oil and salt and sweat and...alive. Half-clunker but all alive. All the human bits that matter anyway.

He pats my back, stiff in my arms like he ain't ever had a hug before. I let him go and knuckle away tears.

"Don't tell Bird Man what a shit I am, yah?"

He smiles a li'l smile.

I wave at him before steppin' out onto the stairs.

The wind's buffetin' me with salt and flecks of water, though we're high above the crashin' waves below. The stairs wind down the jagged cliffside, and the sheer concrete expanse of the Wall juts up past us on the left, cuttin' a neat divide through the world. Just on the other side, even knowin' how huge it is, is home, the Slumland. All we've known and loved. Right faggin' there. As I pick my way down the crumblin' steps, worn from time, water, and the thing Bird Man called "erosion," it feels final somehow. Like we ain't comin' back ever.

"You all right?" David's shoutin' at me, holdin' out his hand. I grab it, the height of the stairs and whippin' wind makin' me unsteady. I teeter on the crumbly steps and then let go of his hand so he can grab Elenbar. The roar of the ocean drowns the scream of my inner thoughts, and we march downward, Elenbar saggin' against David.

Turns out seaplanes can land on water, what with those buoy things on the bottom of them. The plane dips so low it looks like it's gonna bust up on the water's surface, but like a lakeside duck, it touches down and skims a ways before ploppin' into the sloshin' whitecaps. It's beyond the big waves of the shoreline, bobbin' and disappearin' from view with each new swell and curl of water. Looks as far away as the whole Outer World itself. We're standin' on the sand, which is weird and unstable compared to the Wall we've been inside for so long.

"You can see here what is happening." Bird Man points to the foundation of the Wall, and sure as he said, huge portions have crumbled away, creatin' pebbly rivers of debris. The crash of waves sucks against them, and particles and smaller boulders froth in the maw of the hungry ocean.

Like it's heard us, like it senses we're tryin' to leave, the earth suddenly shudders beneath our feet, and I grab Elenbar outta instinct. She holds my arm, and we tremble like we're standin' on a deceptive layer of pond scum, about to plunge into the swill below the sandy surface. There's a deafenin' groan, and I scream because it's the Wall. The Wall bellows and quivers, the concave face of stone lookin' like a tidal wave that's gonna crash down on us. My heart's yammerin' even though it can't, not now, it's not gonna just fall on us right as we're about to leave.

Instead, a chunk of a foundation block breaks away, farther up the beach from where we stand. Like it's nothin' but sand instead of dense material designed to be withstandin' the strain of time. My entire body's shiverin', covered with pickle flesh, because I can't shake my mind's image of the great Wall crushin' down on us.

"Is everyone all right? It's a frightening thing, but it won't fall. Not yet," Bird Man says.

"When? How long will it stand?" David wipes sweat outta his eyes. Might be tears, too.

"It will not fall because the Society will not miss the opportunity to detonate the bomb. They are watching it as closely as I am. When the time comes, anyone close by will not have an opportunity to consider the horror. It will be quick." Bird Man directs himself down the beach, and I see what I missed when we first stepped onto the sand: a boat. It's tethered to the Wall itself, to a ring set deep in the concrete.

"We should run." Elenbar's voice suddenly hisses in my ear. I try to shake her off, but she grips my arm, her eyes shinin' with a mania and fear that scares me deep into my guts. "We should go. We can track the coastline until we find—"

"Find what? What exactly are we supposed to find? Ain't this what you wanted? A military enclave, ready to take on the Society! It's the faggin' help we need! For the Brigade! For everyone!" I grab her arm too, and I'm shakin' her, rage so hot in my face and ears the skin feels like it's gonna blister. "This *is* it. This is all there is. You're not well, Ele. You're weak and confused and—"

"No! There's others! Supposed ta be others here." Elenbar's lookin' away from Bird Man and David, who are still walkin' toward the moored boat.

"Who? Who are the others? What are you talkin' about?"

She turns her gaze to me, and I bite the inside of my cheek because the look's blacker than her single tear at the Farm, more desperate than death or livin' or anythin' that's come before this moment.

"They're supposed ta be here. Jane. And Ennis. Tot-tot. I sent them *here*. Ta reach—ta reach the Outer World. A year ago. They came here. They're supposed ta be here!" She's tremblin' hard, more than the shake of the earth ever had.

"Jane." I'd forgotten about Jane. Just gone out my mind like so many things and people and places. Elenbar's sister. But Elenbar said they'd moved on, that she'd sent them away to be safe in one of the outer quarters, because she was the leader and a target. Jane would always be in danger. "They came here? You sent them through the Wall?"

Elenbar sinks to the sand, clutchin' at it with gnarled white fingers. "She wanted ta come. She—she wanted ta help us. Always wanting ta help. And she's smart. So fucking *smart*." She chokes on the word like it's a wad of splintered glass. "She researched, said she could. Said she wanted ta pay back the Society fer clipping her. And fer me. Ta keep it from happening ta me. Those contacts I told ya about. They were supposed ta meet her here. Supposed to keep her safe."

I wanna touch her shoulder. Wanna tell her it ain't her fault. Wanna...but it ain't gonna help. Ain't that always it? The shit we carry in the black pits of ourselves? The festerin' truths that erode our foundations, that eat at the Wall we build inside our heads.

Goddamn shit junkie-trash-belly-black-junkie.

Elenbar sent her sister to die. Straight into a Wall she couldn't outsmart. Couldn't escape. That we, by faggin' fuck luck, survived. We shouldn't have. Not when Jane died back there in the Wall, because she did. I know it, and Elenbar, ravin' about others bein' here, rantin' about runnin' away—she knows it better than me.

The waves howl against the shoreline, which denies them entrance to the world. Spray and salt and wind chap my face, and I lean into it. Suck it deep into lungs that ain't breathed fresh air since their first squall outside a shriveled whore's womb. Elenbar's crumpled and crouched on the sand, and I let her be. Because I know too, that maybe—that Elenbar ain't ever gonna come back. That her hope got tied to an anchor, an anchor that looked an awful lot like her sister. And her sister's dead. Anchors are funny like that. They'll hold you strong and proper, until you're tryin' to surface for air. Then sometimes, an anchor's a noose you drown yourself with.

The thumpin' buzz of a motor blows to us on the wind. David and Bird Man are leanin' over the boat. They've dragged it into the low surf, and it's chuggin' with life and purpose. Because beyond the waves is the waitin' plane, and beyond that, hope, though it means leavin' behind the hope of a sister, of a secret hideout of Brigade operatives just waitin' for us to show up. Leavin' behind a dream that never was and won't ever be.

Elenbar's still down on the sand, and David's wavin' his arm at us, beckonin' us to come. So I crouch beside Ele, because that's what she is right now, the li'l part of herself still at St. Aggie's, still runnin' with Jane and callin' me a pussy-ass bitch for cryin' durin' sermons. I fold my arms around her shoulders and rest my chin against the tangled mess of her red hair. Words whisper from my lips to the gentle curve of her slightly pointed ear, and I talk to her. I tell her all the things someone should've told me. That maybe a ma somewhere should've told all of us, holdin' us tight against nightmares and the big scary world full of pain and badness. I tell her those things because there ain't a single other thing to be said.

I'm a goddamn shit junkie. Elenbar sent her sister to die. And like so many things in this life, and all the others we might come to live, none of it were our fault.

Not really.

Seaplanes & Freedom

OCEAN MAKES YOU sick.

I ain't ever been on water long enough to learn that, but I know it now. David rubs my back as I heave again over the side of the motorboat, the spray of the waves sprinklin' my face with flecks of my own bile. I tried to hold Elenbar for a while, cradle her as we headed toward the plane, but rockin' horizon does funny things to guts that have only lived on solid ground.

"We're almost there!" David shouts above the roar of the motor and water.

Bird Man directs the boat with the same calm confidence he's done all other things. Wish he'd be confident enough to take us back to shore. Enclave or not, faggin' plane or not, Society killing us all or not, I just want three solitary still moments where I can curl up and die, undisturbed.

The boat slows, the high whine of the motor droppin' off into dull thuddin' as we approach.

"Who goes the boat?" a voice calls to us.

"The free folk who still live!" That's Bird Man.

I force myself to look up at the plane. Standin' on one of the plane's buoy floats are two—well, they're women. Maybe. Clad in leather one-suits, with goggles atop their heads, they mighta just stepped out of an Uppers fashion catalog for models who fly faggin' planes on the vids. Except for the pistols slung at their waists and the white handprint emblazoned on their chests.

The one with slickered short hair grabs the rope David tosses to her, and Bird Man cuts the engine. We're pulled alongside the large bobbin' body of the plane, and I forget about bein' sick for a moment. The plane's small, hardly able to carry much of anythin', and it's a slate-gray color, no markin's but that same white handprint on its nose. It ain't the flashy red, white, and blue flyers on the vids or the tiger jets howlin' through the sky on Patriot's Day. Just a gray slim profile, like it don't do nothin' but spray crop fields.

"We've got to hurry. We've already got a report. Society's got a bead on us. Our scattershield will only cloak us for so long. Is this them?" The other woman, whose long hair's pulled back into a tight bun, looks us over. Wrinkles her nose. We probably ain't a delightful sight. I'm still smeared with sludge and oil from the tunnels, and Elenbar...her ashen face is real corpse chic. She don't even give any sign she's hearin' any of us. Her cheek's smudged against the rim of the motorboat edge, and she's lookin' back at the shoreline.

"Yes, they're Brigade," Bird Man says.

The woman makes a tongue-click sound. "They aren't much. Never are, huh? All right, let's get them inside. Time's running." She cocks a thumb toward the plane.

David extends his hand toward me, but I push it away, strugglin' to my feet and wobblin' over to Elenbar. I grab her metal arm, and David takes her fleshy one. Like a doll with broken joints, she lets us, barely on her own feet. He gives me a solemn look over the top of her head, but I ignore it.

"Wait, is she sick?" The woman with the slicked hair stares at Elenbar. Starin' at her steel clunker arm. The other's lookin' too, brows furrowed like she ain't likin' what she sees.

"No—no, she ain't sick. She ain't! Just tired. It's—look, the Wall, it's hell. They just came through, and she ain't had chance to get her strength back." My words prattle like rands in a gutter fly's can.

"She isn't sick," Bird Man says from behind us. "Damaged and weary, perhaps. As we all were once, Myra. Or have you forgotten so soon?"

Myra—guess that's the one with the bun—frowns and crosses her arms. "Mm. Fine. Can you get her up here?"

"Come on, Ele," I say in her ear. "Let's get outta here."

Elenbar don't say nothin' but does as she's told. Myra grabs her arm to steady her before guidin' her inside the small cabin of the plane.

"Go on, Andi." David motions for me to step up, so I do, if only to get off that puke-smeared boat and away from the nauseatin' swells of the ocean.

I stop and look back at Bird Man. "You're a crazy fagger, you know that?"

He nods, and his bushy beard bristles with a hidden smile. "Indeed. But I think I find myself in familiar and similar company."

"Yah, birds of a feather, huh?"

"Yes. But it's time for you to go forward. And speaking of time..." He winks at me, and somehow I know he knows about the heavy ticker bulgin' in my pocket. "Time is of the greatest importance now—I know you will use it wisely. Remember, there is no going back."

My cheeks burn, but he's right. There is no going back. The Wall rises from the shore like a mountainous skyline, obscurin' the cityscape beyond it. I can see the faint shadows of a few tall buildings, cloudscrapers cloaked in the haze and smog of the suffocatin' Slumland. I wonder if they can see us from there, whoever lives in those lofty towers, high above it all.

"Come on, we need to get moving," David says, his voice a low kindness.

"All right. Take care of Boy and, uh, get outta the way before the Wall goes, keepers?"

"Knockers." Bird Man salutes me.

"Knockers, knockers!" squawks Oliver from inside Bird Man's jacket.

I step up into the plane, followed by David. Then the door slams behind us, and it's done. We're leavin' the Wall, the Slumland, everythin' for good. I look back through the window, but Bird Man is already putterin' the small boat away from us, not watchin' us leave. Seems it's final for him too.

"Hold on tight. It's going to be a bit bumpy," Myra says as she scampers into the front pilot seat. The plane has four passenger seats inside and one large wooden box stashed toward the back of the tail.

The other lady slides into the seat beside Myra and checks the switches and mirrors. Then the motor roars to life, and within moments, we begin to accelerate, the plane's buoys rumblin' over the undulatin' swells. My empty shriveled gut squirms. Elenbar's head's pressed against the side window. I'm feelin' too sick to be mad, but I wish she'd say somethin', anythin' right now.

"Here we go," Myra shouts back over the roar of the engines, and the bumpin' stops, goes completely smooth like we've skidded onto a pool of silk. But it's just us leavin' the water, the buoyed frame up and out, as the plane does as it's meant to do and soars.

We go high, higher than I've ever been in my short cocked-up life. The water fades to a mottled blue, almost black in some places, like there's a dark canyon underneath the white-capped waves. I shiver thinkin' about how deep the ocean is, how wide it goes, all the way into a world I only ever heard terrible stories about. I press my forehead to the glass to see as far as I'm able.

The Wall stretches away on our left side, and it's shrinkin', a curvin' edge holdin' back the swell of the UFS world inside. It's so small from here. Can't believe I was deep inside the guts of it, blowin' up part of it. My pulse quickens at the thought of the bomb, the tickin' danger nestled like an egg deep inside a henhouse. Just waitin' to bring it down. To destroy everythin' bustlin' on the other side. The buildings, cars, people, and all the features once so home to me are just a wash of indistinguishable detail, like a blurry paintin' of a long-ago memory.

"There's the Liberty Bridge! It's right there!" I smile at David who nods, and my stomach does a flip. I press my hand against the cold glass, keepin' the tears tucked inside my eyelids. "It looks so close, like we could touch it." I'm homesick for it all. How long since we passed through the Wall? Was Bosco there still? Were they all dead? Did any of that even matter anymore now that we're headin' to safety, far away from the Society, from the very world that's tried so hard to kill us?

"The Wall is so tiny, so easy from here." David's got his head pressed to the glass too, gazin' at what we've gone through. "Can't see the hell inside until you're actually in it."

"You know what, cuck? Fuck that Wall. Fuck it right to the faggin' depths of a hooker hole."

David glances at me, surprised. "Been a while since I've heard you sound like you."

The slickered-hair woman looks back at me, smilin', and it shows a small gap in her front teeth. "Hey, did you really stop them? From blowing the bomb?"

"Yah, I guess." I shiver, rememberin' the concussive blast rockin' through my head. My own ears still buzz with a faint distant whine.

"That's great work you did. You've bought us time. We're going to need it," she says. "I'm Trina, by the way."

"Hey. You part of the Enclave, then?"

"Yeah, we're Union forces, but specialized for the push into the UFS."

"Well, you guys better fuckin' hurry. That bomb? It ain't gone, and they're gonna come back." There's a hitch in my throat as I say it, because it's the truth. I ain't stopped nothin'. They're still comin'.

She nods and settles back into her seat, mutterin' somethin' to Myra who nods too.

WE MAKE A slight detour as we near the border, makin' wide circles in the air. Trina hops back with us in the main cabin, and David helps her shove the huge wooden box out the side of the plane. It's equipped with its own parachute, which catches the wind, bloomin' like the head of a white mushroom as it sinks slowly toward the ocean. We're just off the shoreline, and a blue pop of flare smoke signals it's been seen. Below, a small motorboat cruises toward the supply drop and eventual lands in the choppy surf. I'm glad I ain't on a faggin' boat anymore. Flyin' is the true magical way to travel. Seems my guts were always meant to fly high above it all because I ain't been sick or quakin' since we left the ground behind. I think about the plane I saw, gazin' up from the prison yard at the Farm, wonderin' where they were goin' and why. Well, now I know. They were goin' to freedom, just like me.

"Who's down there?" I yell over the buzzin' engines as we leave the drop-off location behind.

"Another outpost like Bird Man's. They signal information from the Upper boroughs along the Wall," Trina shouts back.

"The Upper boroughs? Like Concord? And Quincy?"

"Yah, though they collect info from Somerset, too."

I think about those places I ain't ever seen, only heard about from relayed intel told in the quiet muffle of Brigade meetings in the Brick. They might as well be Outer World for all I've ever known of them. But there's people there too, that's what Elenbar said. There's Brigade just like us, fightin' in all those hidden pockets of places we ain't ever been or seen. Somehow the world got bigger than us. The shoreline is stretched out like a map beneath us, and my mind boggles at how small it all really is. How close we are to each other.

The land beyond the Wall changes as we fly farther north, the colors growin' green and thick with forest. Ain't much city at all and I wonder where we are. Wonder who lives in those dense trees and whether the

Society rides them like they do in the cities. Seems harder maybe, like keepin' the tight fists slammin' against people wouldn't work real well, not when they can run and hide deep in those wild-lookin' woods.

It's close to evenin' darkness as we approach the border. I pull out the heavy watch and rub my fingers over the scratches on the surface. The lid of the timekeeper is a clear circle of glass with tiny hatchmarks around the edge, creatin' a funny diagram across the front that looks like it's been scratched on purpose. *Time is of the greatest importance now—I know you will use it wisely.* The hands say it's eight of nine o' clock, the tiny minute hand flickerin' faintly inside the watch. Bird Man is right. We're all runnin' on time none of us got, whether we're here or beyond in the mystery of the north. There ain't no escape. Not really.

Ahead, the Wall's blinkin' indicator lights activate, the same blinkin' red ones we could count time by in the Slumland. Back when all I had was a busted watch and veins bustin' with a jackin' Flow high.

"Hey, you ever seen where the Wall ends?" Trina points ahead through the windshield.

"Where it...ends?" I crane my neck to see, mouth loose like a slack-jawed toad.

The Wall disappears. She's right. It *does* end. There's a blunt cutoff to the long barricade that's traced the entire eastern seaboard. We pass the last blinkin' light, and just like that, we're outta the United Free States, surgin' into the Detachment Zone. We're just past the edge when the plane tips forward, startin' a gradual descent.

"But where's the rest of it? Why does it stop there? Don't Canada got a Wall?" I'm almost in the front seat, ready to grind my ass onto Trina's lap so I can see it all better.

"Because this is the border. The Wall stops right at the edge. There is a fence that extends along the length of our shared border, of course." She smiles as she points at a thin line formin' a sharp corner with the blunt edge of the finished Wall. "But isn't much of a fence along here. Isn't much of anything, really. Guess the Society doesn't fear us friendly neighbors to the north, eh?"

She winks at me, but I ain't got any idea what she's talkin' about. Far as I'm sure, the Society thinks everyone's an enemy.

"Wow, is that it then? Is that where the Enclave is?" David points out the window as I force myself back into my seat. Ahead, sprawled out below us, are the blinkin' bustlin' lights of a city. A sight at least familiar to a gutter punk like me, unlike all the other shit we've seen so far. My chest's too tight for the boomin' drum of my heart.

"Get comfy and hang on for the landing," Trina calls back to us.

Myra's flickin' switches and holds a radio receiver to her mouth, mumblin' somethin' I can't hear.

I look over at Elenbar. Who looks right back at me. Who actually looks right into my eyes as she wrangles a seat belt across her lap.

"Are you ready, Andi? Really ready fer this?" Her voice is hoarse and wheezy, but the words are clear.

A whip of fear snakes through me, and I got some terrible feelin' like we ain't even close, like there ain't nothin' down there but the worst sort of endin'. The kind that never does. But at least I got Elenbar. And David too.

I force my lips to wrench out the word: "Knockers."

The plane's nose dips harder, and my gut wrenches as we begin the real descent. The plane trembles and bounces, wind whistlin' through the seams of my window. We're headed straight down, straight toward the Enclave, headin' toward the future, headin' toward...freedom. *There is no going back.*

My knuckles ache as I clench the arms of my seat. I try not to think about what life, the Brigade, the Farm, the Society, what every part of my bein' born's been teachin' me all along: freedom ain't ever what it seems.

I know that. Don't I just fuckin' know?